MURDER WORTH A THOUSAND WORDS

The Sisters, Texas Mystery Series
Book 12

BECKI WILLIS

Original Artwork for cover by Jeanette Duke
Editing by SJS Editorial Services
Cover by Diana Buidoso dienel96

ISBN 13: 978-1-947686-21-2

CONTENTS

1

September in Texas wasn't the same as in many parts of the country.

Here, the mercury still climbed to the tops of thermometers, as if reluctant to say farewell to soaring midday temperatures.

Here, leaves didn't turn into a kaleidoscope of vivid color to greet the brisk, autumn air; they shriveled up, turned brown, and fell to the ground as testimony to a hot, dry summer. A summer that was still in full swing, often into November.

September in Texas brought with it the time-honored rituals of high school football, street fairs and crafts shows, and a fresh round of the beloved garage sale—or, if the seller hoped for higher prices—estate sales.

On this Saturday morning, Madison deCordova and Genny Montgomery got an early start, hoping to make at least two, maybe three, sales before the day grew too warm. Now seven months pregnant, Genny couldn't take the heat the way she once could. Already, her feet were swelling, and her personal thermostat was on the blink, often drenching her in a full-fledge sweat. She knew to do her errands early in the day, so she could spend her afternoons beneath the air conditioner.

Their first stop was the late Alpha Bodine's grand old Victorian. As expected, the sale drew a large crowd; it was the first time the house had been opened to the public in almost thirty years. Miss Alpha had been one of Naomi's most upstanding citizens and wasn't known to have a single enemy. Her murder here in this very house had shocked the community and reverberated, still.

Even now, no one had been charged for the dastardly deed. There were too few clues and too little evidence to make an arrest.

There were rumors that the bloodstains had never come out of the carpet in the front parlor where poor Miss Alpha's body was discovered. Madison wondered if that wasn't part of the reason behind the big turnout today. People could be morbid, curious about the mysteries of death and all too eager to see the vestiges of murder, up close and personal.

Not Madison, mind you; she had seen enough dead bodies over the past two and a half years to last her a lifetime. She found nothing fascinating about the smear of someone's life substance soaked and dried into an otherwise lovely Persian rug.

The house had stood empty for over a dozen years. Her grandsons, living with her at the time of her death, were shipped off to other family members, and the house was closed up tight. When the youngest of the boys turned twenty-one, the three brothers became rightful owners of the estate and had free reign to the house, even though they spent little time there.

Who could blame them? The house held painful memories for them all. Mostly, the brothers used the rambling old house for storage and a tax write-off.

Madison wasn't sure of the particulars, but rumor had it that one of the men had used the estate as collateral for a business deal and defaulted on the loan. The house and all its possessions had been seized and ordered liquidated.

Hence the estate sale and one of the biggest turnouts The Sisters had ever seen for what was, essentially, a glorified garage sale.

Genny was looking for something special to go in the nursery, some heirloom from the past to remind their children that history should never be ignored. There were lessons to be learned from looking to the past. She didn't have anything specific in mind, but she would know it when she saw it.

For almost two years, Madison had lived in an old Victorian twice the size of Miss Alpha's, but there were still plenty of naked walls and barren nooks and crannies. She was looking for something to fit the time and general feel of the house.

A canvas painting had captured Madison's attention. She didn't normally decorate with Western decor, but the painting was exceptionally done. Something about it spoke to her.

Her late husband had imagined himself something of an art connoisseur, and he always told her to seek works not for what they said to the world, but for what they said to *her*. Their home in Dallas had been filled with art pieces she thought screamed 'ugly,' but they whispered something else to Grayson. For him, the bolder and more colorful, the better. Madison preferred understated pieces.

This one was just that, with its pastoral setting and a single longhorn bull, lazing in the sun.

"Ooh, that one's pretty," Genny said, looking over her shoulder to the canvas she studied. "Where will you put it?"

"I'm not sure. Do you think Brash will like it?"

"Absolutely."

"I may tuck it away and give it to him for Christmas." Her new husband of a year and a half was difficult to buy for, but she thought he would like this. If nothing else, he could take it down to the police station and hang it in his office.

"The carving on this frame is gorgeous," Madison continued. "And I like the detail of the work itself. Look at the shading on the horns and the space between them. You can practically count the individual hairs."

"It is cool," Genny agreed.

"I think I'll carry it around with me. If I don't see something I like better, I'll buy it."

They ventured into the front parlor where most of the lookers seemed to congregate. Everyone was eying the rug, some more pointedly than others.

"I'm not sure that's blood," Madison murmured from the side of her mouth, her tone doubtful.

"Maybe not. But the price is right. Where else could you get a Persian rug for so little? It would be worth the dry-cleaning bill to try."

Madison shrugged. "I suppose so. Even if it has set in for good after almost thirty or so years, there's always the furniture on top of it trick."

They moved around the room, examining knickknacks and consoles. Madison was inspecting a small mantel clock when Genny nudged her arm.

"Maddy," she whispered in an urgent tone. "Don't look now, but there's a guy who's followed us through two rooms now."

"I'm sure he's just following the same clockwise pattern we are. I've seen a lot of the same people over and over again."

"No, this guy has been watching you the entire time. I can see his reflection in that gilded mirror. He's pretending to look at an ivory pipe, but his eyes are on you."

"Do you know who he is?"

"Never seen him before."

Madison casually turned around as if to scan the room for the next great treasure. She saw a man in dark clothing and a ball cap pulled low on his head. He looked in her general direction, but his eyes were riveted upon the painting.

"I think he's interested in this painting. He's probably hoping I'll decide against it and set it down."

"It is a good rendering," Genny agreed.

"I don't know any of the Bodine brothers. Maybe it's one of them, and it has sentimental value. Maybe he came to buy it back."

"I heard they were prohibited from attending the sale and buying back their own possessions."

"That's rather strange, but who knows?" Madison lifted a slender shoulder in bewilderment. "For all I know, he recognizes me from the makeover show and wonders where I'll put the painting. A lot of people don't realize that Kiki and the *Home Again* team only decorated a portion of the rooms at the Big House."

"They seriously think a three-storied mansion only has three bedrooms?" Genny scoffed. "There's more like seven or eight!"

"Yes, but most viewers didn't realize the renovation wasn't for the entire house."

Genny's blonde head bounced up and down like a bobblehead. "Just the ones that made for riveting television."

Madison's lips twisted in thought. "That could also explain the reason that guy keeps looking over here. He may recognize us but doesn't remember from where."

"So? Are you buying the painting?"

Madison looked back to the canvas in question, trying to decide. She sneaked another peek at the man and saw him still eying the artwork.

"Geez, he's obsessed!" Genny muttered.

"Maybe I should buy it. It's not signed by the artist, but maybe it's a lost Rembrandt or something. That guy certainly thinks it's worth something."

"I don't know about a Rembrandt..." Genny said dubiously. "More like a Jean Applegate original."

"Hey, maybe it is!" Madison said, looking down at the painting with renewed curiosity. "It's definitely her style. And she's gained such national attention lately, I hear her early works have skyrocketed in value."

Her friend nodded in agreement. "I hear the library is trying to get her to come for a presentation, but she's so busy, it's hard to pin her down."

"I guess that's what happens when you hit the big time. Hey, look at this pedestal bowl. You could use it in the nursery to put items like ribbons and bows or bottles of lotion."

"That's not a bad idea," Genny agreed, picking up the white milk-glass bowl with interest. "I don't see a price. Do you?"

As Genny held the bowl up, Madison peered underneath to see if it sported a price tag on the bottom. "I don't see anything. Here, let me hold it for a better look," she offered. "That's probably a little heavy for you to hold up so high." Madison set the painting at her feet and reached to take the bowl from her friend.

The man in the ball cap moved in quickly, intent on snagging the painting. He pushed between two women admiring the previously contemplated mantel clock and swooped down, his face obscured by the bill of his cap.

Genny saw him just in time. "Maddy! The painting!"

Madison reacted on instinct. Outraged by his audacity, she cried, "Don't you dare!" She swung the heavy bowl without even realizing she did so.

Startled, the man looked up. He dropped the

painting so he could defend himself, but not before the crimped edge of the glass made contact. It bit into the soft flesh just beneath his eye, leaving an angry red mark in a zig-zag pattern.

Madison was so appalled by her own show of violence, she gasped aloud, dropping the bowl as she did so. The bowl shattered at their feet and drew the attention of other shoppers.

The man stared at Madison for a moment, caught with indecision. She imagined she saw the options as they ran through his mind. Return the blow? Call the police and press charges? Steal the painting outright? She held her breath, waiting for the outcome of his decision.

In the end, he abandoned the painting and ran from the house. He rudely pushed aside anyone in his way. Voices shrieked in surprise, overturned chairs clattered to the floor, and more glass crashed against marble tiles and hardwood floorboards as he weaved through the rooms and the people milling about.

"What—What just happened?" Genny whispered.

"I don't know." Madison put a hand up to cover her horrified cry. "I—I can't believe I did that. I can't believe I hit him!"

"Don't feel too sorry for the guy. Whoever he was and whatever he wanted, he gave me the creeps. Normal people don't follow other people around, trying to snag things right out of their hands."

"Genny's right," another voice said from nearby, joining into their conversation. Pearl Huddleston nodded vigorously, setting her chins wiggly and her gray curls bouncing. "I saw the way he kept eying you. Mark my words, that man was up to no good."

"Do you know who he was?" Madison asked the older woman. When Madison first opened *In a Pinch*, Pearl had been one of her first customers. She hired the struggling young widow to drive her husband Leroy back and forth to the doctor on numerous occasions. Bryan-College Station, the nearest large town to their small community, was about an hour away.

The older woman shook her head. "Don't think so. He kept his head down most of the time, but I could tell he had his gaze on you." She gave a disapproving *tsk*. "It's a darn shame when you can't even come to an estate sale without being harassed! What is our world coming to?" Another shake of her head set off more wiggles. "Don't you fret about putting that pervert in his place. He deserved it and more!"

"Thanks, Miz Huddleston. I appreciate your support."

The older woman made a show of looking around. "Is your grandmother not with you? I figured she couldn't wait to get inside this house again."

"Again?"

"Bertha and Alpha were friends, you know. Not bosom buddies like her and Sybil or Wanda, but close enough to visit on occasion. Alpha's death took us all by surprise, but it hit your grandmother especially hard. She was justice of the peace at the time and had to identify the body. I think the worse part of all for her was that the killer was never caught. Bertha felt partially responsible for not seeing justice done."

"There were no suspects?" Genny asked. "I was barely in junior high at the time and don't remember many of the details."

"I think it happened right before I came to live with Granny Bert and Grandpa Joe," Madison added. Being dumped on her grandparents at such an impressionable age, she had been too absorbed in her own drama to notice anyone else's pain. Had Granny Bert been grieving the death of her friend, on top of raising her irresponsible son's only child? Had

Madison's sudden presence kept her from doing her duties as an officer of the court?

"Alpha was a sweetheart," Pearl Huddleston said, ignorant of the worry clouding Madison's hazel eyes. "Not a single enemy that I know of. There were rumors of someone in the family doing the deed, hoping to get their hands on what was left of her daddy's money. But there was never enough proof. No suspects, either. Eventually, it just became one of those cold cases." She shrugged her shoulders and heaved out a deep breath.

Madison was curious to know more. She would ask Granny Bert, of course, but first, there was the matter of the broken bowl. "I guess I should find whoever's in charge and ask if they have a broom," she mumbled.

"I'd say that uptight-looking woman coming your way is in charge." Pearl chuckled. "Don't worry, girl. I got your back if she bothers you about clocking that man with the bowl."

"Maybe no one noticed that part," Madison hoped aloud.

"Oh, they noticed, all right. But don't worry, we protect our own," the older woman assured her. "That lady yonder is an outsider, sent down from some bank's corporate office. Just say you dropped it."

The woman in question wore a tailored navy suit and high heels. *Yep, definitely an outsider*, Madison surmised. She stopped in front of the mess, glaring down at it with flared nostrils.

"I suppose that man did this, too. He left a trail of destruction all the way to the door!" the woman huffed.

For a brief second, Madison considered taking the easy way out. But then she thought of what she always told the twins about owning up to their mistakes and taking responsibility for their actions. Brash had raised Megan with the same values. Madison wouldn't shirk her duties as a parent and decent human being over something as insignificant as a broken bowl.

"I'm afraid he wasn't to blame," she admitted. "Not directly. He startled me when he grabbed this painting from me, and I—I'm afraid I dropped the bowl."

Okay, so maybe that was only half the story. Did that make her only a half-decent human being?

"I'll pay for the bowl, of course," she added quickly.

"Very good. I believe that is part of a set," the woman said, consulting the electronic tablet she carried with her. "Yes, here it is. A set of rare pedestal bowls, embossed with alternate ruffled lace and crimped edges. The pair was priced at $125."

"For two bowls?" Madison gaped.

"That is correct." The woman glanced down at the painting. "If you're taking the artwork, I'll cut you a deal. $175 for the remaining bowl and the canvas."

Madison sighed. "Then let's find that other bowl and get out of here. I can't afford to stay any longer."

Looking unimpressed with her plight, the woman sniffed. "If it were signed, the painting would be worth at least three times as much."

After locating the other half of the pair and paying, Madison and Genny waved goodbye to Mrs. Huddleston and hurried out to the car. Madison took care to nestle the over-priced 'rare pedestal bowl' in a safe spot. Then she dusted the canvas free of any remaining shards of glass, stashed it behind her seat, and pulled out of the driveway.

Unnoticed, the man in the ball cap started his car and pulled out behind them.

2

"I still can't believe I did that," Madison lamented, shaking her head in dismay. "What will Brash say? And how will that look if the police chief's own wife is arrested for assault?"

"The way that man ran out of there, I don't think he'll be filing a police report. Something was up with him."

"Maybe you're right. So, where to next? Are you up for another round?"

Genny couldn't help but tease her friend. "Is that boxer lingo?"

Madison wrinkled her nose. "Very funny."

Rubbing her rounded tummy, Genny sighed. "Would you mind terribly if we called it quits? I know we just got started, but this one is doing somersaults and doesn't care what she kicks in the process. Namely, Momma's bladder."

"We're closer to Granny Bert's house than we are to the ranch," Madison said.

"A few more blocks," Genny pointed out, "and we'd be at *New Beginnings*."

"But then you'd feel obligated to stay and work, and today is your day off."

Genny saw through her thinly veiled ruse. "You're just anxious to ask Granny Bert about Miss Alpha's murder!"

"I'm just thinking of you," Madison insisted with faux innocence. "Those train tracks into Naomi are murder on the bladder. And what if we get caught by a train?"

"Then we could go to your house. It's on this side of the tracks," she pointed out. Before Madison could sigh in defeat, Genny's dimples flashed. "I'm just messing with you. Take me to Granny Bert's."

"You're sure? I am curious, but it could wait another ten minutes while I run you to the café."

Genny looked appropriately appalled. "And chance those tracks? Not a chance, girlfriend!"

A few minutes later, they pulled into the drive of Granny Bert's rambling old Craftsman. Lumbering out of the car, Genny reminded her friend, "You'd better lock up. That's one expensive bowl you have in here."

"You're telling me!" Madison clicked the key fob and slipped it into her pocket. Like most citizens of the small community, she left her purse in plain sight. Most people didn't even lock their cars, but Genny had a point. That 'rare' bowl had cost her.

"So rare," she muttered under her breath as she trailed behind her friend, "that there happened to be two of them there."

Accustomed to drop-in visits from unexpected guests, Granny Bert didn't seem surprised to see the duo. While Genny made a mad dash for the bathroom, Granny Bert led her granddaughter into the kitchen for iced tea.

"I could add a splash of ginseng if you like," the older woman offered, her back to Madison. "I hear it's good for a strong right punch."

Madison sighed. She should have known her

grandmother would have already gotten wind of the morning's incident. "Who called you?" she asked in resignation.

"Oh, I've already had a half-dozen calls or so." Her grandmother turned around to bring the tea, a smirk on her wrinkled face. "Coach Luna wants to know if you'd like to sponsor the boxing team, seeing as you have an affinity for the sport."

"Ha, ha." Madison's voice lacked mirth.

"I hear you wallop a pretty good punch. I'm proud of you, girl. I didn't know you had it in you."

Propping her elbow on the table, Madison cradled her forehead with her hand. "I can't believe I did that. It—It was just instinct. I didn't even know I reached out, until I felt the bowl smack against his face."

"From what Pearl said, he deserved it. She said he'd been following you around, leering at you like you were a slice of ripe, juicy watermelon."

Madison wasn't sure she appreciated being compared to a round, shapeless fruit, but she understood the sentiment.

"Actually, I think he was leering at a piece of artwork I was buying, rather than me."

Her grandmother whistled lowly. "That must have been one doozy of a piece! What was it? A naked woman?"

"Hardly. It was of a longhorn. I thought it would make a good gift for Brash."

"Brash might like a painting of a naked woman better," her grandmother suggested, "but whatever." She cut a sly look at her companion. "What about that rare bowl you bought? What are you planning to do with it?"

"The gossip mill didn't leave out a thing, did they?"

"I've trained my crew to be thorough," Granny Bert said, no small amount of pride ringing in her voice. "If you're going to tell something, you may as well tell the whole story."

"Speaking of whole stories…" Madison allowed Genny time to shuffle into the kitchen and get settled into the chair opposite her before continuing. "What's the story on Alpha Bodine's death?"

Her grandmother's eyes clouded. "Now, that's a sad tale, for sure and certain."

"Have a seat and tell us about it."

Bringing her own glass to the table, Granny Bert sat with a heavy thud. Not for the first time, Madison noticed how much her grandmother had aged. She wore her eighty-three years well, but there were times, like now, when they seemed to catch up to her without warning.

"Alpha was the sweetest soul you ever did meet. That woman had a heart of gold. Needed it, too, with that no-account husband of hers and that flighty daughter. She came from money, but it didn't take her family long to plow through it."

"Who was her husband? I've never heard anyone mention him before," Genny noted.

"Lester Bodine." She said the name like it left a bad taste in her mouth. "He was from Louisiana. Hightailed it back there, too, from what I heard. Right after he cleaned out their bank account, that is. Left Alpha to raise those two children on her own."

"What happened to her children?" Madison wanted to know. She knew their situations were different—Gray had died, whereas Lester had abandoned his wife—but she could sympathize with Alpha Bodine's plight. In a way, Gray had abandoned her, too, long before the fatal accident that took his life.

"The boy chased after his father at the first chance. He joined his daddy in the shrimping business, but they were both lost at sea, so the story goes. I wouldn't put it past either one of them to fake their own deaths, but that's neither here nor there. Alpha never heard another word from either one of them. Sylvia, though, was another matter. That girl gave her momma nothing but grief. Alpha had tucked away a tidy little sum Lester didn't know about, but Sylvia found out about it and made it her life's mission to spend it all."

She paused to take a noisy slurp of sweet iced tea. "She ran away a half-dozen times before she 'found' herself at some hippy camp. Claimed to have found Jesus, too, but between the skimpy clothes, the steady parade of men in her life, and the drugs, it was hard to tell. She eventually had three sons, but then she flew the coop and left them all high and dry."

"That's how the boys came to live with Miss Alpha," Madison surmised. That, too, sounded all too familiar. Her parents had gone through their own 'free-spirited' days, choosing a nomadic lifestyle over parenting. When her father got a hankering to become a race car driver, they had more or less dumped Madison with her grandparents and took off.

"Alpha did her best by those boys, but they were a handful. When she died, they were shipped off to live in a foster home. No one knew where their mama was, or who their daddies might be."

At least my parents loved me and talked to me about their decision, Madison reminded herself. *They were selfish, yes, but they also knew I deserved better than what they could give me. It turned out to be the best thing that ever happened to me, even though I didn't see it that way at the time. Maybe in her own warped way, Sylvia Bodine thought the same thing, but she went about it the wrong way.*

Getting back on track, Madison said gently, "Miss Alpha didn't just die, Granny. She was murdered, right there in her home. Were there never any suspects?"

"There was plenty of speculation if that's what you're asking. Some claim it was Sylvia's doing. Reasoned she probably came back needing money and killed her momma in a fit of rage. Or maybe it was Lester or Benny, believing their names were still in the will. Neither one was bright enough to realize that if the courts proclaimed them legally dead, they couldn't inherit a thing."

"And the police? What did they think?"

"At that point, we didn't have a fully appointed police department. Otis Perry was our only officer, and he was still wet behind the ears."

"Leave it to Berry Perry to blotch the case," Genny muttered. There was no love lost between the cantankerous officer and any of the women at the table. It only made matters worse that Madison was now married to his boss. The man still held a grudge about being overlooked for the leadership position.

"I imagine he did do a few things wrong, but the truth is, we were all rattled," Granny Bert admitted. "It was a gruesome scene, and she was our friend."

"Didn't the River County sheriff's office step in to handle things?"

"Yes and no. Budgets were tight, resources were few and far between, and it appeared to be an isolated incident. Without momentum, the case just fizzled."

"And people were content with that?" Genny asked.

"Officially, the sheriff's department claimed it could have been a vagrant just passing through. That seemed to appease most folks. And of course, that was before the internet, so there was no one to be offended and stir up a big stink."

Madison chewed on the inside of her lip. "So, it's a cold case? Still open, but in a perpetual state of limbo?"

"I reckon so." Granny Bert cocked her gray head to one side. "What's all that racket? Sounds like a car alarm going off."

Madison and Genny looked at one another, their eyes wide.

"The painting!" Madison cried, sprinting from the table. She headed out the front door, while her grandmother took the side exit. Genny came in a distant third, battling the sudden urge to empty her bladder again.

The man in the ball cap stood beside Madison's SUV, a long piece of pipe in his hand, poised to strike.

"I don't think so!" Madison bellowed, charging down the walk. Her only weapon was her blazing glare.

"Yeah?" he sneered. "Who's going to stop me? You're not armed with a deadly object this time."

He drew back to swing, but Granny Bert's authoritative voice stopped him. "No," she said in deadly calm manner. "But I am."

The unmistakable sound of a shotgun chambering a shell crackled through the air and froze the man's arm in midair.

The man's eyes widened, but he backed away from the vehicle. "You broads are crazy!" he snarled, before ducking inside his car and peeling away on a squeal of rubber.

"Granny Bert!" Madison cried. "What do you think you're doing?"

"Getting riffraff off my property," she answered proudly.

"Put that thing away before someone sees you!" her granddaughter hissed.

The older woman shrugged. "It's aimed at the sky. No danger in that."

"It's also full of rock salt, not real ammunition."

"That's true," her grandmother said. With a cunning smile, she added, "But he didn't know that."

Madison grumbled all the way back to the kitchen.

"I swear, you are going to outlive us all," she complained, "because you'll send *us* to any early grave!"

"You're losing sight of what's important here," Granny Bert sniffed. "I got rid of him, didn't I?"

"What's important is that there is some man out there just crazy enough to try stealing a painting from me, twice in one day! And my guess is he'll keep trying until he's successful."

"And now he knows we're as crazy as he is, so maybe he'll think again before he tries anything else."

Exasperated, Madison shook her head. "Your logic makes absolutely no sense."

Ever the peacemaker, Genny broke in, "Granny Bert, can you think of any reason someone might want to steal a painting from Alpha Bodine's estate? Was she an art collector?"

"Once they inherited it, I heard her grandsons used the house for storage as much as anything else," Genny said. "Maybe it belonged to one of them?"

"Possibly. Word is that one of the boys got tangled up in something bad and used the house as collateral," Granny Bert said. "For all I know, it could have been stolen in the first place. Maybe the guy in the baseball cap was just trying to get back what rightfully belongs to him."

"Are you trying to make me feel even *more* guilty?" Madison wailed.

"Not at all. That guy deserves a black eye and then some." The older woman huffed with a renewed sense of ire. "Imagine! Coming onto my personal property and pulling a stunt like that!"

Genny dragged herself to her feet again. "Sorry. Nature keeps calling my name."

Madison watched her friend shuffle from the room. Soon, she would be waddling.

"I don't envy her," she murmured. "As the mother of twins, I know how difficult it is to have two babies at once. At our age, her situation will be even worse."

"And you'll be there for her, the same way she was there for you," Granny Bert assured her.

"Plus, she has Cutter's family for support. A mother-in-law and sisters-in-law willing and eager to help." With a wrinkle of her nose, Madison recalled her own mother-in-law's lackluster response to Bethani and Blake's births. "Annette wasn't about to get spit-up on one of her designer blouses or dirty her hands with a poopy diaper."

"Her loss."

"Absolutely. At least she's trying to make amends now. And she's been wonderful to Megan, considering there's no blood between them."

"Megan is a charming girl. And you know that hunk of a husband of yours has Annette wrapped around his finger."

Madison shook her head in wonder. "I don't know how he managed it, given that Annette always believed Gray walked on water. She's been amazingly supportive of my marriage to another man. Particularly when she never supported my marriage to her son."

As Madison pondered the irony of it all, Genny

slugged back into the room. She had just settled into her chair again when her cell phone jingled.

"It's Tatiana," Genny said, her face lighting up at the call. She was always anxious to hear news from the other expectant mother.

"It's time!" Tatiana's frantic voice said on the other end of the line. "My water just broke!"

Genny froze, suddenly unable to remember the checklist she had made for just this purpose. Her mind went blank.

After trying unsuccessfully to get pregnant the first year of their marriage, she and Cutter believed they couldn't have children naturally. When nineteen-year-old Tatiana Gomez approached them about adopting her child, Genny fell in love with the idea of a dark-haired baby. They committed to adopting just before her own pregnancy was discovered. Now, they were expecting almost-twins, two months apart.

Think, Genny. Think.

Her hand fluttering in confusion, Genny said into the phone, "Uhm, okay. Take a deep breath and just breathe in. Try to relax."

They both practiced the breathing exercise as Genny visualized the list they went over at least once a week.

"Do you have your suitcase?"

"Yes. It's in the car."

"Is the car full of gas?"

"Yes. Mom has it running."

"Have you called the doctor?"

"Yes. He'll meet us there."

"Have you called Genny and Cutter?"

"Uh... yeah. I'm talking to you now."

Genny laughed at her own foolishness, but the sound came out in a quiver of nerves. "Oh, yes, how silly of me. Okay, let me grab Cutter, and we'll meet you at the hospital."

"Got it. Oh, and Genny?"

"Yeah?"

She could hear the bittersweet smile in Tatiana's voice, a mixture of sadness and joy that this moment had finally come. Nevertheless, the girl squealed with excitement. "You're about to be a mommy!"

3

Cutter was already at the restaurant, waiting for his wife to arrive. Madison saw her friends off before driving home. A happy smile lingered on her face. She couldn't imagine better parents than Genny and Cutter.

"Okay, so maybe Brash and I would give them a run for their money," she amended aloud. "We've done a good job with our own three, if I do say so myself." Punching her code into the gate and pulling into the driveway, she added, "With help from Gray, I suppose, and definitely from Shannon and Matt. It may have taken all five of us, but we've produced three very fine young adults."

Before she could obsess over the fact that her babies were now seniors in high school—*seniors*, when just yesterday they were toddling about, speaking in their own language that only the two of them understood—Madison forced herself to focus. Brash wasn't home, so that meant she had time to stash the painting somewhere in the house.

With a house so huge, it should have been an easy feat. But everywhere she thought of seemed too obvious. Just as she heard the bing alerting her to the gate opening again, inspiration hit. She would hide it in one of the house's many secret passageways. The sliding panel beside the fireplace in the library-turned-office should be perfect.

"Maddy? You home, babe?" His deep voice spoke through the intercom system.

"In my office," she answered, pressing the intercom there. She still had to slide the panel in place. Even his long legs couldn't cover that much space in a matter of seconds.

By the time he appeared in the doorway, she looked convincingly busy.

"Where'd the bowl come from?" he asked, nodding to the pedestal dish she fussed over.

"Genny and I went to an estate sale this morning."

"I may have heard about that," Brash said, crossing his arms and leaning against the door frame. She couldn't tell whether the slight twitch around his mouth was from suppressed laughter or anger.

"Don't believe everything you hear," she was quick to say. "Isn't that what you always tell me and the kids?"

"I back it up with 'Let me hear your version of events,'" he reminded her in a wry tone.

"Uhm, maybe we should sit down for this."

"That bad, huh?"

"Not at all," she said smoothly. "I just thought we could have a cup of coffee while we visit." She slipped her arms around his waist and presented him with a kiss, hoping to delay the conversation for as long as possible.

He was on to her gimmick. "You're stalling."

"I kiss my handsome husband hello and get accused of stalling?" She managed to look appropriately offended.

The lines around his mouth twitched again. "Better

than being accused of battery and assault."

Madison visibly paled. "He—He filed charges against me?"

"He, *who*, Maddy?" He dropped his arms, clearly not amused.

"I'm being completely honest when I say I have no idea. But let's go to the kitchen and continue this conversation there." She tugged at his waist, dragging him along with her.

She knew when his tightly coiled body relaxed. "Are you sure it's safe?" he asked. "There are knives in there. Worse, by far, are the cabinets filled with an arsenal of bowls."

She looked up to see his brown eyes twinkling with laughter. "Oh, you!" she said, jabbing at him with her fist. "I told you. Don't believe everything you hear."

"How can I, with a weak punch like that?" he teased.

"Weak, was it? How about this one? Or this?"

"Ouch," he said, easily deflecting her punches with one hand around her wrist. "Now you're just being mean."

"I'll let that remark slide, since I have news." She danced away from him, excitement in her hazel eyes. "Tatiana went into labor! Genny and Cutter are on their way to the hospital now. She'll give me an update when she gets there."

"Are we going today or waiting until they get home?"

"I'm not sure. I've never been in this situation before. These are all new waters, having a birth mother and an adoptive mother, and both being like one big, happy family. I don't want to intrude on Tatiana. I know this must be an emotional time for her. At the same time, I want to be there for my best friend. She's waited for this day for so long."

"Maybe you can take your clues from her," Brash

suggested. "See what she wants or expects you to do."

"That's what I thought."

They took the shortcut to the kitchen, foregoing the elaborate front entry and famed dining room mural in favor of the less than glamorous back hall and laundry room. Both paths led to the kitchen and to the cozy breakfast nook everyone favored.

"Coffee or tea?" Madison asked.

"Answers."

"Okay, okay. But we need something to drink."

"Water is fine."

And quicker, she grumbled silently.

"Spill it, Maddy," her husband said as she brought the glasses to the table. "And no, I don't mean the water. I mean the truth. What happened this morning?"

"What did you hear?" She often found it was best to find out what he knew before volunteering unnecessary information.

"About the confrontation at the Bodine mansion or about the shotgun incident at Granny Bert's?"

"I see your grapevine is about as thorough as my grandmother's is," she muttered.

"This is The Sisters, sweetheart. There's no such thing as a secret. The juicier the news, the faster it travels. Let's start with the estate sale."

"There was a *huge* turn out! Which is no wonder, really, when you consider it was the first time the house was opened in over a decade. I think people came out to be nosy more than anything, hoping to see the rumored blood stains. Personally, I don't think—"

"Personally," Brash broke in dryly, "I think you're stalling again."

"No, I'm not. Why haven't you ever told me about the case, Brash? I hear it's still open."

"It's a bit of a legend here. I thought you knew."

"I think it happened just before I moved here. Besides, I was too caught up in my own misery to worry about the misery of others, my grandmother's included. Now I'm feeling terribly guilty, not realizing how much she was going through at the time. That was *on top* of suddenly having a teenager to raise again."

"We'll have a therapy session later. Right now, you're telling me about the estate sale and why a half-dozen people thought it prudent to call me this morning, 'just so I knew' what was happening with my wife."

"We live in such a caring community, don't we?"

He refused to be sidetracked. "That's one way of looking at it. Now talk."

"Fine!" she huffed out. "I broke a bowl. It was part of a pair, and I had to pay for both. Is that what you wanted to know?"

"You may have left out a detail here or there. Like how, exactly, you broke that bowl. The way I heard it, it was on a man's face."

"Not so," Madison said with a small note of triumph. "It broke when I dropped it." The triumph faded as she admitted, "*After* I hit the man in the face."

"Over a *bowl*, Maddy? What was so special about it?"

"Is... that what they're saying?" she asked cautiously. She was trying to determine if this were some sort of trap, or if his intel hadn't included news of the artwork. All the better for her if the latter were the case. It was intended as his gift, after all.

Memories of another gift and another mystery flashed through her mind but discovering the chair had turned out to be a blessing for the entire community. The gold-plated sign on the newly expanded medical office was evidence of that. 'Sitting on a fortune' took on a whole new meaning after that gift.

"The way I heard it," Brash scoffed, "there was nothing special about the bowl to begin with."

"Not according to the seller. She claimed it was part of a very rare set and worth every penny she extorted from me."

"I heard you could have taken the easy way out and blamed it on the crazed man running through the rooms, but you did the honorable thing and 'fessed up." He put his hand over hers and gave her one of his heart-melting smiles. "For what it's worth, I'm proud of you, babe."

Madison looked glum. "A hundred and twenty-five dollars' worth of proud? Because that's what my honesty cost me."

"That does sound like extortion!" he agreed. "How many bowls were in the set? For that price, I hope a dozen or more!"

Madison shook her head and held up two lone fingers.

"Two? For a hundred and twenty-five bucks?"

"Just one, now," she pointed out.

"So, walk me through this. A man tried to grab the bowl from your hands, so you just clocked him with it?"

"More or less."

"I'll take the more version, please."

With a sigh, Madison told him everything she could without specifically mentioning the painting. "Genny had already noticed the man following us around from room to room, watching us. I thought maybe he recognized us from *Home Again*. You know, the gift that just keeps on giving." Her tone was sarcastic. "Anyway, we noticed the pedestal bowl, but Genny couldn't find a price. I offered to help her when the man made his move. You pretty much know the rest."

"Not really. I don't know what possessed you to *hit* a man in the face with a bowl, Maddy! That's not like the woman I know and love.”

“I know. I know it’s not,” she bemoaned. “And in my own defense, I don’t know what possessed me, either. It’s not like I intended to hit him. I—I just... did.”

“And you have no idea who the man was?”

“None. To my knowledge, I’d never seen him before.”

“And what did he do after you hit him?”

“For a few seconds, he just stood there. I’m not sure who was more surprised. Me or him.”

“Probably him,” Brash guessed. “I hear you left a mark.” His mouth twitched again, but he refused to smile at the images flashing through his mind.

“Laugh all you want, mister. I was horrified at what I’d done!”

“I’m not making light of the situation, sweetheart. Not at all. Technically, you assaulted the man.”

“Technically,” she shot back smartly, “he was harassing me. I have witnesses.”

“The same witnesses who saw you strike the man in the face with a blunt object. You may not want to go there, sweetheart,” he warned, a slight edge to his voice.

“I don’t suppose there’s anywhere *to* go,” she said. “He seemed to debate the situation for about five seconds, and then he ran out of there, leaving a trail of broken and damaged items behind him. I doubt he’ll come forward, for fear of having to pay for damages. And believe me, it will cost him a lot more than a hundred and twenty-five dollars!”

“Okay,” Brash seemed to agree. “We’ll assume you’re right about that. What about the shotgun incident?”

“Wh—What about it?”

“Neighbors called to report Granny Bert had a shotgun. You remember that neighborhood watch program you instigated, don't you?" His smile wasn't exactly sincere.

"Don Beevis," Madison said with a sigh. She may have 'pulled a Granny Bert' on him as the kids called it, conning him into giving her information in a ruse that touted starting a neighborhood watch. Who knew the man would take the concept and run with it? "And what did Mr. Helpful have to say about it?" she asked.

"Just that a car alarm went off, you ran out yelling at the top of your lungs, and Granny Bert came out with guns ablazin'."

"I wasn't yelling at the top of my lungs," Madison said primly. "But I was using a very stern voice."

"And how did that work out for you?"

"Fine. Once he heard the sound of a shotgun being loaded."

By now, Brash was openly laughing. "Mr. Beevis was so worked up, I didn't have the heart to tell him the gun was loaded with rock salt."

"Worked up? As in livid or just excited?"

"Oh, he's convinced he lives on the safest block in Juliet," Brash assured her. "He's offered to start an appreciation program, where everyone gets together and mows your grandmother's lawn for free. He has no doubt she would protect any of her neighbors with the same sass and vinegar—not to mention salt—as she did you today."

"Which she would," Madison pointed out.

"True. But all this is beside the point." His laughter dried up as he gave her a hard stare. "*Why* was the man trying to break into your car, Maddy?"

"Again, I honestly have no idea. I suppose he's as stubborn and determined as my grandmother."

"Over a *bowl*?"

Madison avoided a direct lie by offering an exaggerated shrug. "Your guess is as good as mine."

"Why did you want the bowl, anyway?"

"It wasn't for me. I suggested it would be cute in the nursery, filled with baby stuff."

"So, now that you own one very expensive pedestal bowl, what are you going to do with it?"

"What do you think?" She grinned. "I'm going to fill it with bottles of baby lotion and butt cream and give it to Genny at her baby shower!"

Later that night, as Madison slathered moisturizer on her legs and feet and crawled into bed, she pointed something out to her husband.

"You never did answer my questions today."

Closing the book he was reading, he placed it on the nightstand. "I'm not entirely sure you answered all mine, either. Turnabout is fair play."

He had a point, so she proceeded carefully. "Is it true? Is Miss Alpha's case still technically open?"

"It may have glazed over now with a thick coat of ice, but technically, yes. Her murder remains unsolved."

"Would you mind if I take a look at it?"

"Why?"

"Why, what? Why would you mind, or why do I want to look at a cold case?"

"Both."

"I'd like to know more about it," she said honestly. "Miss Pearl mentioned how upset Granny Bert was about the whole thing. Like I said, I feel guilty now, not realizing she was suffering in her own way, in something that went beyond our dysfunctional family unit."

"The Charlie and Allie Cessna branch of it is. Or at

least it was. I think they've finally grown up and become responsible adults, but it was touch and go there for a while. I didn't think I'd ever get them raised!" She pretended to jest, but he saw the pain in her eyes and lifted an arm so she could snuggle in by his side.

"Granny Bert put up such a brave front on my account," she went on, "that I never realized she was going through something difficult, both in her professional life and her personal one. From what I hear now, I understand she took her friend's death especially hard. She felt guilty for not being able to bring the killer to justice."

"It's a tough spot to be in," Brash agreed. "Sometimes, there's just nothing you can do."

"That's why I'd like to take a look at it. Plus, it will help sharpen my skills for when and if I ever do decide to pursue my private eye license."

"I thought you'd ruled against that."

"I'm keeping my options open. For now, I'm content being an amateur sleuth." She flashed a mostly innocent grin. "Besides, I have a lot more freedom this way. Not as many rules and regulations to keep up with."

"Given your knack for getting into trouble, that's probably a wise decision."

Ignoring his comment, she continued, "And I figure there's no reason for you to object to me looking at a cold case. A fresh set of eyes may be just what you need."

"Agreed. But don't expect Deputy Perry to be much help. This case is still like a thorn in his side."

"Worse than Genny and me?"

"Yes, and that's saying something."

"I may not need Berry Perry," she predicted. "I have a much better source of information."

"Granny Bert." It wasn't a question. It sounded more like a terrified realization.

"Yes, Granny Bert." Madison giggled. "And I think this may be good for her. With Sticker gone so much lately, she's been a little down in the dumps, even though she'll deny it with every breath. She claims she's hardly noticed he's gone, but I know that's not true. This will take her troubles off herself and give her the chance to settle an old debt."

"Are you sure this is about her or about you?" Brash asked knowingly.

"A little of both," she admitted. "I still feel guilty for my teenage ignorance."

Brash trailed a finger down her arm, setting off shivers of delight and lighting tiny fires with his smoldering gaze. "This is where that therapy session kicks in," he murmured.

4

"Are you on your way?" Genny wanted to know.

"Yes, Genny, we're on our way," Madison returned with a laugh. "Church just got out, and we're headed to the hospital. I did make the mistake of letting the lawman drive, though, so don't expect us there anytime soon." She shot a teasing look at the man behind the wheel.

"You had no complaints about me taking it slow last night," he replied smoothly.

Scandalized, Maddy covered the phone. "Brash! You can't say that!"

"Why not? You're my wife, and it's true," he reasoned.

Waving him into silence, she removed her hand from the mouthpiece and spoke to her friend. "Anyway, we'll be there as soon as we can, Gen."

"I can't wait to introduce you to Hope!" her friend gushed with excitement. "She's absolutely gorgeous!"

"I'm sure the pictures don't do her justice."

"They don't. Be careful coming over."

"Will do. See you soon." Hanging up, Madison told her husband, "I've never seen Genny this excited before."

"She's never been a parent before. It brings a whole new level of joy into your life."

"I can't believe my best friend is having her first child, and mine are about to go off to college."

"They aren't going off to college, Maddy. They'll be at home for at least another ten or eleven months. Instead of spending that whole time in tears, why don't you decide to make the most of it?"

"Easy for you to say," she grumbled.

"Easy? They're my kids, too," he reminded her. "Megan may be my only biological child, but I love Blake and Bethani like they were my own."

"I know you do, sweetheart," she said apologetically, rubbing his arm. "Ignore me. It's just a mother thing."

"No. Dads have it, too," he informed her, his voice rough with emotion.

"I can see this year'll call for a lot of therapy sessions," she teased, hoping to lighten the morose mood she had created.

"You got that right." Brash glanced into his rearview mirror. "What is that joker back there doing? I think he wants to pass, but there's a curve up ahead." They traveled a two-lane highway with narrow shoulders.

"I know Genny wanted us there ten minutes ago, but we're not in that big of a hurry. Let him pass."

"If he ever makes up his mind. Now he's pulled back in behind us."

"Probably saw the curve ahead."

"Or not. Here he comes again."

"Uh-oh. I recognize that car. It's the one from yesterday."

"What one from yesterday?"

"The one the guy in the ball cap was driving. He's bound to have a bald spot on his tires, the way he peeled away from Granny Bert's curb."

"What is he doing out here?"

"Looks like he's following us."

"No, it looks like he's pulling up alongside us." Brash tightened his grip on the steering wheel, alternately his gaze between the upcoming curve and the side mirror. "Hold on, Maddy! He plans to run us off the road."

"There's a guardrail ahead and that steep ditch! We'll wreck."

"Unclip my badge from my belt," he instructed. "And hand me my piece from the glove compartment."

"You think you need a gun?" she asked in alarm.

"I'm not taking any chances. I'll try showing him the badge and see if he backs off."

Following his instructions, Madison suggested, "Maybe he thinks I'm in here alone."

"Then he's in for a surprise," Brash replied grimly.

The car pulled up even with the SUV. Brash flashed his badge in the window, keeping his other hand steady on the wheel.

It could have been seeing a man behind the wheel. It could have been the badge. Either way, the car let up on the accelerator and fell behind again, tucking in meekly behind the larger vehicle. The sedan slowed even more, until it reached a gravel driveway and turned sharply into it. As Brash made the curve, he saw the car make a U-turn in the road and speed off in the opposite direction.

"What's going on, Maddy?" Brash growled.

"I don't know! At this point, I think he may be holding a grudge."

"I don't suppose you got a license plate number? I could only see the first two letters." He was already punching numbers into his phone.

"Who are you calling?"

"The station. I'll have someone stationed in town,

waiting to intercept him."

"What if he turns off before then?"

"Good point. I'll send a unit out to meet him."

After speaking to the dispatcher for several minutes, Brash hung up with a muttered comment beneath his breath. It sounded suspiciously like a curse. He was trying to break the habit, but some words had a life of their own.

"What's wrong?" Madison asked.

"Not sure anyone's free for surveillance. There was a hit and run in front of the *Bumble Bee Bed and Breakfast* and reports of a prowler around Myrna Lewis'. That leaves Perry, and he's not answering his radio. Probably taking his lunch break and doesn't want to be disturbed."

"You're his boss! He has to answer."

"Remind him of that. I've learned to pick my battles where Perry is concerned."

"But this could be something crucial! How does he know it's not an emergency?"

"If it were, I'd make him answer the radio, even if it meant going back and keying down his mic for him," Brash said with a determined glint in his eyes. "But at this point, it's not crucial. We've got nothing on the guy other than poor judgment, trying to pass with an upcoming curve. There wasn't even a stripe on his side of the road."

"What about yesterday?"

"Did you see this man's face? Can you say without doubt that it was the same guy?"

Madison blew out a frustrated sigh. "Just drive," she said irritably. "I need to see my new niece."

Never mind that she and Genny weren't technically sisters. They were, in all the ways that mattered. They were sisters by heart.

"Oh, Gen," Madison breathed in adoration as she held the newborn in her arms. "And Cutter. Your baby is absolutely gorgeous."

"Told you!" Genny beamed. "Did you see her lashes? Can you believe them? They're so long and thick!"

"And her hair has just the right amount of curl," Madison proclaimed, allowing a dark, silky tendril to curl around her finger.

"She's going to be a heartbreaker," Brash agreed.

"I'll be beating the boys off with a stick," Cutter predicted. "Absolutely no dating until she's seventeen."

"And only if we're available to tag along," Genny added.

"You want her to like you, don't you?" Brash teased. "I said the same thing when Megan was born, but that didn't last long. It's amazing how much it hurts to be shunned by your own child."

"Hush. Don't let her hear you," Cutter said in mock horror. "She may subliminally store the information to use against us one day."

"You don't have to worry about that," Brash assured him blithely. "Girls have a built-in radar when it comes to twisting their daddies around their little fingers. I know I still fall for it, even with Bethani."

"Come on," the new father said. "I'll buy you a cup of coffee in the cafeteria and let you give me a few pointers on how to raise a little girl."

Before leaving the room, the rugged cowboy firefighter dropped a kiss onto his wife's lips before tenderly kissing the top of his new daughter's head. "Daddy will be right back, princess. But Mommy and Aunt Maddy will take extra good care of you while I'm gone with Uncle Brash. I won't be long."

"Ah, he's a goner already," Madison said when the men were gone.

"Absolutely!" Genny couldn't have looked more pleased.

After a moment of marveling over Hope's coloring, Madison asked, "How is Tatiana dealing with all this?"

"She's sad, naturally. I think it's harder than she imagined, but she's been amazingly strong. She was released about an hour ago. Since Hope needs to stay one more night, they said we could keep her room and stay here with the baby."

"Wow. That was nice of the hospital."

"I think Laurel had something to do with it." Her dimples flashed. "It's nice to have a friend on the inside."

"I was hoping we'd run into her while we're here."

"If not, she promised she and Cade would both visit when I deliver this one." Genny put a hand to her rounded belly and rubbed. After a moment of silence, she asked quietly, "Am I crazy, Maddy? Having a baby at my age? And not just one, but two?"

"It's a little late to be worried about that, isn't it?" Madison laughed. "And it's not crazy. It's wonderful. What you're feeling is perfectly normal. It's also hormones, which will only get worse before they get better."

"If this is your idea of a pep talk, you suck at it," Genny grumbled.

Madison's eyes sparkled in playfully malicious glee. "I didn't even point out that about the time *your* hormones level out, your daughters' hormones will kick in. Those are especially fun."

"Again. Not helping."

The teasing left Madison's eyes, but the twinkle remained. "The truth is, Genny, things are going to be crazy and they're going to be hectic. You'll do without sleep, and you'll go without a shower for days. But you know what? You wouldn't change a minute of it, even if you could. You'll be the happiest you've ever been, and you'll discover a love you never knew existed. Not just for your children, but for their father. Parenthood is an awesome thing, Genny. And you're a natural."

Genny closed her blue eyes and practiced her deep breathing techniques. "Thanks, Maddy. I needed to hear that right about now."

"You'll need to hear it a hundred more times, too. And I'll be right here beside you to say it a hundred more."

Genny took the sleeping baby from her friend's arms and cradled her in a gentle embrace. "See, Hope?" she crooned to the child. "I told you your aunt was something special."

A nurse peeked into the room. "Mom? Can I borrow your baby for a few more tests?"

"Only if it's necessary," Genny said, reluctant to give up the sleeping infant.

"It is. Just a few routine blood tests. Nothing to worry over." She scanned the I.D. bracelet on both the mother and child's wrists, as well as her own name tag. "Just for reassurance," she explained. "These days, you can never be too careful. Why don't you ladies stretch your legs and visit the cafeteria? We'll be about a half hour. If you're not back yet, we'll tuck her into a crib in the nursery."

All the way down to the cafeteria, Genny fretted over a new batch of worries. She had never considered the possibility of child abduction before, but now the terror loomed large in her mind.

"Maybe I should go back," she worried.

"Genny. Everything will be fine. You know you can't have your eyes on her 24/7."

"No, but I don't have to leave her alone, either!"

"She's not alone. She has an entire team of nurses fussing over her. Didn't you hear them in the hallway? They were all saying what a beautiful baby she is with such a sweet disposition. Trust me. She'll be fine."

Seeing them come into the cafeteria, Cutter leapt from his chair. "What's the matter? Is something wrong?"

"Nothing like that. They needed to run some standard lab work is all," Madison assured him.

"They're going to poke her *again*?"

Finding herself caught between two anxious first-time parents, Madison was happy to change to subject. "Oh, I see you found Laurel!"

"More like she found us. Cade is here, too." Cutter led them back to a table that was already crowded with the four of them.

"Genny! Congratulations on the birth of your daughter!" the petite ER nurse for *Texas General Hospital* said, getting up to hug her friends. "I can't wait to come up and meet her. And Madison, this is an added treat. I didn't expect to see you today."

"I had to come meet my niece." She glanced at the scrubs the other woman wore. "I see you're working today."

"Yes, but Cade brought me a bite to eat. We just happened to see your two guys in here, so we asked to join them. If you'd rather, we can move to our own table."

"Are you kidding? I have pictures!" Genny said, whipping out her phone.

"Hey, Cade," Madison greeted Laurel's boyfriend, who was a detective with the College Station Police Department.

Since first meeting the pair several months ago, their relationship seemed to have solidified and be off to a good start. Madison thought they made a cute couple, even though their careers sometimes put them at odds. Laurel was a dedicated nurse and wasn't about to back down for anyone when it came to her patients' wellbeing, even if that person wore a badge. Cade was an equally devout officer of the law who wouldn't allow suspects to hide behind the excuse of a hospital gown. Madison knew that if their relationship were to survive, it would be because both were determined to make it work.

"Madison." The blond-haired detective smiled. "Please, take my seat. I'll grab more chairs." Brash had already given his to Genny, whose feet looked painfully swollen.

"I'm not sure what strings you pulled to get it done, but thank you for arranging our stay," Genny told the nurse.

"We aren't too full right now, so it worked out for the best," Laurel said with a smile. "And I was happy to do it."

"Well, whatever you did, it's greatly appreciated."

"Just don't stay up all night, admiring your baby. You need your rest," she cautioned.

"I was a little nervous when they wanted to do more tests. She's already staying a day longer than expected because of elevated bilirubin levels."

"That's not uncommon," her friend assured her. "It's normal to run more tests to check levels and liver function before releasing a newborn."

"But she's so tiny, and they keep poking her," Genny whined.

"Just assuring that she's healthy and thriving and not jaundiced."

"Heed my advice," Cade said, leaning across the table in a conspiratorial manner. "Take Laurel's word for it and don't argue. You won't win."

"Very funny," the curly haired nurse said, wrinkling her nose. "But when I'm right, I'm right."

Cade spread his hands wide. "See what I mean?"

"We men never win," Brash said sympathetically.

"Hey, no ganging up. Two lawmen against the rest of us," Madison protested.

"You've proved to be a good detective yourself," Cade commented. In her eyes, it was high praise. "Got any more big cases up your sleeve?"

"Not big, but I do have a new project I'm about to start. A cold case. Have any tips for me?"

"Have patience. Lots and lots of patience. People's memories tend to fade with time, and evidence gets lost or degraded. But, when and if you do finally manage to crack a cold case, there's a special satisfaction in seeing justice finally served."

"Thanks. I'll keep that in mind."

Cutter glanced down at his watch. "Maybe we should get back upstairs," he said worriedly.

"Help me to my feet and lead the way," Genny answered.

"And I suppose I should get back to work," Laurel said. "I'll come up when my shift is over and see that little beauty for myself."

Brash and Maddy remained at the table while Cade walked Laurel back to the ER entrance, and the anxious new parents returned to the maternity ward. "We'll just go up and say goodbye when the baby gets back to her room. Genny said she'd text me," Madison said.

"No problem. Actually, there's something I wanted to talk with Cade about."

"That sounds like my chance to visit the gift shop," she quipped.

"Pace yourself, woman. You've already bought a dozen outfits and one very expensive pedestal dish, and there's still another baby yet to come."

"Whatever." She waved away his concerns. "Pretend it's a fishing lure or a box of ammo."

His dark eyes lit with amusement. "Are you suggesting I buy some? Because I know where all the sporting goods stores are here."

Cade returned in time to overhear the exchange. "Uh-oh," he said. "I recognize a stare-down when I see one. Should I go?"

"Not at all," Madison chirped. "Brash was just insisting I visit the gift shop. You guys visit, and I'll shop."

"Good to see you again, Madison."

"You too, Cade. The Montgomerys may have their hands full for the next few months, but maybe you and Laurel could come to the house one night for supper."

"Sounds great. Let us know when."

Madison left the men with a wave and made her way to the gift shop. After browsing the aisles and finding an adorable stuffed rabbit she couldn't do without, she paid and left, purchase in hand.

She rounded a corner and ran straight into another person coming from the opposite direction. Her eyes widened first in surprise, then concern, as she recognized the man from the estate sale.

He must have turned back around and followed us, after all, she thought.

"Pardon me, ma'am," the man said politely, making a point to step out of her way.

Madison couldn't help but frown. *That's it? After stalking me, trying to break into my car, and then trying to run me off the road less than two hours ago, you're suddenly a gentleman? You're no longer angry? You don't even seem to recognize me!*

"Uh, n—no problem," she mumbled, waiting for the other shoe to fall. Any minute now, he would realize who she was, and he would reveal the nasty side to his personality.

It never happened. The man sidestepped her and went about his way, never once looking over his shoulder. Madison stared after him, wondering what had just happened.

"I don't get it," she muttered aloud. "Granted, today I'm dressed for church, but did I look that bad yesterday? So bad he didn't recognize me now?"

Madison put her hand to her face, wondering how she must have looked yesterday. Perhaps a little sweaty, even in the mild morning heat. She had remembered to fix her hair and wear makeup, hadn't she?

As her fingers touched her cheekbone, Madison had a startling realization. The man didn't have a black eye. Not even a red streak, nor a bruise where the bowl hit his face.

She brightened with a smile.

"See? I didn't hit him as hard as I thought. Maybe he did forgive and forget, and I was wrong about the car today. Just a crazy coincidence and a bad driver."

Straightening her shoulders, Madison was going with that rendition, even if she didn't quite believe it.

5

Monday morning was a flurry of activity.

"Mom, where's my blue blouse?" Bethani wailed through the cell phone.

Already in the kitchen making breakfast, Madison broke another egg into the bowl as she put the phone on speaker. "You have a dozen blue blouses. Which one is missing?"

"My new one with the sweetheart neckline that matches my eyes. The one Trenton says is his favorite."

"I have no idea which blouse your boyfriend likes the best."

Joining in the conversation from where he manned the toaster, Brash said, "It better have a high neck and long sleeves. And buttons in the back."

"Hardy-har-har," his stepdaughter said sarcastically. "You're such a *dad*." She didn't mean it as a compliment, but her stepfather's chest puffed with pride, just the same. "Seriously, Mom. Have you seen it?"

"No. Did you do your laundry this weekend like I told you to do?"

"I didn't have time!"

"And neither did I. Wear something else."

"You are no help," the teen huffed. "Whatsoever."

"Breakfast in ten," her mother reminded her before she hung up.

Brash turned with a smirk. "Sounds like someone's in a mood."

Madison shrugged. "A typical Monday morning."

Her phone rang again. "Yes, Blake?" she asked her son, hitting the speaker button again.

"Do you know where my practice jersey is?"

"I thought the school washed them there."

"There was some sort of plumbing issue in the field house," he said. "They told us to bring the practice jerseys home and wash them ourselves."

"And did you?" his mother asked.

"I thought you did."

"I gladly cook for you, son. I take care of you when you're sick. Your father and I pay for your clothes. But I don't pick them up off your floor, and I don't wash them. That's the least you can do."

The boy sounded horrified. "Do you know how much they're going to reek?"

"Unfortunately, I do." Madison grimaced at the thought. "Bring them down, squirt them with fabric freshener, and toss them in the dryer while you're eating breakfast."

"Is it ready? I'm starved."

"Of course you are. Be down in five."

As she disconnected, Brash smiled. "No wonder Genny wants to take notes. You have this mothering thing down pat."

"Almost eighteen years of experience," she said modestly. "Thirty-six, if you give double credits."

As her own words registered, Madison turned melancholy. "Just think about it, Brash. In a blink of an eye, our children have gone from babies to almost adults. Another blink, and they'll be married and having children of their own! We'll be old and gray, and I'll be cooking for our grandchildren." She looked stricken.

"Sweetheart, you're doing it again. You're stressing yourself out. Take a deep breath and imagine it's one of Blake's sweaty uniforms."

The visual snapped Madison out of her mood. "Why on earth would I want to do that?" she asked.

Her husband grinned. "Because that smell is one thing none of us will miss."

With her family fed and scattered for the day, Madison cleaned the kitchen before going into her office to work. After checking emails and returning a few calls, she made her own call down to the police station.

"Good morning, Vina," she said to the woman in charge. Everyone knew that without the veteran dispatcher and clerk, the whole department would fall apart at the seams.

"And how are you today, Madison? Calling to speak with your husband?"

"I'm fine, and no. I'm calling to speak to you."

"Oh?" There was a note of surprise in her otherwise professional voice. Vina could be a bit intimidating at times, with her clipped tones and air of strict protocol, but Madison had learned she was a softy at heart.

"I'm consulting with Brash on a cold case. The Alpha Bodine case. You're familiar with it, I assume?"

"Of course."

"Do you happen to know if any of the files are there at the station, or are they all at the sheriff's department in Riverton?"

"The hard evidence is at the county. We have a copy of all the paper files here."

"How hard would they be to put your hands on?"

"Not hard at all."

"Could you pull those for me, please? I'll swing by around noon to pick them up, if that gives you time to locate them."

"I know exactly where they are." Was that a sniff of offense Madison heard? "Officer Perry goes through them quite often." After a slight pause, Madison detected a distinct note of caution in her question. "Does he know you're looking into this?"

"No."

The professional coolness slipped from the dispatcher's voice, and the warmth of the real Vina came through. "Don't expect him to take this well when he finds out."

"Why? What does it matter to him?"

"You've met Otis Perry, right? He's a bit proprietary when it comes to his job. He doesn't take defeat well, nor does he warm to opposition."

"But I'm not opposing him. I'm trying to help solve a cold case!" As usual where Otis Perry was concerned, exasperation flooded through Madison. It came out in her voice.

"*His* cold case," Vina pointed out. "One of the very first of his career, and the one he could never solve. It's been a point of contention with him for over twenty-five years. Don't expect him to feel grateful when you start poking around in what he'll deem as none of your business."

"I never expect him to feel grateful toward me," Madison huffed. "But there's nothing he can do about me reviewing the files and consulting on the case. Not if I have his boss' approval."

"Another thing he hasn't warmed to."

Vina couldn't see it, but Madison made a face. "I don't suppose there's any way we can keep this from him?" she asked hopefully.

"We can try. But remember where we live."

Madison sighed. "Maybe you should put the file on Brash's desk, and I'll get it from him. At least Perry won't know right away."

"I'll have it there and waiting by noon. Is there anything else I can help you with?" Already, her professional persona took over.

"Just one thing. Do you have any suggestions where I should start? Anyone I should speak with?"

"Your grandmother is always the best bet. And maybe Virgie Adams."

"Thanks. I appreciate your help."

"Anytime."

The line went silent.

Madison had been dismissed.

Madison stopped by the new sandwich shop in town and picked up lunch to go, which she then carried to Brash's office.

"Knock, knock," she said as she stood outside his door. "Delivery."

"It's open."

She walked in to find her husband at his computer, busily punching in a digital report. "Hey, sweetheart. Just give me a few more minutes, and I'll be done. Have a seat on the couch, and we'll eat there."

"Did Vina leave a file for me?" she asked hopefully.

"Right there on the corner."

"Great. Take your time. I'll look through this while I wait."

Madison laid their lunch out on the coffee table before settling into the cushions with the file on Alpha Bodine. She couldn't help but notice that the manila folder was worn and smudged from repeated use. They hadn't been kidding; judging from the looks of it, Otis Perry was obsessed with this case.

The details were stark and cold. The grandsons had arrived home from school to discover their grandmother lying in a pool of her own blood on the parlor rug. A wooden-handled butcher knife was stabbed into her chest. Just one violent upthrust had punctured her heart and drained her veins.

The photocopied black-and-white photos were hard to look at. Her hair was wound in a neat, gray bun, with only a few strands gone astray. She wore an apron, and a dust rag laid nearby, suggesting she was interrupted while cleaning house. If not for one leg turned inward and the blood around her, it looked like she could have simply lain down to take a midday nap. Madison recognized many of the knickknacks and the mantel clock in the background, having seen them at the estate sale on Saturday, but she saw no artwork on the walls.

"What really happened?" she whispered aloud. "Who killed you?"

"If you get an answer from that photo, I'm hiring you on the spot," Brash said.

She looked up in surprise. "Oh. I didn't hear you. I thought you were still on the computer."

"All done and ready for lunch with my beautiful wife."

"I'm not sure I have much of an appetite now," she said, waving the photo in her hand. "These are hard to stomach."

"Murder is never pretty," Brash agreed. He looked at the picture she indicated. "Tell me your observations."

Madison studied the print in question. "Alpha Bodine appears to have been a well-dressed, well-groomed woman in or around her mid-sixties. Favored an old-school bun and apron while she worked around the house. Her house was nicely appointed and well-kept. The only thing out of place is the body on the rug. No apparent sign of a struggle, if her hair and clothes are any indication. I think the killer may have taken her by surprise."

"Very good," Brash said with approval. "Not everyone would have made the hair connection."

"See that tendril there? It was intentional. This one, on the other hand, got mussed when she fell. If she had struggled with her attacker, her whole head would probably look like that."

"Well noted. Anything else?"

"The clock on the mantel says the picture was taken at 4:27. I don't know what the time of death was, but it appears the blood has had to gel and thicken. That doesn't mean a lot to me, but I'm sure it gave the investigators an estimated time of death."

"It should have," Brash agreed. "But the main investigator was new and untrained and easily excitable. And things aren't like they are on television, especially not here in a small town, and especially not then. It took weeks to get the autopsy results. By then, a lot of key evidence was gone."

"That new and untrained investigator was Otis Perry, wasn't it?"

"None other. But Maddy, he's come a long way since then. I know he has bad social skills, and we like to give him grief, but the truth is, he's a good officer. He regrets how his lack of knowledge and experience may have impacted the case. I believe it's driven him to become the best officer of the law that he can be."

"Are you telling me to tread softly?"

"I'm just asking you not to stomp on the man's pride."

Madison considered his words before nodding. "I can live with that."

"Good. Then you have my blessing to do what you can with the case. Within parameters, of course."

"Of course." She rolled her hazel eyes to the ceiling, waiting for a lecture that never came.

"Now. Let's eat!" her husband said, rubbing his hands together in anticipation.

"Geez. Two days in a row," Madison mumbled under her breath.

"What two days? What row?"

"Uhm, nothing. It's just that this is the second time in two days that I've braced myself for a rant that doesn't come."

"You *want* me to rant?" he asked uncertainly. "Because I can give you a full lecture if you like. Remind you of all the dos and don'ts and lines you can't cross. I can rant all you like."

"No. No need. Forget I said anything."

"Okay." Distracted by the sandwich, he all but salivated. "Is this bad boy mine?" He picked up the biggest of the two hoagies, its paper bulged from an overload of toppings and meats.

"Yes. And your favorite chips." She pushed the package toward him.

"So? Who was the other rant-less soul?"

"Uhm, actually, it was the guy from the estate sale."

He paused from unwrapping his sandwich. "What? You saw him again? When?"

"Yesterday. At the hospital."

"So, he turned around a second time and followed us to *Texas General*? Who does this guy think he is?"

"I think I was mistaken about the car," she admitted. She told him about the encounter in the hospital corridor, and how the man had no apparent recognition of her. "Best of all," she added, "he also had no mark on his face. I guess I didn't hit him as hard as I thought. Just enough to scare him off."

"And you're just now telling me this?"

"Sorry. By the time I got back to the cafeteria, Genny called and said the baby was back in the room. And then we went up, and I got caught up in those adorable dark eyes again, and... well, I forgot."

"You forgot?" He sounded skeptical.

"Holding that sweet baby, it just didn't seem as important anymore."

Brash looked at his wife for a long moment. "But you'll tell me if you see him again? If anything else happens? Rant, let down, or otherwise?"

"I promise."

He returned her words to him. "I can live with that." He finished unwrapping his sandwich as she tucked papers and photos back into the file. "*Now*, can we eat?"

Madison nodded. "Now we can eat."

6

In the hallway of The Sisters High, Trenton Torno tugged on his girlfriend's arm. "Come on, Bethani. It will be fun."

"It's an *art* class!" the girl said in something sounding very near a whine.

"Yeah. You know I'm into design."

"You want to be an architect."

"But it all stems from art. Painting is just a different form of design."

"But it's so... dorky." Not so long ago, she had been guilty of calling him Dork Face, along with half the school. No need to dwell on that now, though. "What if we took photography, instead?" she suggested.

"No one is offering a photography class now," he pointed out pragmatically. "Remember, the guy broke his arm? They're offering a painting class, instead. Besides, aren't you from Dallas? Home to dozens of art galleries? There's nothing dorky about that."

"But they're professionals," Bethani argued.

He flashed his killer smile. "Hey, they had to start somewhere." When she shifted her feet uncertainly, he went on. "Come on, Beth. You know how much I love that mural in your dining room. This is your chance to learn about those brush strokes and shading techniques I'm always raving about."

"Sometimes, I think you're only dating me because of that mural," the blonde pouted.

"Not true." Behind his glasses, his crystal-blue eyes twinkled. "But it does sweeten the deal."

She swatted at him playfully, which he took as a sign that she was softening.

"Didn't I go to the mall with you?" he pressed.

"We were shopping for school clothes."

"Didn't I carry all your packages?"

"Well, yes."

"Didn't I ooh and ahh in all the right places and tell you how beautiful you looked? And when you tried on that hideous purple top, didn't I skillfully draw your attention to the blue one, instead?" her boyfriend cajoled.

"I guess so."

He gave her an amused look. "Did you *really* think I was blown away by a day of shopping at the mall?"

"But you needed clothes, too!" she protested.

"I'm a guy, Bethani. If it's clean and semi matches, it's good enough for me."

"My twin doesn't even care if it's clean," she grumbled. She straightened the collar of Trenton's button-down shirt. "But you have to admit. You've become a much sharper dresser since we started going out."

"Because you tell me what to wear," he snorted. "Again. Clean and near-match is good enough for me." Not to be distracted by the hand lingering on his chest, he said, "Now. What about the art class?"

"I don't know..." She was still reluctant to agree.

"It's something we can do together," Trenton said, tucking her blond hair behind her ear.

"We went to the mall together."

"That was something you wanted. This is something I want. Can't you do it for me?"

Bethani huffed out a breath. "When you put it like that..."

He smiled at her again, charming her all over again with his brilliant smile. "You'll see. This will be fun. You may come to appreciate shading techniques as much as I do."

"You are such a dork!" she accused him, pushing on his chest.

"Not just any dork," he reminded her smartly. "The dork with the hottest girlfriend at Sisters High."

"You can lay off the hard sell. I'll sign up for classes with you."

"No hard sell," he insisted. "Just the truth."

Bethani shook her head in mock exasperation, but secretly, she was thrilled. Trenton was right. He wasn't just any dork. He was the smartest, cutest dork she had ever known, and she was proud to be his girlfriend. Not for the first time, she thanked her lucky stars that Mrs. Hathaway had 'stuck' her with the unwanted partner during health class last year. Bethani still didn't know how it had happened, but quite unintentionally, she had fallen hard for Trenton Torno. Dork face and all.

"Where do we sign up?" she asked wearily.

"Right through here." He took her hand and pulled her into the nearby classroom.

He had hoped to find the room empty, so that he could steal a kiss and show her how much he appreciated her sacrifice. He knew Bethani was a cheerleader and had better things to do than attend art classes with her boyfriend.

It was a new program the school had implemented this year, where people from all walks of life taught mini sessions on their area of expertise. The classes were optional, and the services were on a volunteer basis, but a last-minute cancellation left their very first offering unfilled. Trenton felt sorry for the poor photographer with the broken arm who was originally scheduled, but he was glad an artist had volunteered to take his place. The teen hoped this class would make Bethani appreciate art the same way he did.

Instead of finding an empty room with a clipboard and sign-up sheet, they found a man sitting at the desk.

"May I help you?" the man asked.

"Is this where we sign up for the art class?"

"Yes." Perhaps realizing it wasn't the warmest of welcomes, the man added, "I hope you're here to join?"

"Yes, sir, if there's still room for two more."

"I think we can fit you in."

The teens approached the desk, where they found a clipboard with only a handful of names on the list.

"Good. A small class," Trenton said. "I like more one-on-one attention, anyway."

The man smiled at the boy's obvious attempt at politeness. "Pardon the shades," he apologized. "I had a long drive last night, and my eyes are sensitive to the light."

"I'm just glad you came," the teen said. "I'm Trenton, and this is my girlfriend Bethani. We'd both like to sign up. Right, Beth?"

Her smile was just a little too bright. "Sure."

"I'm Mr. Raymond. Welcome to Painting with Purpose."

After spending the morning going through the photocopied files, Madison admitted defeat. She picked up her phone and dialed.

"I need your help," she said.

"The words every grandmother longs to hear."

Something in Granny Bert's weary tone didn't match the claim.

"Seriously," Madison said. "I need your help. With a case."

She heard an immediate perk in her grandmother's voice as she cackled gleefully, "Hot dog, it's about time! I told you we'd make a great team. What do you need me to do? Are we going on a stakeout? Do I need to load my shotgun with real buckshot?"

"What? Of course not! But I do need you to help me with some research."

The glee faded. "Research? That sounds boring."

"Not at all. It's just like poking around in other people's business. You're a natural."

"At least you've finally come to appreciate my talents."

"I've often come to you for help with my cases. Particularly for help understanding the background dynamics of my clients. I need your expertise more than ever on this case."

"What's the case?"

Madison didn't want to discuss it over the phone. "I want to talk to you about that. Can I come over?"

"Since when do you ask?" She heard the suspicion in her grandmother's voice. "It's something I won't like, isn't it? Did one of Sticker's ex-wives hire you to investigate his shenanigans? Does he have some girlfriend checking up on him?"

"This has nothing to do with Sticker, Granny. Fix me a glass of iced tea, will you? I'll be right over." She hung up before her grandmother could protest further.

As she drove the few blocks to her grandmother's, she noticed a dark car following at a moderate pace behind her. For caution's sake, she went two streets past Live Oak Street, made a loop, and came down from the other direction. She wasn't surprised to see the dark sedan idling at the corner.

Remembering her promise to Brash, Madison reached for her phone to tell him of this newest development. Before dialing, she also remembered that her husband was at the county courthouse today. The car would be long gone by the time he drove there from Riverton. And so far, all the car was doing was sitting there, pulled over at the curb.

She decided not to put her grandmother at risk. She continued down the street, turning in front of the car and heading back toward the Big House. She tried to see the driver, but the person had their head down, consulting their phone. She couldn't determine whether it was a man or a woman.

With a sense of relief, she also noticed a dent in the sedan's front bumper. She was relatively certain that the car from the weekend hadn't had that.

"You have an overactive imagination," she told herself aloud.

Even so, she watched in her rearview mirror as she took a long and convoluted route back to her grandmother's house. By the time she arrived, there was no dark sedan in sight.

"It's about time you got here!" her grandmother chided. "What took so long? All the ice has melted in your tea."

"I'm sorry. I thought I saw the car again, but I guess I was mistaken. Just in case, I took the long way around." She sat at the scuffed kitchen table, stalling by taking a sip of watered-down tea.

"The tea is fine," she reported. She took another leisurely sip, trying to find the right way to approach her grandmother.

"Well? You may as well spill the beans!" Granny Bert said impatiently. "What is it, girl?"

"I'm working on a new case. Which is actually an *old*

case. A cold case, to be exact. One that I know you may be particularly interested in."

The other woman was quiet for a moment before asking, "It's Alpha's murder, isn't it?"

"Yes, ma'am, it is. I know now that it holds a special significance for you, and I thought you might like to help me with it."

Her grandmother appeared to be caught between skepticism and grief. "You think I can do now what I couldn't do then?"

"I think a lot of things have changed in twenty-nine years. There's new technologies, new techniques."

"You have access to those?" Her grandmother pinned her with a look.

"Not exactly. But if we find enough new evidence, Brash could officially re-open the case, and *he* has access to those."

"And how are we supposed to find this new evidence?"

"I don't know yet. That's why I need your help."

Granny Bert pushed back from the table to pace the floor.

"Don't you think I tried? She was my friend, and I failed her. I did everything in my power to get her case properly investigated. I called in favors. Pushed buttons. Pulled strings. The sheriff's office spent less than two weeks here, questioning witnesses and collecting evidence. Then a bigger case came along, and they hightailed it out of here, faster than a jackrabbit running from a hound." She slid her hands against one another with a smack and an exaggerated motion.

"After that, it was just me and Otis working the case, and you can imagine how that went. He resented me for bringing in outside investigators and was so busy pushing me away, he hardly had time to get any real work done. It all went downhill from there."

"Is that why the two of you have always butted heads?"

"Well, that, and the fact that he's an idiot."

"There is that," Madison agreed.

"I just don't know what we can do now, girl. Not after all this time."

"Emotions were running high then. Everyone was understandably shocked by her violent death. I know time has a way of dimming memories, but it also has a way of softening the pain. Maybe in retrospect, someone will come forward with new evidence. Something that was overlooked before."

"I'll do what I can to help," Granny Bert said, "but I hate to see you getting your hopes up. It's been over a quarter of a century."

"Yes, I know that. But it won't hurt to try, will it?"

Her grandmother drew in a weary breath. "Okay, sign me up." Her voice sounded a bit shaky when she asked, "Where do we start?"

7

"Aunt Genny, she's gorgeous!" Bethani enthused, staring down at the baby in her arms. "I'd give anything for that coloring."

"You've held her long enough," Megan protested. "It's my turn."

"Don't worry, girls," Genny laughed. "I see many, many hours of babysitting in your very near futures."

"I'm game," Megan assured her. "You can ask my mom. I was always a good sitter for my little brother."

"I'm sure you were."

"Mom never would give us a little brother or sister," Bethani pouted, shooting her mother an accusing glare.

"Two babies were plenty for me!" Madison insisted.

"It's not too late, you know," Genny said with a sweet smile. "You and Brash could have a baby of your own. It would be fun to raise our children together."

"You had your chance, sister, and you missed it," Madison quipped. "I'm too old to start over now."

"You're not too old to go through the motions, are you? Don't think I didn't hear Brash's comment in the car the other day."

"Genny!" Madison cried as color flooded into her cheeks. "There are children present. *My* children."

"Come on, Mama Maddy," Megan teased. "We're old enough to know the score. Don't think we don't see those scorching looks that pass between the two of you."

"Or how early you go to bed some nights," Bethani added knowingly.

Madison feigned innocence. "We both work hard. Plus, we're getting older. We need our rest." Defying her claim of old age, she hopped agilely to her feet. "I'm thirsty. Is anyone else thirsty? Why don't I go to the kitchen and fix us something to drink?"

"I'm not sure Mary Alice will let you in," Genny warned. "She's barred me from my own kitchen. Imagine what she'll do when I actually give birth."

"Enjoy the pampering. You're entering the last phase of your pregnancy, and it may be rough, especially with a newborn to care for."

"I've barely gotten to hold her," Genny sulked. "Hope has entirely too many aunts, cousins, and one very greedy father."

Madison laughed. "That, too, will fade. Enjoy the help while you have it."

"You want your baby back, Aunt Genny?" Megan offered, though reluctantly.

"Oh, don't mind me. It's just my hormones getting the better of me. I can share."

"While you're sharing," Madison said, moving an ottoman toward her friend, "why don't you put your feet up and relax?"

"Now you sound like my mother-in-law!"

"We speak from experience."

Genny rested her blonde head on the back of her chair for about ten seconds. "Has anyone been by the café? How are things going? Are they taking care of things? Remembering to write the daily specials on the board?"

"I haven't been by," Madison told her, "but you have an excellent staff. You've trained them well. I have no doubt everything is running like a well-oiled machine."

"Trenton and I dropped in yesterday after school," Bethani said. "Other than a bunch of dirty tables and a newly installed jukebox, everything looked fine."

"What!" her 'aunt' cried in alarm.

The teen flashed a cheeky smile. "Just kidding. Not a dirty table in sight. And no jukebox, either. Although, you might consider adding one."

"No, thanks. I like to set the mood for the diners with music I select myself."

"Hey, speaking of music," Megan said. "I heard next semester a couple of members from the Cowboycandy Band have volunteered to teach some of those new alternative classes at school."

"Wow. I bet that classroom will be packed!" her stepsister and best friend replied. "There's only going to be like ten or eleven people in our art class."

"That's because it's art," Megan said with a twinkle in her eye.

"What I said. But Trenton is so excited about it, I just couldn't say no to him."

"You'd better be able to say no to your boyfriend," her mother said sharply.

"Mo—om! What a thing to say! I thought you liked Trenton."

"I do. And as much as I adore my newborn niece, I have no intentions of becoming a grandmother, anytime soon."

Bethani rolled her eyes. "I think I'll take my chances and brave the kitchen. Now *I'm* thirsty!"

Megan relinquished the baby and went with her stepsister, leaving Madison and Genny alone with the swaddled infant. After more oohs and aahs over Hope's delicate features and sheer beauty, Genny managed to talk about something other than her newest love.

"Any more trouble with your mystery stalker?" she asked.

"As a matter of fact, something else did happen. With all the excitement around the baby, I guess I forgot to tell you."

"So? Don't keep me in suspense! What happened?"

"After you and Cutter left the cafeteria to check in on Hope, Brash and Cade were talking cop shop, so I made a visit the gift shop. I rounded a corner, and who do you think I ran into?"

Genny's surprised gasp startled the sleeping infant in her arms, but Genny rocked her gently back to sleep. "The man in the baseball cap?" she guessed.

"Bingo. But get this. He didn't even recognize me. And he didn't have a black eye, either."

"How can that be?"

"I'd like to think I didn't hit him as hard as I thought and therefore didn't leave a mark. Going with that option, I was mistaken about him being in the car behind us and trying to run us off the road, and after Granny Bert's stunt with the shotgun, he decided to let bygones be bygones."

"Wait, wait, wait. What car? When did someone try to run you off the road?"

"Oops. Guess I forgot to mention that, too." Madison gave an apologetic grimace before explaining, "On our way to the hospital that day, there was a black car behind us trying to pass. I thought it looked like the same car the man from the estate sale drove. It appeared he was trying to run us off the road or, at the very least, was a terrible driver with a bad case of depth perception."

"Could you see the driver?"

"Not really. But when Brash flashed his badge, he— or possibly she, if I was mistaken— backed off and turned around in the middle of the road."

"Wow. I had no idea," her friend murmured. After mulling over this new information, something else Madison said registered in Genny's mind. "And your other options?"

"There's a rumor the man ended up in the hospital with a concussion. Going with that option, maybe it messed with his memory, and he simply didn't recognize me."

"Was he wearing a hospital gown?" Genny quizzed.

"No. Regular street clothes, no cap."

"Did he looked injured or confused?"

"No. Come to think of it, he had a bag in his hand. Takeout of some sort."

"Most people don't pack a lunch to visit the ER. And patients don't run out to get their own food."

"That leaves us with Option Three."

"Which is?"

Madison threw both hands up in a gesture of helplessness. "I have absolutely no idea what is going on!"

"I agree. Three is the most likely bet. None of this makes any sense."

"None at all," Madison agreed. "I have no idea why some random man wants to get his hands on that painting badly enough to stalk me, break into my car, run me off the road, and then act like he doesn't even recognize me, not two hours after the road incident!"

"I know it doesn't make you feel any better, but maybe he's some sort of a psycho. Or a druggie."

Madison shot her friend a sardonic smirk. "You're right. It doesn't make me feel any better."

8

Two days later, Granny Bert's living room was filled with some of her dearest and oldest friends. Literally. Other than Madison, there was no one under the age of seventy-five in attendance.

The smell of BenGay and liniment mingled with the more enticing aroma of pumpkin bread, lemon cookies, and salsa queso with tortilla chips. While Granny Bert manned the coffee station, Madison moved among the attendees, passing out glasses of iced tea and mint-sprigged water. She interrupted more than one woeful tale of some woman's latest surgery or a debate over the best place to buy denture paste. The favored topics of the day were who was in the hospital and the juiciest rumors floating about town this week.

When everyone had a filled plate, Granny Bert called the meeting to order.

"I know you're wondering why we're all here today," she began.

"It's about getting Jean Applegate to speak at the library, isn't it?" Verna Bishop guessed. "I spoke with her daughter-in-law just this morning, and—"

"This isn't about Jean," Granny Bert cut her off.

"Is it about finding volunteers for the new career

program at the high school? None of the teachers are certified, mind you, but volunteers who've promised to give classes two days a week on their chosen profession. It's something they're trying with the curriculum this year. My son-in-law is the new vice-principal, you know," Cora Sikes said proudly.

"You may have mentioned that a dozen or so times," their hostess replied dryly. "No, this isn't about the new curriculum."

"Oh, I know!" Harriett Evans bounced up and down from her place on the sofa. It was no easy feat for a woman of her size, and it nearly upset Cora's overflowing plate. "It's about Arlene Kopetsky's new support duck!"

That gave Granny Bert pause. "What in tarnation is a support duck?" she asked.

"It's like a support dog, except it waddles. And quacks," the woman offered helpfully.

"I know what a duck is!" Granny Bert snapped. "What I don't know is how that qualifies as support."

"It's for emotional support," Wanda Shanks pitched in to educate them. "Poor Arlene's gone through such a rough patch lately, what with breaking her leg and that ordeal with her daughter. And then there was that mishap on the cruise... She says she's nervous going out in public these days. Her therapist suggested she get an emotional support animal, so she chose a duck."

Madison sidled up to her grandmother and whispered, "Should I even ask what happened on the cruise?"

"No!" her grandmother hissed. "Don't get her started. And leave it to Arlene to choose a duck. She always was a bit of a quack."

"I think it's helped," Wanda went on. "I saw her out in her yard yesterday, walking her duck on a leash. She's very well trained."

"Arlene, or the duck?" smirked Granny Bert's best friend Sybil. She and Granny Bert were still miffed at Arlene for taking Wanda along on the cruise for free, while asking them to pay their own way.

"The duck. Her name is Lucky. Lucky Ducky."

"Now I've heard everything," Granny Bert huffed. "But, no, it's not about Arlene and her latest shenanigans for attention. This is about something far more serious. Something important."

"If it's about your granddaughter's heroic act, disarming that thief at the estate sale," Pearl Huddleston broke in, "I'll gladly act as a character witness if it goes to trial. I was there. I heard the man wound up in the hospital and was threatening to sue. But the way I see it, she did us all a favor."

Madison barely heard the murmurs of agreement or the wave of support washing through the room. Her mind snagged on something Mrs. Huddleston said.

Was that why he was at Texas General *on Sunday?* She wondered. *Had he been at the hospital to check in? Did he have a concussion? Is that why he didn't recognize me?* Her imagination raced with new worries.

Madison wasn't too distracted to notice that Granny Bert didn't deny the claim. Instead, her grandmother used it to steer the conversation in the right direction.

"I'm glad you brought up the estate sale, Pearl, because that's what I want to talk to you about. Alpha Bodine."

"Oh!" Harriett said with sudden inspiration. "You want to put a statue up in her honor. Why, I think that's a lovely idea!"

Beside her, Janet McSwain straightened her original 1960s pillbox hat and smiled serenely. "Alpha Bodine. Why, I haven't heard that name in ages! I surely do miss her." She shook her gray head, rattling a few memories loose and tangling the past with the present. "I had lunch with her just last week. We were having a lovely visit, until the principal stopped by our table."

When her friends would have downplayed the gaffe, something about the statement intrigued Madison. She encouraged the former schoolteacher to go on. "Oh? Did the principal bring bad news?"

"There was some sort of trouble with that grandson of hers. Again. I swear, that Garwin is always in a peck of trouble! He's a troublemaker, that's what he is. And *mean*. I'm telling you right now, that boy has a mean streak a mile wide." She nodded her head emphatically, threatening to send her headpiece toppling.

Eager to hear more, Madison asked, "Really? Why do you say that?"

"There's a look in his eyes. After so many years in the classroom, I can just tell. You mark my words. That boy is nothing but trouble. He's dealt poor Alpha nothing but heartache, and I fear there's more to come." She turned to Lavonne Wynn. "You know the boy, right? Isn't he the one who killed your cat?"

"I had forgotten all about that," the other woman said in wonder. "But yes. We always suspected it was him. We didn't have proof, but he seemed to enjoy torturing animals and giving them grief."

"Grief." Janet echoed the word. "That boy is nothing but grief. By the way, Lavonne, how's your little boy doing?"

An uncomfortable silence filled the room. Everyone knew Lavonne's 'little boy' was now expecting his first grandchild.

For her part, Lavonne handled the situation with grace. "He's fine. Here, can I take that for you?" She indicated Janet's empty plate. "Now, let's hear what Bertha has to say, shall we?"

"Thank you," Granny Bert said, clearly exasperated with all the distractions. "As I was trying to say, I know we all remember the tragedy of Alpha's murder. It rocked our small community, and a shadow of sadness still hangs over us today. I don't know whether any of you remember this or not, but tomorrow would have been Alpha's birthday. With her home going up for auction and her belongings sold for piecemeal, I thought this might give us an opportunity to keep her memory alive."

"It *is* a statue!" Harriett squealed in excitement, clasping her hands together.

"No, it's not a statue. Even if it were, some blame fool would just vandalize it or tear it down. What I'm talking about is a monument of sorts, but an intangible one. I thought we could keep her legacy alive by telling stories here today and sharing our memories of her."

"What a sweet gesture," Janet said, tears gathering in her eyes. "I can't wait to tell Alpha about it."

After an uncomfortable silence, Sybil raised her hand. "I'll go first. I remember the time Alpha and I decided to go over to Louisiana to try to track down that no-good husband of hers. Lawdy, at the sights we saw in those New Orleans swamps! We had us some good eatin', too. Cajun food that was out of this world!"

She launched into a tale about wading through grassy bayous and alligator-infested swamps, en route to a shack where Lester was said to be holed up. All they found was trash and evidence of a recent and hasty departure, but Alpha swore the place held the lingering stench of her absentee husband. The two women took their time returning home, enjoying an extended weekend on Bourbon Street. Sybil claimed some details were too embarrassing to share, although she eventually allowed her friends to coax them out of her.

"I'll go next," Wanda offered, waving her arm in the

air like she was back in a classroom. "Bertha, do you remember the time the three of us took that painting class from Jean? We got more paint on us than we did the canvas, but, boy, did we have fun!" She went on to tell a few of the humorous incidents that happened during the sessions.

"You know," Granny Bert's sister-in-law Lerlene Hamilton pitched in, "Alpha once told me that was what inspired Gordon to start painting. Bless her heart, she never lived to see it, but he went on to become a very good artist. I hear he opened an art gallery in Austin and was very successful for several years."

"Until he got in some sort of financial trouble and lost the whole thing," Virgie Adams tsked. "I hear that's what this whole estate sale and auction stems from. Settling old debts."

"It's a shame to see it all torn apart like this," someone else agreed.

"Sounds more like something Garwin would have done," Janet insisted. "He was the mean one, not Gordon." It was unlike the normally sweet-dispositioned schoolteacher to be so negative. Madison made a mental note to drop in for a visit and hope she found her on a lucid day.

That was what today's meeting was all about. It was all a ruse, of sorts, while still serving a higher purpose. Not only was it to honor Miss Alpha's memory, as Granny Bert said, but it also let Madison glean information into the woman's past without tipping her hand. The last thing she wanted was for the grapevine—the very root of it gathered here today— to get wind of that fact she was investigating the cold case. Depending on what was shared, she would follow up privately with the women she felt could best likely shed more light onto the case.

It was a stall tactic, at best. It wouldn't take long for

one woman to share news of Madison's visit to the next, and soon the entire town would know. Including Otis Perry. But it was worth whatever time she could buy herself. Madison only hoped she could find out some valuable information before the temperamental deputy attempted to shut her down.

"Too bad Arlene couldn't be here today," someone else said. "I know that she and Alpha were friends. There for a while, Lana and Alpha's youngest grandson were sweet on one another."

"Lana Kopetsky was sweet on anything in britches!" Virgie snapped.

"Gregg, I believe was his name," Sadie put in helpfully.

"Garwin, Gordon and Gregg?" Madison questioned, her eyebrows high. "Sounds confusing."

"Alpha used to get their names all tangled up!" Aunt Lerlene recalled fondly. "At one point, she resorted to calling them all three 'boy.'"

"I remember that. Just like the time..."

Stories circled the room, flowing from one person to another. The more she heard about her, the more Madison was convinced that Alpha was one wing short of being an angel. She had certainly earned her halo if all her friends' tales were to be believed.

"That Sylvia was a tonic," Granny Bert said. It was an old expression that meant she was hard to handle and a bit of a headache. The expression amused Madison, who thought that dealing with someone like that *required* a tonic, as in the medicinal kind.

"Poor Alpha didn't know quite how to deal with her," her grandmother continued. "It was always one thing or another with that girl. And then she ran off and left those poor little boys, leaving Alpha to pick up the pieces."

"Whatever became of Sylvia?" Madison asked.

"Does anyone know?"

"I heard she eventually settled down and joined a convent," one woman said.

"Convent?" another smirked. "That girl was no more of a nun than Lana Kopetsky! No convent would have her."

"I heard she wound up somewhere up north. Chased after some man, who left her high and dry with no way to get back home."

"I'm sure he left her high, all right," someone else snickered. "She had a bad addiction. That's why Alpha cut her off the way she did."

"I always did believe that's what happened to Alpha," Cora confided to the group. "I think Sylvia came back, demanded more money from her mother, and killed her in a rage of anger. She was probably too high to know what she was even doing."

"I believe it was a break-in," Virgie said. "I went to locking my doors after that. Which didn't turn out well when I forgot to tell Hank about the locks. He had to replace the doorjamb the next day."

"I never warmed to that theory," Lerlene said. "By all accounts, nothing was taken. Not even her jewelry."

"I remember that gorgeous broach she had!" Janet McSwain said. Her memory may have been hazy, but some details remained sharp in her mind. Fashion was one of them. Remembering the hideous orange and white leather recliner the woman had once 'misplaced' and hired *In a Pinch* to find, Madison thought it a shame that her fashion sense didn't extend to home decorating.

"I still say Lester faked his own death and came back for more money," Wanda Shanks huffed. "He would do anything for a quick dollar. Probably found a way to cash in on his own life insurance policy."

"Or his boy's," Verna said. "They say both of them

died on that boat, but my first husband had a cousin down in the bayou. Swears he saw Benny years later, running a shrimping rig and going by the name Henry Boudreaux."

Madison discreetly entered the information into her phone, along with the other notes she had taken.

"Lord, help us if there's another man like Benny Bodine running 'round!" Sybil said. "I know where his nephew got his mean streak from. Benny was as ornery as they come."

"What would he be now if he had lived?" someone mused. "Sixty, sixty-five?"

"That means Sylvia would be in her mid-sixties, too," someone else observed.

"Old enough to have settled down and straightened her life out, with any luck."

Madison jotted down more notes. She would do a search on both of Alpha's children. And on her grandsons, as well.

"Does anyone know what became of the boys?" she asked.

"Gregg, the youngest, became a therapist of some sort," one of the ladies volunteered.

"He's a school counselor!" Cora corrected, clearly miffed by the confusion between the two occupations. "Down in Port Aransas."

"Not anymore," someone else corrected her correction. "The school was wiped out by that hurricane, and I hear he moved inland, somewhere over by Baytown."

"I hear Gordon is still in the Austin area. After his gallery closed, he went to work for one of those newfangled breweries that are popping up everywhere."

"And Garwin?" Madison asked.

No one seemed to know for certain. Someone

thought he was living down along the coast. The person next to her insisted it was the Texas panhandle, some six hundred miles in the opposite direction. Someone else heard that he went in search of his mother, and the two were now con artists out in Vegas. (That woman had been in the little girl's room when the conversation went around the first time.) Someone else was convinced he was in the state penitentiary. A fifth person believed he had died in a motorcycle accident.

"To be honest," Verna Bishop said, "I don't think anyone ever cared enough to keep up with him. Like Janet said, he was nothing but trouble."

9

With her family gone for the day, Madison made a large cup of coffee and fueled herself for a day at the computer.

The case file on Alpha Bodine's murder was scant, at best. There were statements from a handful of local citizens, none of which contributed any viable information. The coroner's statement, confirming death by knife wound. A few well-defined fingerprints retrieved from the scene, all belonging to the victim or her family. The same photographs Madison had seen in Brash's office. A very short, inconclusive list of suspects. Even fewer interviews. A few jotted notes of speculation, but no hard proof of guilt or innocence for any person of interest or suspect.

The folder also included a rap sheet for her daughter, Sylvia Marie Bodine. *Did that mean she had been a suspect in her mother's death?* Madison wondered. There was no shortage of ink on the report.

On her eighteenth birthday— the very day she lost the anonymity of being a minor— Sylvia was arrested for disturbing the peace, establishing a pattern that would continue for the next three to four years. She was often named as a participant in a peaceful protest rally gone wrong. She was cited for various misdemeanors and small crimes. Damaging public property. Petty theft. Instigating fights, primarily at bars and nightclubs. One count of solicitation. Two counts of fraud. Two counts of forgery. Possession of marijuana. Criminal trespassing.

Madison had to wonder how many times her name had been withheld for similar events during her early years.

After a tumultuous end to her teens and early-twenties, there was a sudden improvement in Sylvia's arrest record. Madison assumed it correlated with the time she spent at the 'hippy camp' Granny Bert mentioned and Sylvia's new relationship with Jesus.

Clipped behind the rap sheet were two pages of photocopied pictures. One was a shot of three women selling fresh vegetables at a roadside stand. The taller woman in the middle was circled in red ink. Another shot featured a group of people handing out pamphlets outside an abortion clinic in Waco. Again, red ink encircled a tall woman with dark hair. There were two more photos of the same or similar group engaged in community-service type activities: working to man the lines at what appeared to be a mission and providing water during some sort of marathon race. Red circles made it easy to spot Sylvia Bodine among them.

While such acts were commendable, something about the photos bothered Madison. She noted that all the women looked the same. Faces scrubbed clean, hair hanging long and free except when held back with a flower. Their clothes were simple and loose fitting, most often made of light-color woven fabrics. She couldn't help but notice how many of the young women looked pregnant in the photos. The men by their sides were carbon copies of one another. Long hair, beards and mustaches, tunic-styled shirts and jeans, with sandals upon their feet.

Granny Bert may have called it a hippy camp, but to Madison, it looked more like a cult. Not only was it during the decline of the social movement, but there was a uniformity and oneness about the photos that defied the very essence of the hippy lifestyle. While traditional hippies strove for freedom of expression and to break free from the binds of conventional standards, these pictures smacked of repression. These people lacked individuality and reminded Madison of a flock of well-matched sheep.

On a whim, she searched for cults active in the mid-to-late seventies in the general vicinity of Central Texas. Only two looked like possible candidates. She earmarked the pages for later perusal, an uneasy feeling settling between her shoulder blades.

What if Sylvia Bodine had been involved with a cult, and Miss Alpha's death were somehow connected? The thought was unsettling.

Skipping forward to research the brother, Madison found far less on Benjamin (Benny) Bodine. He played Little League as a child and was on the baseball team once he reached high school. There were a handful of sports articles and photos in the local newspaper that came up when she entered his name, along with details of the memorial service after his presumed death. Outside of that, Benny's life in The Sisters had been largely unremarkable.

She followed the link to an article that appeared in the Louisiana newspaper at the time of their boating accident. According to it, the Benny and his father were last seen as they set out for a day of shrimping. A storm blew in by afternoon, upsetting the Gulf and creating a strong undertow. A distress call from their boat went out at 6:17 that evening, but the connection was soon lost. Rescue search teams were unable to locate the boat, and there was no sight of either man in the turbulent waters. After an extensive search, the vessel was feared lost at sea, and the men were eventually presumed dead. Seven years later, the courts made it official and declared them both deceased.

Madison used an age-progression app to imagine what Benny Bodine might look like at his current age of sixty-three.

"Definitely not the guy from the estate sale," she assured herself aloud.

"Are you talking to me?"

The sound of Derron Mullins' voice startled her. She hadn't heard her employee come in. "Derron! Where did you come from?"

"Well, now, that's debatable," the petite man answered, propping one hand upon his slender hip. Always a sharp dresser, his artful pose could have come from the cover of a sleek fashion magazine. He tapped a manicured finger to his delicate chin in fake contemplation.

"Rumor has it I was born, but I can't imagine any man actually sleeping with the Dragon Lady. Or with her sleeping with a man, for that matter." He wagged his blond brows suggestively. "Therefore, I'm currently vacillating between my mother being impregnated by artificial insemination, my tiny little self being delivered in a cuddly velvet blanket by a well-groomed stork, or the crude but humble possibility of being found beneath a cabbage leaf."

"I think you can safely mark those last two off your list," Madison remarked dryly.

Being deliberately obtuse, he said, "I do thank you for asking, however." He flashed her a charming smile as he sashayed over to his desk.

"I didn't hear you come in."

"You were busy talking to your computer screen.

What has your rapt attention this morning? And do remember not to frown so, dollface," he advised. "We have to watch those frown lines, you know." He rubbed at the smooth area between his own eyes, the wrinkles no doubt erased by one of his favored beauty products.

Since Derron was known as the go-to fashion guru around town, she let his remark slide. "I'm working on a new case. Sort of."

"That's what I like about you," he said with a sardonic jeer. "You're so precise."

"For your information, it's a cold case. New to us but old to the rest of the world."

Intrigued, Derron rubbed his hands together in giddy anticipation. "Ooh, how exciting! Just like on television!"

"You may want to put on mittens and make a cup of hot chocolate. I'm talking ice cold."

He ruffled his hands along his peach-colored silk shirt. "I feel the chill all the way over here."

"Jest all you like. I can see why this case was never solved. There's like zero leads."

"What's the case?"

"The unsolved death of Alpha Bodine. She was murdered in her living room over twenty-seven years ago."

"Is that what yesterday's meeting at GB's was all about? I may have been out of town, but I heard all about it."

"With Wanda Shanks as a roomie, I'm sure you did." The thirty-something, openly gay male rented a room from her grandmother's eighty-something-year-old friend. The pair made for unlikely housemates, but the living arrangements suited them both well. "And in answer to your question, yes. I have follow-up visits planned with some of the attendees, but today I'm scouring the net for leads I may want to chase down. So far, the list is depressingly short."

"I can pump Wanda for any information she has," he offered. "If Miss Arlene knew her, that's two less you have to interview."

"That would be great. And yes, your next-door neighbor knew her quite well, from what I understand. By the way, what's this I hear about her having a support duck?"

"Lucky Ducky? Cute enough duck if you go for the waddling sort, but she and Tango aren't compatible."

"So, parrots and ducks aren't compatible?"

"You know Tango has a flair for dramatics. Beautiful coloration. A glorious wing span. Impressive intelligence. A growing vocabulary. Lucky Ducky is just so... ducky." His slender shoulders shivered ever so slightly in judgmental disdain. "He just waddles and quacks. There's no foundation for friendship," he all but whined.

"Miss Arlene must have seen something special about him," Madison pointed out.

"No," Derron argued. "She just wanted to be the first person in The Sisters to have a support duck."

Madison cringed at the thought of it becoming a fad among local citizens. "I think—I hope—we can safely assume she'll be the *only* person in The Sisters to have a support duck."

"One could hope." Derron yawned, signaling he had tired of the conversation.

Each went to work at their own desks until a familiar *bing* signaled someone was at the public entrance gate. Derron engaged the intercom to speak with them.

"May I help you?"

"Yeah," a man's voice said from the other end. "I, uh, I'm here to spray for cockroaches."

"I can assure you, sir," Derron told him in a frosty

voice, "we do not have cockroaches."

"If you wanna keep it that way," the man shot back, "you'd better let me in."

Derron deferred to his boss. "Dollface? You know anything about an exterminator coming this morning?"

Following another faint but possible trail on the computer, Madison looked up in surprise. "What was that?"

"Bug service. Do you have one scheduled for today?"

"I have no idea. I thought you handled that."

"I do. According to my notes, he's not due for another two weeks."

"Tell him to come back then."

Derron turned back to the intercom. "We're not scheduled for service for another two weeks. I'm afraid you'll have to come back then."

"You don't have sugar ants like everyone else in town?" the man persisted. "We've seen an outbreak of them in the past week. And fleas. Fleas are hopping all around, with or without pets. It's your house, but if it was me, I'd want to stop 'em before they got started."

Nostrils flaring in distaste, Derron looked at Madison with beseeching eyes. "He has a point, dollface. I detest fleas."

"Why didn't he call before now?" she asked irritably. "And I wish he would make up his mind. First it was cockroaches. Then sugar ants. Now it's fleas. Does he even know what he's spraying for?"

"Do I look like the man's keeper?" Derron complained.

"That depends," she taunted. "Is he good looking?"

"I can't tell. He has on a ball cap. It's pulled too low to see his face."

Something about the words *ball cap* set her senses

on alert. "Let me see!" She whirled around to consult the hidden screens behind a built-in panel. She tapped a few buttons to pull the image in closer.

She couldn't tell for certain, but she thought it might be the man from the estate sale. "No!" she hissed. "Don't let him in! Call the extermination service and ask if they sent someone to this address."

Addressing the man again, Derron asked him to please wait for a moment.

"I ain't got all day," the man snarled. "You want me to spray for bugs, or not?"

"We'll take the not option. Good day to you, sir." Derron clicked the intercom off, not bothering to hear the man's reply. Able to read his lips, Madison knew he had a colorful reply.

For one moment as he idled at the gate, she feared he considered ramming through the bars. After a long inner debate, he jerked the gears into reverse and gunned the engine. His flair for peeling out of the driveway was all too familiar by now.

"The nerve of that man!" Derron huffed.

"I think that was him. The man from the estate sale."

"The same one who showed up at GB's? The one who followed you and Brash to the hospital?"

Madison's nod was vigorous. "I can't be certain, but I think it was him."

"What is it with that man? He's certainly persistent!"

"I think the real question is *what is it about that painting?*" Madison said, her lips pursed in thought. "I don't think it's *me* he's interested in. It's the painting."

Derron let out a low whistle. "That must be some painting!"

"It is good," she allowed. "Very good. But not worth all this trouble he's gone to, trying to steal it out from under me."

"Maybe it's one of Remington's early pieces. Or a Charles Russell original."

"There's no signature, so I have no clue." Glancing at the screen once again to assure herself the intruder was gone, Madison stood and went to a panel alongside the fireplace. Applying slight pressure, she eased the hidden panel aside until it tucked in behind a bookcase. She carefully pulled the picture from her secret hiding spot.

"How'd you do that?" Derron demanded. "Since when is there a hidden panel in the wall?"

"For about a hundred years now," she answered wryly. "This is just one of many." Seeing the intrigue light his blue eyes, she immediately squashed any notions he might have. "Don't! Don't even think about searching for the others. And don't you dare go around tapping and poking at walls. Forget you just saw this."

"Sure. That would be like forgetting I saw Wanda and Arlene in their itty-bitty, polka dot bikinis. Trust me. It's not a pretty sight!"

Madison cringed. "Thanks a lot. Now I have that image in my mind."

"No problem. Just forget it, like you told me to do." His smile was flippant.

"Fine," she relented. "But you have to promise me. Do *not* tell a soul about the secret passage."

"That's a *passage*?" he squealed in delight. "Where's it go?"

"Never mind. Juliet Blakely had a thing about hidden passageways between rooms and little hidey holes everywhere. Some have been blocked for safety purposes." She shuddered, recalling the twisted staircase leading from the master bedroom down to a crude sub-basement room. The reason for the passage had been as twisted as the stiles. It, along with the hidden tunnel entrance in the main basement, had been permanently disabled. Hoping to divert his attention, Madison asked, "Do you want to see the painting or not?"

"Of course I want to see the painting!"

She carried the framed canvas to his desk, deliberately placing her body between him and the visible passage entrance. Derron was easily distracted by shiny objects and, with any luck, a well-done painting.

"Wow," he said. "I'm no fan of Western art, but that's an exceptional piece!"

"It is. Look at the shading and the way the shadows are perfectly aligned. It's very well done."

"I know enough to know the big names. Remington. Russell. Terpning. Are you certain this isn't an original piece?"

"I know nothing about it. It caught my eye, so I bought it for Brash."

Derron examined the piece more closely, the same way Madison had done a dozen times. He even looked at the back, hoping to find some missed clue or piece of evidence.

"Nothing," he reported.

"Exactly. I have no way of knowing who may have painted it."

"Either it was done by one of the masters when they first got started," Derron surmised, "or there's a hidden message painted into it."

Madison frowned. "Message?"

"Sure. Just like the hidden code in that flower drawing the little girl gave you at the airport. Maybe this had a hidden code, too."

Madison retrieved a magnifying glass from her desk and approached the canvas. She tilted her head from side to side, trying to decipher a pattern she may have previously missed. "I don't know what I'm looking for," she admitted.

"Maybe you can't see the forest through the trees," Derron murmured. "Look in those tree trunks. See anything there?"

"Yes. Minute details like bark and spidering branches. No words or codes."

"What about in the grass?"

She traced over each section, still coming up empty.

"Maybe we're supposed to connect the dots on the bull's hide. Look. That one's shaped a bit like a heart."

"So is that one. That one, too, even if a bit deformed." Madison shook her head. "I don't think that's it."

"If it's not in the hide, maybe it's in the horns."

Madison went over them from tip to tip, examining them through the magnifying lens. "I don't think so. Honestly, if it's a message, it's so well hidden, I can't see a thing!"

"If not a message and not a famous artist, what could it be?" Derron pondered. "The frame is nice, but that's not real gold."

"Maybe it's stolen. Maybe it came from a famous museum or a private collector, and this man is desperate to get it back."

"We could do an internet search, I suppose."

Madison flashed him a bright smile. "That's a great idea. Thanks for volunteering!"

"Wait. I didn't volunteer. I meant *you* could do an internet search."

"I can't. I'm working on the cold case. Remember?"

"I'm starting that display case project for Lamont Adams," he countered. "Remember?"

"I sign your paycheck," she one-upped him. "Remember?"

"Tiny as it may be," he grumbled.

"You don't start the display cases until Monday. That means you have the entire weekend to dedicate to your search."

"I may have plans this weekend."

"You don't," she reminded him sweetly. "Just an hour ago, you were whining about being bored with Lover Boy out of town this weekend. By the way, who is it this week?"

"His name is Nate, and he's divine," Derron answered, getting a starry look in his eyes. "Ramon was fun, but sometimes I think he only wanted me for my hair. He said it was the perfect palette for his color and style creations. He was so shallow, always wanting to talk about himself."

Does he even hear himself? She wondered silently. *This, from the most self-absorbed person I know.*

"Sounds like your perfect match," she muttered.

He looked aghast. "Are you serious? He was more into himself and his hair designs than he was me. Nate, on the other hand, is smitten with me." Crossing his hands over his heart, he sighed dreamily. "I think he could be The One."

"I think I've heard this before. Like maybe ten or twelve times? I've lost count."

"Since when did you become so jaded?"

"Several boyfriends ago. Yours, not mine," she clarified. "Tell me this. What's Nate's full name."

Derron hesitated for a fraction of a moment. "Nate Hot Stuff Cutie," he replied smugly.

"You don't even know this last name! And you think he could be The One?" she hooted.

"I've said it before, and I'll say it again. Now that you've met and married your soul mate, you've become cruel to those of us still searching." With a sniff, he stood from his desk and assumed a wounded expression. "I think I'll raid your refrigerator. Maybe

I'll find something to soothe my wounded soul."

"Good luck with that. You know Blake. My son doesn't believe in leftovers."

"I'll make that determination for myself," he said, sweeping from the room with his nose still in the air.

Madison simply shook her head with patience, waiting for him to be good and gone. Hearing his footsteps retreating, she returned the painting to the hidden passage and slid the panel back in place, out of sight and out of Derron's mind.

If he weren't so good at his job, she wouldn't tolerate his antics. But the truth was she couldn't do all she did without him. The prissy little man was personable and possessed excellent people skills. He was a whiz at organization and keeping her life straight. In addition to his prowess in the office, he was a superb carpenter and gave each job the same thought and attention he gave to choosing his wardrobe. Obsessing over perfection was just one of his specialties.

Returning to her desk and the digital trail she had been following, Madison glanced again at the alarm panel. The man was long gone by now, but a shadow remained on her mind.

Whatever this man wanted, it surely meant trouble.

10

If Friday nights stood for high school football in the South, Friday afternoons stood for high school pep rallies.

Bethani and Megan were both cheerleaders and Blake was on the football team. As a proud parent, Madison attended as many of the rallies and actual games as she could. Today was no exception.

With the painting stashed out of sight and Derron back from his foraging expedition, she concluded what little research she could do on the computer. She and Derron reviewed the next week's schedule before she left for the afternoon.

Madison grabbed lunch from *New Beginnings* and took it to Genny's house, where she was able to get in cuddle time with baby Hope before the pep rally started. Caught by a train, the gymnasium was already packed when she arrived.

Lucky for her, Shannon Aikman had saved her a seat in the bleachers. The perky blonde waved to catch her eye as Madison scanned the sea of excited faces. As she wove her way toward Megan's mother, she marveled for the hundredth or so time how strange it sometimes felt, being so close to her high school nemesis. Time did, indeed, change one's perspective.

During her time at The Sisters High, Shannon Wynn had been her arch rival. It seemed that everything Madison was interested in—classes, extracurricular activities, the legendary Brash deCordova—Shannon was interested in, too. The two girls ended up competing with one another for almost everything. Brash was two years ahead of them in school, his reputation bigger than life on and off the football field. Like practically every girl in school, Madison had a huge crush on him, but it was Shannon who caught his eye. For that, Madison could never forgive her. It simply reinforced Maddy's immense dislike for the snooty blonde.

It wasn't until she came back to The Sisters— according to her grandmother like a hound dog slinking under the front porch, tail tucked between its legs and ears hanging low—that she finally saw Shannon in a different light. Without the lens of rivalry coloring her vision, she discovered Brash's ex-wife was completely different from the girl she remembered from high school. Shannon was warm and gracious, and she had done an excellent job co-parenting the daughter she and Brash shared.

Megan was a confident, well-rounded young woman. Best of all, the vivacious, auburn-haired beauty had four parents who adored her and who all got along well with one another. Ironically, Shannon was now married to Matt Aikman, Brash's best friend since grade school and Madison's ex-boyfriend. The vicious cycle of high school rivalry had come to an end and, as unlikely as it seemed, Madison now considered Shannon one of her closest friends.

"Hey, girl," Shannon greeted her. "I was about to give up on you."

Madison slid into the empty seat with a breathless

explanation. "Running late."

The blond looked sympathetic. "Busy day?"

"Aren't they all?" Madison countered with a smile.

"And then some! Business has picked up at the studio. I'm having trouble keeping up."

Shannon had recently opened *Moments in Time* in one side of Juliet's old movie theater. Adjacent to the photography studio, none other than Carson Elliot now held dance lessons and recitals on the other side. The renowned dancer had a long list of accomplishments to his name, including coaching contestants for television's popular *Dancing with Dreams* and serving as a judge one season. Already, their foray into the arts was a big success in the small community, drawing customers from all around the state.

"I can see why. You're a very talented photographer."

"Thank you, Maddy. That's such a sweet thing to say." Shannon touched her arm affectionately, just as their attention was drawn to center court. The cheerleaders came out one at a time, cartwheeling their way into the limelight.

Halfway into the program, Madison felt the eerie sensation of someone watching her. She looked discreetly around to find the culprit. All eyes were on the court. No one seemed to take notice of a mom sitting in the stands.

Noticing how she squirmed, Shannon shot her a strange look. "Are you okay?"

"Uhm, sorry. These seats aren't as comfortable as they used to be."

"Crazy, isn't it?" Shannon agreed. "Especially since we now have more padding on our backsides. Or I do, at any rate."

A few minutes later, Madison spotted a lone figure leaning against the gymnasium wall in a far corner. She couldn't be certain, but the man seemed to be about the same size and height as the man from the estate sale.

"Shannon?" she asked, nudging her friend with her elbow. "Do you know that guy standing down near the concession stand?"

The other woman peered across the distance. "I don't think so. Should I? Who is he?"

"No idea. But he reminds me of the guy from Miss Alpha's estate sale. Megan told you about that, right?"

"She didn't have to," Shannon said, the edges of her mouth itching with a grin. "My great-aunt Lavonne beat her to it. I hear you wallop a mighty punch, girlfriend. I'm glad you and I never got into it in high school!"

"I still can't believe I did that." Madison put her hands to her inflamed cheeks.

"Sounds like he had it coming." Already taking pictures with her zoom lens and professional-grade camera, Shannon swung her focus to the man in question. She snapped a few shots in rapid succession. "I'll get these sharpened up and send them to you. Maybe they'll help you identify the creep."

"Thanks. I appreciate it."

"Ooh. Here comes the girls' new pyramid routine," Shannon said, drawing their attention back to the cheerleaders.

When Madison looked again, the man was gone.

The game was out of town that night. Ever the faithful parents, Madison and Brash drove the hour-plus distance to watch the Cotton Kings battle against the Leon Cougars. It was a close game, but the Kings came out the victor by a narrow margin of three points.

It was late when the bus arrived back in The Sisters from Leon County. By the time the team showered, deposited their uniforms in the locker room, and dispersed to their vehicles, it was well after midnight.

Blake crawled into his pickup and turned the key. Nothing happened.

He tried again.

Still nothing.

He pulled out his phone and dialed Brash. The teen knew that one or both of his parents were still up. His mom made it a habit to stay up until her children were safely tucked inside their nest each evening. Game nights were no exception. On the rare occasion she went on to bed, Blake knew Brash took his turn as mother hen. He took a chance that tonight was his stepfather's turn.

"Daddy D? Can you come to the field house and pick me up? My truck won't start."

Brash never let on that he had already fallen asleep. He cleared the sleep from his throat and said, "Sure. Be right there."

"Thanks."

"Anytime. You know that."

Seeing her husband throw back the covers and pull on his jeans, Madison put away her electronic reader and asked, "What's wrong? Are you going on a call?"

"That wasn't dispatch. It was Blake. His truck won't start."

"I hope it's nothing serious."

"If it's not an easy fix, we'll just leave it there and go back for it tomorrow." Tucking his t-shirt into his jeans and fastening his belt, he said, "Why don't you go on to sleep? We'll be fine."

"Are you sure?"

"Absolutely. If I don't see the problem right away, we'll just wait till daylight. He may only need a jump for his battery."

Stifling a yawn, Madison murmured, "If you're sure…"

"I am. Get some sleep. Love you."

"Love you, too. I may just doze here until you get back. Text me to let me know what's going on."

"Will do." He brushed a kiss across her lips and headed for the door.

She heard him engage the security locks as he left. Hoping not to fall into a deep sleep, she settled back against the pillows and closed her eyes. A few winks wouldn't hurt.

A few minutes later, a beep roused her. She sat up in bed when she heard the second beep. Had she missed Brash's text? A glance at her phone told her he hadn't been gone long enough to be returning already.

Someone or something triggered the alarm, she realized, *and it wasn't Brash.*

The state-of-the-art security system had been compliments of the *Home Again* team and was one of her favorite features about the remodel. The alarms were very sophisticated and were set in stages. The closer an unknown entity came to the house, the more intense and the more frequent the beeps became.

At the third and decidedly more piercing beep, Madison got out of bed and padded over to the built-in armoire which hid, among over things, a command station identical to the one in her office. She pulled the monitors up to see where the breach occurred.

The flashing monitor focused on the rear of the property, past the old caretaker's cottage that was currently in a state of disrepair. She and Brash had vague plans of someday redoing the small structure as a guest house or office, or perhaps an apartment if one of the kids wanted a place of their own during or after college. The trees were denser in the rear, but the gardener kept the briers clipped and the foliage trimmed. Cameras kept the area under surveillance.

Someone, however, had managed to breach the metal fence and drop onto the grounds of the Big House. Any minute now, they would come close enough to trigger the floodlights. A few more steps, and a silent alarm would call the police station.

Madison wasn't waiting that long. She hit redial on her phone.

"Brash! Someone scaled the back fence and is on the property!"

"It's a setup, Maddy." His voice was intense. She heard him turn his head to bark out orders to their son. "Blake, call 9-1-1 and tell them there's an intruder at the Big House." To her, he said, "Someone tampered with Blake's starter. They wanted me out of the house. What can you see?"

She peered into the monitor, squinting to make sense of the shadows. "A figure in black, moving alongside the old caretaker's cottage." Her eyes traced the person's movements.

"We've got dispatch on the line. They'll be there in less than four minutes. Have the floodlights come on yet?"

"No. Wait. Yes! Right now."

"What's the person doing?"

"He pulled back into the shadows. I can barely see him."

"Can you tell anything about him?"

"He's wearing a baseball cap." Fear invaded her heart and tampered with its rhythm. "Brash, I think it's the man from the estate sale! And I think I saw him today at the pep rally."

"Try to keep him in your sight. We're leaving Blake's truck here and are already headed your way. So is Officer Schimanski."

"Hurry but be safe!"

"I'll stay on the line with you. Can you still see him?"

"I think so. It's hard to tell, even with the floodlights. I think he's slipped around the cottage."

"Another monitor should have picked his movements up."

"What if he gets inside the cottage?"

"Then we have him cornered."

"There!" Brash couldn't see her, but she pointed to one of the other screens. "He's gone around behind the cottage and headed back toward the fence."

The Big House encompassed a full city block. Accessing the rear of the property would be easy enough. "I'll try to cut him off. Blake, take over while I call for backup."

Blake caught the phone mid-air as Brash tossed it his way. He was already on his police radio, barking out orders for someone to cover Randolf Street. For all they knew, there were two intruders on the property.

"Hey, Mom. You hanging in there?" the teenager asked his mother.

"I am. What happened to your truck?"

"Daddy D says someone tampered with the starter. Nothing that can't be undone, but we're leaving it for tonight, especially after getting your call."

"I'm sorry, Blake. I never meant to drag you into this."

"Into what?"

"Honestly? I have no idea!"

"Then how can you be sorry?" he reasoned. "We're not far from home now, Mom. We'll be there in just a few minutes."

"And Schimanski is turning onto Second," Brash broke in. "Perry will come in from the rear."

"He's having trouble getting over the fence," Madison reported. "The lights have come on back there, and I can see him." She watched as the man struggled to latch onto a rope dangling from the top of the fencing. "He has a rope tied from the other side, with a handhold. He can't quite reach it. Oh, wait. No! He did! He managed to grab it and pull himself up!" In dismay, she watched the man shimmy up the railing and disappear over the top. "He's getting away, Brash! I can't see a car, but he's gone over the top and is on foot. He's running toward the library."

Brash relayed the news through the radio.

"They'll get him, Mom," Blake assured her. "One way or another, Daddy D will get him."

11

As a former college football coach, Brash liked to analyze each play from the night before at Saturday morning's breakfast table. He and Blake would create strategies and scenarios for different reactions and subsequent outcomes. In Madison's eyes, it was overkill, but she loved seeing their heads—one blond, one dark auburn—bent together in a moment of father/son bonding. Gray had always been too busy to even come to the kids' events, much less relive them in minute detail the following day.

This Saturday, however, there was little talk of the night's previous game. All talk was about the events taking place afterward.

Despite the best efforts of the Sisters police, the intruder escaped. It was as if he vanished in the night. One moment, Madison saw the dark figure running into the darkness, and the next moment, he was gone.

"I think he either knows the area well," she told her husband again that morning, "or he staked it out before scaling the wall."

Brash wore a grim expression as he lowered his coffee cup. "I imagine it was a bit of both," he said. "He had to have studied the timing and placement of the security lights. I'll change the settings to do a random rotation."

"You can do that?" his wife asked in surprise.

His signature half-arch of the brow/half-smirk was answer enough.

In the process of finishing the last of the eggs, Blake paused before stuffing his mouth. "Why do you think he's local?"

"He knew exactly how to escape," Brash answered.

"Couldn't he have scoped that out, too?"

Brash hesitated before answering. "There's a few escape routes only locals know about. Old-timers, mostly."

Madison shook her head in rebuttal. "This guy wasn't an old-timer. And are you saying there are *more* tunnels around here? More than the secret one in our basement?"

Brash put his hand over his heart. "I plead the fifth."

Blake perked up, his blue eyes sparkling with intrigue. "Secret tunnels? Where?"

"Some secrets are best left secret."

"Come on, Brash," Madison protested. "You can't dangle that kind of information and not give us something more."

Rather than answer, he masterfully redirected the conversation. "We're getting off track here. We were discussing the intruder. No matter how he escaped, the fact is that he did. Now we have to find him. Can you remember anything else about him? Any pronounced limp, or a guesstimate of his size?"

"I can't even be certain it was a man. Like last time, it could have been a woman."

Blake broke in with a sardonic, "Does anything about that sentence strike you as strange? Like, are we the only people in town that attract danger? This is the second person to scale the fence and get into the yard.

Does that happen to other families? You're already a dead-body magnet, Mom. Was that not enough for you?"

Madison closed her eyes and drew in a calming breath. She didn't dare admit to her son that she had often wondered the same thing herself. Why *did* these strange things keep happening to her?

"Eat your breakfast, Blake." It took great effort not to snap out the words. She turned to her husband, intent on getting more information out of him about the tunnels. A cacophony of noise broke her attention. Her cell phone rang, Blake's phone buzzed with a message, and Brash's police radio squealed as a static-filled voice came over the air.

Madison tuned out the radio as she answered Bethani's call.

"Mom! You'll never believe what happened!" The teen sounded breathless.

Since Bethani had spent the night with Megan, Madison hadn't filled her daughter in on the previous night's excitement. Now it sounded as if she had some news of her own to share. "What happened?" she asked.

"Someone broke into Shannon's car last night! They did something to the battery so the alarm wouldn't go off when they busted her driver's side window."

Mention of the disabled battery put Madison on high alert. Sitting up straighter, she caught enough of the dispatcher's words to know it concerned a call at the Aikman house. "That's terrible! Did they steal anything?"

"Mama Matt went out to get Shannon's camera bag and found the window broken. Apparently, they took her whole bag, camera and all!"

Remembering the photos Shannon had taken yesterday at the pep rally, Madison couldn't help but gasp. "They—They stole her camera?"

"And it was brand new!"

"That's terrible," she murmured again, her mind already in a whirl. Whoever the man in the baseball cap was, he hadn't taken kindly to having his picture snapped. More than simply donning dark clothes that blended into the night, he had gone to great lengths to keep his identity hidden.

Who was this man, and what did he want? The thought distracted her attention as Bethani rattled on about the break-in.

She was hesitant to tell her daughter about their own troubles, but she had a right to know. As chilling as the thought was, Bethani could very well be the man's next unwitting target.

"I need to tell you something, Beth. Something happened here last night, too, and I think it was the same guy. Someone tampered with Blake's truck in the school parking lot. When Brash went to help him, a person—presumably the same one—scaled the back fence and sneaked onto our property. The motion lights scared him away before Brash or the deputies could get here. He didn't do any damage, but I'm pretty sure it was the same guy that broke into Shannon's car."

"Why, Mom? What's going on?" Madison could hear the fear in her daughter's voice.

"I don't know, baby girl. But I want you to stay extra vigilant. Watch your surroundings. Tell Megan to do the same. Try not to go anywhere alone."

"Now you're scaring me!"

"I don't mean to scare you. I just don't want to take any chances. Until we know who this guy is and what he wants, we have to take every precaution." She accepted Brash's hurried kiss as he fastened his service belt and clamped his cowboy hat onto his head.

"I'm coming home!" the girl wailed.

"How about if I come get you? Matt and Shannon need to be there when the police arrive. Brash just went out the door."

"Okay but bring Blake with you. You don't need to be out alone either," Bethani reminded her.

"Don't worry about me, sweetheart. Let me clean up the kitchen, and I'll be right over."

Disconnecting, Madison blew out a deep breath. *What, indeed, was going on?*

With the twins in tow, Madison swung by her grandmother's to make certain nothing had transpired at her house the night before.

"Nope," Granny Bert reported. "Me and the girls went to *Montelongo's* for fried fish and 'ritas. After that, we went back to Sybil's for a game of rummy and more margaritas. I got back here in time to catch the news and know the team won." She turned to Blake. "Good job last night, boy. You got in some good yardage."

Madison patiently waited as the two discussed the game. The elderly woman promised to be at the next game, which was slated to play on the home field. When she turned her attention to Bethani, asking about new cheers, Madison helped herself to coffee.

"How's that new program working out?" Granny Bert wanted to know. "Cora Sikes is going around bragging about how her son-in-law thought up the whole thing, turning career day into a class all its own. I hear you're taking art."

The teen lifted a shoulder. "It was Trenton's idea. You know he's into that sort of thing."

"Learned anything yet?"

"I now know how to properly hold a paintbrush. Who knew there was a right way and a wrong way?"

"Wow," her brother scoffed as he bit into an apple. "Showing real genius there, sis."

"You study how to hold a stupid ball, so what's the difference?" she shot back.

"The difference is a career."

Bethani's reply dripped with sarcasm. "Because there's never been a famous artist before."

"You can barely draw a stick figure. Don't stake your future on an art career."

Using a stern voice, Madison broke in, "Knock it off, you two."

"Ah, let 'em go," her grandmother grinned. "I've missed their daily squabbles."

"You can borrow them anytime you like," Madison replied sweetly.

"I really do want to know more about this new class," Granny Bert said. "Who's the teacher?"

"His name is Mr. Raymond. The first class was supposed to be photography, but the original guy was in some sort of car wreck and broke his arm. Shannon didn't hear about it in time to volunteer to take his place. Somehow, this Mr. Raymond heard about the program and said he'd do a painting class, so they switched up the schedule."

"Is he any good?"

"I've seen some of his work. I guess he's okay," she said with a shrug. "Trenton was impressed."

"But we all know Trenton has questionable taste," Blake muttered. "Look who he's dating."

"He's gracious enough to overlook the fact that you're my brother," Bethani retorted. She spared his comment little attention, turning back to Granny Bert. "He says he's sold enough of his works to get by. The place he worked at closed, so he's sort of between jobs.

His aunt or somebody lived here like a hundred years ago."

Madison eyed her daughter skeptically. Bethani was known to exaggerate. "Literally a hundred? Or just before your lifetime?"

"At least twenty or thirty years ago. He says a lot has changed since he used to come here. Since it seems to me like both towns are stuck in time, I'll have to take his word for it."

"He's right," Granny Bert said. "A lot *has* changed. Not the least of it is this crime wave we're having! I think your mother messed up the karma when she punched that guy in the face last week."

"You're blaming this on me?" Madison balked.

"You gotta admit. A lot has happened since then." She ticked off the items on her gnarled fingers. "Someone tried to break into your car, right outside on my curb. Now they've broken into Shannon's car and taken something. Somebody tampered with Blake's truck. Somebody tried to run you and Brash off the road. Somebody jumped the fence at the Big House and trespassed on your property. Somebody cut wheelies in Lavonne Wynn's yard and crushed her petunias. And all of this since your little boxing match last Saturday!"

Madison was incredulous at her grandmother's accusation. "How could I have possibly influenced some kid to ruin Miss Lavonne's yard?"

"Never said it was a kid," her grandmother sniffed. "Could have been this fella in the baseball cap."

"Who ran you off the road?" Blake asked, eyes narrowed. "And when?"

Madison glared at her grandmother. "Thanks, Granny. I hadn't told them that." To her children, she played down the facts. "It was last Sunday, and it was nothing. Really. Some guy trying to pass us on a curve. Brash flashed his badge, and they backed off. I'm sure it was all a coincidence.”

Her son looked dubious. “I know I made a crack this morning about you being a magnet for danger, but I was just kidding. I’m not blaming you or anything,” Blake said, darting a frown toward Granny Bert. “But I do kinda agree that this could all be connected. It sounds like this could be the same guy.”

“We can’t rule out the possibility,” she agreed. “That’s why I want everyone to remain extra vigilant. I have no idea who this man is or what he wants. If this is his idea of carrying out a grudge, he has serious anger issues, and I don’t want you two anywhere near him.”

“All because of something at a garage sale? That’s crazy,” Bethani insisted.

“About as crazy as Arlene Kopetsky having a support duck,” Granny Bert grumbled. “Wanda wanted to invite her for fish last night, but I told her I was allergic to down. Whoever heard of a support duck, of all things!” She shook her head in disgust.

“That reminds me,” Madison murmured, almost to herself. “Derron is following up a few leads for me today.”

“What’s Derron have to do with it?” her grandmother barked. “I thought Tango and that duck didn’t get along.”

“They don’t. But you mentioned Miss Wanda, and he *is* her roommate. Anyway. He’s looking into the possibility that the painting was stolen. That, or if there are any known unsigned, early works from one of the masters floating around out there.”

“I still can’t imagine why Alpha had a Western painting in her home. It just wasn’t her style.”

“But her grandsons used the house for storage after that, and one of them did own an art gallery. Maybe that’s where it came from.”

“That would make sense,” Bethani said, pitching

into their conversation. "Maybe the artist wanted his painting back. Maybe he felt cheated out of it when the gallery closed."

"He's going to rather drastic measures, don't you think?"

"Maybe he stole it originally," Blake offered, "and the mob is after him to get it back."

Madison hastily protested. "Let's not get carried away!" She had enough to worry about, without entertaining thoughts of organized crime.

"Where was the art gallery?" Bethani asked. "Mr. Raymond may know something about it. I don't remember where he said he lived before, but it wasn't around here."

"You're just trying to suck up to the teacher to impress your boyfriend!" Blake accused.

"I don't need to suck up to my boyfriend. We're already dating," his twin reminded him.

Madison made an exaggerated effort to look at her grandmother. "And you missed this? Seriously?"

"Give it time," Granny Bert said sagely. "You'll know what I'm talking about."

12

Derron's investigation turned up no relevant information. Nothing tied the longhorn painting to any known lost or stolen piece of art. With that angle at a dead end, Madison went old school.

Armed with the notes she had taken at Granny Bert's and the scant details gleaned in the case files, she started the next phase of her investigation on Monday morning.

"Thank you for letting me drop in like this," she said at her first stop.

"Oh, I'm happy to see you, dear," Lavonne Wynn insisted. "We didn't get time to properly visit at Bertha's. There was too much hub-bub going on."

With a wry smile, Madison agreed. "It was a rather talkative group, wasn't it?"

"Some of the girls don't get out much anymore, I'm afraid. When they do, they take advantage of some quality gossip time. And that was such a thoughtful gesture for your grandmother to make. A wonderful tribute to Alpha." A smile lingered on the older woman's face as she remembered her late friend.

Madison almost felt guilty about the subterfuge and the true reason behind her visit today. Not enough to come clean, of course, but badly enough to feel a twinge of regret. She put extra effort into visiting with her grandmother's old friend for no other reason than to visit.

After a good chat, Madison subtly shifted the conversation. "From what I understood at Granny Bert's, you had some interaction with one of Miss Alpha's grandsons. Garwin? Is that right?"

"Yes. That's right." Her face tightened, as if she had tasted something sour. "Our places butt up to one another in the back corner. For years, Alpha wasn't only one of my closest friends, but one of my closest neighbors. After those boys came to live with her, though, things changed between us."

Madison was sincere when she said, "I'm sorry to hear that."

"She had her hands full, that's for certain. It couldn't have been easy for her, raising those boys alone. I only had the one myself, plus the girls, but Allen was a handful. I can't imagine how she did it with three." Lavonne shook her head in wonder before continuing, "Allen was friends, of sorts, with the older two, but more so with Gordon than Garwin. There was just something about that one... The kids took to calling him Garwin the Barbarian, given his tendency to brag about trapping and killing small animals."

"As in... kittens?"

"Not at first. He preferred small game like rabbits and squirrels. I'm not talking about setting snares and enjoying your kill over a campfire. Those are common enough rites of passage for any country boy. But Garwin seemed to gain an unhealthy pleasure from torturing his prey before putting it out of its misery. Allen said he was obsessed with animal cruelty."

Madison's nose curled in disgust.

"I kept a couple of momma cats around, so we were

prone to have a litter of kittens at any given time. After those boys came to live with Alpha, I noticed my kittens disappearing at a faster rate than normal. I didn't think much of it at first. Allen accused Garwin a time or two, but to be honest, I thought it was more a case of childish bickering than anything."

"What changed your mind?"

"The junior high science class had a pet gerbil. The students took turns caring for the animal, and on Garwin's week, the gerbil came up sick."

Even before hearing the details, Madison knew she wouldn't like what she was about to hear.

"There was some question of what he may have fed it, mostly because of comments he made in the lunchroom. Something about experimental feeding habits. No one could ever prove he deliberately harmed the pet, but it died shortly after that. At any rate, he took credit for its death, apparently making a big joke of the whole ordeal."

"That's horrible!" Madison cried.

"My boy thought so. Garwin didn't take kindly to his judgment and, soon after, we had another litter of kittens come up maimed or missing."

"Maimed?"

Lavonne nodded, a grim expression on her face. "One had its ear bloodied and torn. We figured it got tangled up in barbed wire or brier bushes. A few days later, another kitty came up with a deep cut on its paw. Knowing how curious the little critters can be, we just thought they had found something interesting to explore and gotten themselves into some close scrapes."

"I assume something more happened?"

"The last two went missing for a few days. Only one came back. By the time it reappeared, its leg was maimed, and the poor little guy was in serious shape."

The older woman cleared her throat before lowering her voice and admitting, "The, uh, marks on it looked deliberate."

Madison was appalled. "Garwin?"

"Like I say, the boy liked to brag. I suppose he thought it made him look rough and tough, picking on innocent animals. He kept making remarks about it in front of Allen, until finally it ended in a fist fight."

"Did you ever talk to Miss Alpha about it?"

"I did. She admitted Garwin was having a particularly difficult time adjusting to his mother's abandonment, even though he had been with Alpha for quite a while by that time. She said he had been acting out and that she would have another talk with him."

"Did it stop after that?"

"In a way, I suppose it did." Almost reluctantly, Lavonne admitted, "Halloween wasn't far away. Someone must have thought we didn't have enough decorations in our yard because they decided to string my black momma cat up from a tree."

"That's terrible!"

"After that, Allen didn't have much to do with any of the Bodine boys. The truth is, it put a strain on all our friendships, mine and Alpha's included. I had no proof that Garwin was responsible, and Alpha had enough to deal with as it was. If his bragging was to be believed, the boy graduated to bigger and more challenging prey. He took to the woods and shot anything that moved." Lavonne put up a hand. "Don't get me wrong. There's an ethical way to go about hunting and putting meat on the table. But there's nothing ethical about killing for the sheer fun of it. Nothing was safe around here. It wasn't just birds and deer. More neighbors started to complain. First a rooster was stripped of its feathers and strung up on a fence. Then a pig was tied and tortured in a pen."

"No one reported it to the authorities?" Madison asked, aghast.

"Sure, they did. But there was no proof of who did it. Before long, folks started to say it was the work of a cult. Rumor had it that most of the animals had a similar mark on them. Folks said it was a cult sign. About a month before Alpha's murder, an entire herd of Jerry Don Peavey's goats were slaughtered in the field. They said the sign was there, too, and looked a lot like the crude tattoo Garwin had carved into his own arm."

"Surely, the police questioned the boy!"

"That's the trouble. He was a boy. A minor. I know Alpha believed she did the right thing but protecting the boy may have done more harm than good. He never paid for the damage he inflicted."

"So, he never learned to become a decent human being," Madison deduced.

"It would appear that way."

"And the other two brothers?"

"The youngest, Gregg, was the best of the lot. He went on to lead a normal, productive life. The verdict is still out on Gordon. He did well for himself opening that art gallery and all, but there's the matter of the failed business. It can happen to the best of us, but I don't understand why he would risk Alpha's home place like that."

Maybe because his grandmother was dead and gone? Madison thought to herself. *Maybe because it was his and his brothers' inheritance to do with as they pleased? None of them lived there. None even used it as a vacation home. Why not use it as collateral?*

Madison glanced down at her watch. "I've taken up enough of your time, and I still have several errands to run. Thank you for talking with me."

"Anytime, dear. And bring Bertha with you next time."

"I'll do that," Madison promised.

The next stop was Janet McSwain's. Madison could only hope she caught the former schoolteacher on a lucid day.

"I was just making cookies, dear. I know how much you and your classmates love them, and they're a good incentive to study harder."

Okay, so maybe not so lucid, Madison thought as she stepped across the threshold. "If this is a bad time, I can come back," she offered.

"If you're hoping I'll give you the answers to tomorrow's test, you're out of luck. I haven't started on my lesson plan yet."

"I wouldn't dream of cheating," Madison assured her.

"Oh, I'm not accusing you of cheating, dear. I know Bertha and Joe raised you better than that. Have a seat, and I'll fetch those cookies."

"Please, I don't want to bother you."

"No bother. I'll be right back."

Madison didn't smell any cookies baking, but she politely waited for her hostess to return. A few minutes later, Mrs. McSwain came back with two glasses in her hands.

Without missing a beat, Madison smiled and took the frosty glass. "Perfect."

"You wanted to talk to me about something?"

Her direct question unsettled Madison. Was that a good sign, or a bad? "Uhm, yes. The other day at Granny Bert's—Bertha Cessna," she added, just to be clear, "you mentioned some sort of trouble with Garwin Bodine."

"Garwin Bodine. Now, that's a name I haven't heard in years! Whatever happened to that boy after his grandmother's unfortunate death?"

"I have no idea. I hoped you might know."

"No, I can't say that I do. He was a peck of trouble, though. I can tell you that."

"What kind of trouble?"

"Always into mischief. The older he got, the more serious the trouble. Some said he was a devil worshiper and liked to sacrifice animals at the altar."

"I hadn't heard that before." She had to question the validity of the statement, given Mrs. McSwain's compromised memory.

"Following in his mother's footsteps, I say. That cult she joined was nothing but a bunch of heathens. She tried getting her hooks into her son and lure him into the cult with her."

While Lavonne Wynn had mentioned a cult, she hadn't mentioned Sylvia being part of it.

"What can you tell me about Sylvia? Did you have her in class, as well?" Madison asked.

"Oh, yes. I taught her and her brother. Sylvia was bright enough, but she lacked ambition. She didn't care about her grades or making a good impression."

"And Benny?"

"Let's just say he was less fortunate than his sister," the former teacher said diplomatically. "But he was good at baseball. He played with my son, before Donny Ray went off to college on that football scholarship. Benny had a good arm and a strong, steady swing."

Not for the first time, Madison marveled at how some facts remained lodged in the woman's memory banks while others, like the absence of her late husband's atrocious recliner, completely escaped her attention.

"Someone mentioned that Lester and Benny could have faked their deaths. Do you think that's possible?"

"Absolutely not! Neither was bright enough to carry through with such a complex scheme."

"What else do you remember about the Bodine family?"

"I remember that Gordon was more subdued than his brother. Don't misunderstand. He wasn't an angel, by any means. I do believe he had a devilish streak of his own, but he layered it behind good manners and a winning smile."

The hallmarks of any good con artist, Madison silently noted. *Maybe he* was *guilty of shady business dealings.*

"Oh?" she asked the former teacher. "How do you mean?"

The question seemed to fluster Mrs. McSwain. "Well, I, uh, remember a time... That is to say... Will you excuse me, dear? I think I smell my cookies burning." The elderly woman came easily to her feet and hurried into the kitchen.

Curious, Madison followed her to the door and peeked inside. She watched as the woman stopped and looked around, seemingly to remember her intentions. After a moment, she went to the refrigerator and took out a package of Oreos. With a smile, she sniffed the package and deemed them done. As she transferred them into a plastic container, Madison knocked on the door before intruding in her space.

"I can see you're busy, so I'll let myself out. Thank you for the lemonade."

"Are you sure you don't want a cookie? Fresh from the oven," the older woman beamed.

"Thank you, but I'm good. You have a nice day."

"You, too, dear. See you in class tomorrow."

As Madison turned away, she discreetly wiped a tear from her eye. Mrs. McSwain's oscillating mental status was hard to watch.

She didn't dare imagine how difficult it must be to live with.

13

Madison's last visit of the day was to see Virgie Adams, who was certainly no stranger to Madison. The older woman's husband Hank had grown up with Granny Bert and had been a pallbearer at her grandfather's funeral. Despite a few bumps in their relationship—including the nasty matter of their son and grandson trying to kill Madison while renovations were underway at the Big House—the couple had remained good friends with the family. Madison had no problem with dropping in unexpectedly for a visit.

"Maddy! What a nice surprise! Is Bertha with you?" Virgie peered around her, hoping to catch sight of her old friend.

"Just me this time. I hope I'm not interrupting anything?"

"Not at all," she insisted. "Come on in."

"Something smells good."

"I've got a roast in the crockpot. It's still too hot to fire up the oven, but the crockpot does a good enough job to suit Hank."

"I love my crockpot," Madison agreed. "And it definitely beats heating up the kitchen."

Virgie wrinkled her nose. "My husband also has a

weakness for cookies, and those aren't so easy in a pot. I've mastered a decent microwavable cake in a cup, though. Top it with some good old Blue Bell Homemade Vanilla ice cream, and he's a happy man."

"I'll have to get your recipe for that." Thoughts of the former schoolteacher crossed her mind. "I went by to visit Janet McSwain earlier. I hadn't realized she was quite so bad. She thought she was baking cookies in her refrigerator. It's a wonder she's still living by herself."

"It's a downright shame, that's what it is!" Like Granny Bert, Virgie believed in speaking what was on her mind. "I don't know why Donny Ray allows her to live alone. She needs constant supervision. It's a wonder she hasn't burned that house down around herself."

"Does he realize how bad she is?"

"It's hard to imagine how he could miss it. But living away like he does, he may not realize how far-fetched some of her tales are. When she talks about her students in present tense, he may believe she still substitutes from time to time." She pondered the thought for a moment. "Maybe you're right. Maybe someone should intervene. I'll bring it up at Bunko. Maybe if we all went to him, he would understand how serious the situation has become."

Madison didn't point out that she had made no such suggestion, even if she had been thinking it. "Mrs. McSwain said something that I wasn't sure how to take. She mentioned something about a cult. She said Sylvia Bodine was in one, and that one of her boys was following in her footsteps. Do you know what she was talking about?"

"She probably meant Garwin. I suppose it's human nature to try to understand someone's worst traits. Explanations may make us feel better, but they don't change the facts. And the fact is that some folks, like

Garwin, are just flat-out mean. Rotten plumb to the core."

"There's no truth to the cult?"

"I didn't say that. Would you like some tea, dear? Now look who's forgetful!" Virgie berated herself for failing her hostess responsibilities.

"Thanks, but I'm fine."

"Are you sure? It's mighty hot out today."

Relenting more for Virgie's sake than her own, Madison nodded. "A glass of water would be nice."

"I'll just be a jiffy."

When the older woman returned, Madison guided the conversation back on track. "Are you saying there was some truth to the cult rumor?"

"There was always the rumor. Like I say, folks have a way of trying to make sense of things we don't understand. No one could understand how Sylvia could just run away the way she did, even after those boys were born. It was easier to believe some evil force influenced her. Even easier to think it took hold of her boy, as well."

Without mentioning names, Madison pressed forward. "Mrs. McSwain wasn't the first person to mention a cult. I heard something about dead animals. Several were found with disturbing signs carved into them."

"That was the talk at the time," Virgie agreed. "I never saw them for myself, but I wouldn't doubt it. I figured it was more the work of a bunch of kids. Garwin was smart enough to play on people's fears and create a panic for his own amusement."

"But you don't think it had to do with a cult?"

"Just meanness," she said with confidence. "He was a bully from the word go. Took pleasure in seeing other folks' reaction. Truth is, some of his meanness was predictable. That brother of his was the sly one. With

Garwin acting out all the time and getting most of the attention, Gordon knew he could sit back, speak politely, smile nicely, and he could get by with just about anything he wanted."

"You're saying that while Garwin was mean, Gordon was devious?" Madison clarified.

"Exactly! It wouldn't surprise me one bit if he was the one to use his grandmother's house as collateral on a deal gone bad."

"He wouldn't be the first person to use his inheritance that way," Madison pointed out.

"True. But it wasn't only his inheritance. From what I hear, he cheated his brothers out of their portions, too."

"From the conversation the other day at Granny Bert's, I wasn't clear whether Garwin was still living or not."

"Bad weeds like that are hard to kill." It sounded so much like something Granny Bert would say that Madison had to bite back a smile.

Virgie wasn't finished with the subject of Gordon Bodine. "I'm not telling tales out of school," she insisted. "And I'm not sucking on sour grapes. We had some first-hand dealings with Gordon. Trust me when I say he can be charming but cunning."

"Can you elaborate?"

"It's no secret if that's what you're asking. When Alpha's estate was finally turned over to the brothers, Gordon approached Hank about doing some work over there. Years of neglect had taken their toll, and a few things needed the touch of a handyman. Hank was happy to do it. But when it came to paying the bill, Gordon was all kinds of slippery. He had a half-dozen sob stories before he worked out a deal that Hank was satisfied with. Hank could have some of the tools from the old shed out back as payment, plus some of the implements. None were in very good shape, and some qualified more as antiques than equipment, but Hank likes to tinker around and get things running, so he was good with it. Until things went south."

"What do you mean?"

"I went with him to collect the things, and we found Gordon there, already hauling off half the promised items. He talked a real good talk, saying he didn't realize how this one thing had a special emotional attachment for Gregg, or how that thing belonged to someone else and wasn't his to give. He had a fine tale for anything of value. Hank got aggravated and said to just forget it. Give him cash and be done with it."

"But?" Madison sensed there was more to the story than a happy ending.

"He handed him a fifty-dollar bill and promised to mail a check for the balance. Instead, we got papers from a lawyer, claiming we tried to exhort money from him for services already paid. He went so far as to threaten a lawsuit. Hank said it wasn't worth the bother and to just let it go. Every now and then, he still grumbles about it."

"That took a lot of nerve on Gordon's part."

"You're telling me! After that," Virgie continued, "I kept my sights on Gordon Bodine. These days, the internet makes it easy to follow a person's career. I can cite five or more failed business ventures for that boy. Each time, he came out without a scratch, but his partners can hardly say the same. He scammed them the same way he scammed Hank. Most people naturally assume it was Garwin who lost Alpha's estate, pandering it away on booze or drugs, but my money is on Gordon. Mark my words, he used the house as collateral on that art gallery, and for once, he couldn't talk his way out of it."

"I had no idea," Madison murmured. "And the

other brother? Gregg?"

"To my knowledge, he didn't take after his brothers. He's done Alpha's upbringing proud."

"Just to circle back to something we talked about earlier. To your knowledge, Sylvia was never involved in anything suspect?"

"Oh, I never said that!" Virgie hooted. "I don't think she was into devil worship or any of that nonsense with occults, but I do believe she was mixed up with drugs and the whole hippie lifestyle. Romanticized communists, as far as I'm concerned. The meek and lowly sheep believe they're working for a common good, when all they're doing is serving a greedy shepherd."

Like Granny Bert, Virgie was known to go off on a rant. Madison knew to steer the conversation along safer lines while she still could.

"Do you know where the commune was, or anything about the father or fathers of her boys?"

"Nothing at all. It made Alpha sad to talk about it, so we all avoided the subject the best we could."

"And no word at all on where Sylvia might be now?"

"I'd say it's anybody's guess. Even with the internet, some folks can stay lost when they want to. I'd say Sylvia is one of those lost souls, still out there wandering about, trying to find herself."

"I thought my father was one of those same lost souls," Madison admitted, "but he finally came around."

Virgie hesitated after her admission, seeming to decide whether to make one of her own. After an inner debate, she made up her mind and spoke.

"There's something else, too. I know it's a sore subject between us, but there's no getting around the truth. Our boy Gerald was friends with Alpha's boy. Even when Benny went chasing after his no-count father, the two kept in touch for a while. I guess that spilled over to the next generation. Our Paul was friends with Sylvia's boys, especially Gordon. You know how our grandson had a way of twisting the truth and seeing things through his own distorted filter, something I'm sad to say he learned from his father. So, believe me when I say there's a reason Paul and Gordon were friends. Despite a few years difference in age, they had a devious nature in common."

"I appreciate your candor, Miss Virgie."

"I mentioned this at Bertha's, but I heard that Gordon is settling old debts. It's been my experience that not all debts are of a financial nature. Maybe there's something to it, maybe not. But knowing Gordon and my grandson, I'd say it's smart to study all angles before making an assumption. You can't double-cross people without making a few enemies. And you usually can't dig your way out from these kinds of messes without taking up with the wrong sort of people. Keep that in mind when doing your investigating."

Madison's eyes didn't meet hers. "In— Investigating? Who says I'm investigating?"

Virgie put her hand on Madison's arm. "Being a terrible liar is a good thing, girl. Just be careful. Know what kind of people you're dealing with."

"I'll keep that in mind," she promised.

"Gerald and Paul got mixed up with Barry Redmond, and you see where that landed them."

"You know I don't hold what they did to me against you and your husband."

"That's mighty generous of you, Maddy. Not everyone would be so understanding."

"I have children. I've raised them the best I knew how but, ultimately, I have no control over how they behave or what they do. I can hardly expect anything different from you and Mr. Hank."

"Thank you, dear girl."

She made certain to hug her hostess goodbye, reinforcing her claim of forgiveness.

Actions, she knew, often spoke louder than words.

14

After the week of unexplained bad fortune and close calls, a full week slipped by with no surprises. When a second week with no relative drama rolled around, Madison decided the man with the baseball cap had either gotten over his vexation, had gone back wherever he came from, or both. At any rate, he no longer tormented the people of The Sisters, and the only surprises in Madison's life were the routine crises that came with raising teenagers.

Amid last-minute changes in schedules, spats with girlfriends, boyfriends, and siblings, aunt duties with baby Hope, and fulfilling promises to actual paying clients, Madison squeezed in time to work on her cold case. She felt freer to move about town now, following what few leads she had on Alpha Bodine's murder. There was still the matter of inciting Otis Perry's wrath, so she proceeded as stealthily as possible.

When her internet search for Henry Boudreaux led to nothing but dead ends, Verna Bishop tracked down the number for the person claiming to have seen Benny years *after* his supposed death. Madison called at her first opportunity.

"Yeah, this is Dom Hebert. Who's asking?" a gruff

voice demanded in a heavy accent.

"This is Madison deCordova. I'm a consultant working in conjunction with The Sisters Police Department, and I'm hoping you can help locate someone who once lived here."

"Why? They come into an inheritance or something?" he scoffed.

"Something like that."

"What's in it for me?"

"That depends on how gracious our recipient is feeling," she hedged.

"Our *what*?"

"The person we're looking for."

"Who ya lookin' for?"

"While living here, he went by the name Benny Bodine."

"Benny Bodine died a long time ago."

"But I was under the impression you saw him, some years later. I believe he may have been using the name Henry Boudreaux."

"I remember Henry. Ain't seen him in a month of Sundays, but I 'member him well enough."

"You haven't seen him recently?" she asked in disappointment. "Do you happen to know where he might be by now?"

"Well, now lemme see. Lemme think about this." After a long, roundabout explanation that involved one of his favorite barrooms, two ex-wives, and a brief stint in the county jail, the man decided he knew someone who could possibly help. Between his rambling and his thick accent, Madison had trouble following the conversation.

"You give 'im a call and tell him Dom says you was okay. Tell him he still owes Dom a frosty one."

"Uhm, okay. Thank you for speaking with me."

"If you find Henry, or Benny, you 'mind him who

put you on his trail and the road to fortune."

"I'll do that. Thanks again."

Her buoyant feeling lasted until she made the next phone call. The number the man gave her had been disconnected. There was no one listed in the directory with his name, and she couldn't find him through an internet search. She resorted to asking Brash for his help locating the man, but even that was a dead end. The last known address was no longer valid, and the phone number was the same one she had.

"I don't know what else to do, Gen," she complained to her friend. With Cutter home with the baby, she had volunteered to drive Genny to her doctor's appointment in College Station. They now sat in a restaurant, enjoying a late lunch.

"It sounds like you've done about all you can. You followed up on the leads from the meeting at Granny Bert's. Even if Brash can help you locate the daughter or this man who may or may not know how to contact Henry Boudreaux, neither has any obligation to speak with you. And what will you ask them? 'Excuse me, Sylvia, but did you kill your mother?' Or 'Excuse me, sir. Is your friend Henry really a man named Benny? A man who's been named legally dead for over a decade or two?'" Genny shook her blond curls. "I'm sorry, but I don't really see either conversation going so well."

"I know," Madison agreed miserably.

"And let's say you do somehow manage to locate this Henry Boudreaux and he is, indeed, Benny Bodine. What does that prove? Do you have any reason to believe he killed his mother?"

"No. Not really. It's all just speculation at this point," Madison admitted.

"So don't stress yourself out on trying to chase down a random possibility. I say concentrate on what you do know."

"Very little."

"How little?"

"Fits inside a thimble little." Her voice sounded glum. "There were no viable prints at the scene. No forced entry. No witnesses. No threats or known enemies. No obvious explanation as to why someone would have wanted Miss Alpha dead."

"With nothing missing from the house, it doesn't sound like a theft," Genny agreed, "even though officials tried to sell it as a random break-in."

"There's nothing that points to a jealous ex-lover, so the next-best guesses are financial gain or settling a personal vendetta. Sylvia is the obvious choice, but a hand-written note in the file places her in Waco at the time of death."

"No other relatives?"

"None that I'm aware of. More importantly, none that the gossip mill is aware of. If Granny Bert doesn't know of any, I doubt they exist."

Genny voiced the thought running through their heads. "That leaves her grandsons."

Madison nodded, her expression grim. "A disturbing thought, at the least."

"Could they have done it?" Genny asked.

"Garwin and Gordon were teenagers. I suppose they were strong enough to overcome their grandmother, but why? What motive would they have had? Normally, their mother would inherit the estate. Even if they knew the details of Miss Alpha's will, they couldn't touch the money or the house until the youngest boy turned twenty-one. He was only like eleven at the time."

Genny made a face. "So, we can probably mark him off the suspect list."

"I agree. Which leaves the older two, Gordon and Garwin. Everyone talks about how mean Garwin was, but now I'm hearing that Gordon wasn't exactly an angel, either."

"What does Brash have to say about it? Didn't he know the boys in school?"

"Not really. The one was several years younger than him. Garwin was maybe three grades above Brash, and Gordon a grade above that. They ran in different social circles."

"Can't he run a background check on them? Find out where they're living now?"

"Sure," Maddy said. "But then what? He agreed to intervene if I found something solid, but what little I've learned is very shaky. Bringing them in for questioning now would equal harassment."

"Not if it was posed as an opportunity to find their grandmother's killer," Genny argued. "Normally, most grandsons would be eager to see justice served."

"Which they may be. Considering them suspects is pure speculation on my part, based solely on gossip from a bunch of busybodies."

Genny's dimples puckered. "You'd better not let Granny Bert hear you say that! She's quite proud of her 'network,' as she refers to them."

"I'm sure most of what they've told me is true. It just doesn't prove anything."

"What's the plan, then? What's next?"

Madison leaned back as the waiter placed a large chef salad before her. With a sigh, she admitted, "I have no idea."

"That looks yummy," Genny said. "And healthy." She rubbed her rounded belly. "But this one has a hankering for enchiladas. I know I'll pay dearly for it later, but a craving is a craving."

"I craved Mexican food when I was pregnant with the twins," Madison recalled. "It gave me heartburn something terrible, but what babies wanted, babies got."

"I remember you craving chocolate milkshakes."

"Those, too," she admitted guilelessly. "And fresh blueberries. I haven't cared for blueberries before or after, but during my pregnancy, I couldn't get enough of the little things."

"Poor Cutter. Right now, even the thought of apple turnovers makes me ill. He's going through withdrawal. I tell him to go down to the café and get some, but he says no one makes them the way I do. He claims it's the least he can do, giving up his beloved turnovers, when I've given up the ability to see my toes."

"Only a few more weeks now, my friend! That little one will be here before you know it, and you'll be able to see your toes once more. You'll even develop ankles again!" Madison promised brightly.

Pausing with a forkful of gooey cheese en route to her mouth, Genny frowned. "Are you saying I'm so fat I no longer have ankles?"

"You *have* them. It's just hard to see them." Her best friend's brutal honesty was softened by a look of empathy. "We've all been there, Gen. Don't let it get you down."

Genny scarfed down the cheese and dove in for more. "I'm not. I don't even think of these extra twenty-five pounds as fat. I'm calling them baby love."

"Yeah, I really loved my babies. All forty-seven pounds of them." Madison touched her trim waist, remembering a time when it had stretched beyond what seemed humanly possible. "Just remember. The weight picks up in the last month."

"Which is all I have left now. Less, actually. I can't believe she moved up my due date!" That thought made Genny set down her fork. A stunned expression crossed her face. "Maddy! I only have three weeks left. This baby will be here before I know it. I'm not ready!"

"Of course you're ready. You have everything you can possibly need, and you still have one baby shower left."

"But I'm not ready to give up my time with Hope. She still needs me!" Genny wailed.

"You aren't going anywhere, Genny. And you aren't giving up your time with her. You'll still be the same loving, devoted mother you are now."

"But with another baby to care for, she may think I'm neglecting her!"

"She's an infant. I promise, she won't hold it against you. She may even appreciate being able to lie in her bed for more than ten minutes at a time. I swear, you hold her more than anyone I've ever seen," Madison teased.

"Not so. Have you seen how Cutter hogs her whenever he's around? Why do you think he asked you to take me to this appointment? He saw an opportunity to have her all to himself. I never knew the man was so selfish," Genny sulked. She crossed her arms childishly, propping them upon her extended belly.

"Stop pouting and eat your lunch," Madison advised. "Trust me. Once this second one is born, eating an uninterrupted meal will become a true luxury. You may not have another chance for months. Years."

"With so many greedy relatives sitting around, waiting for a chance to put their grubby hands on my babies? I'll be lucky to hold one, much less both at one time!" Genny continued to grumble about her many sisters-in-law, nieces, and one greedy but well-meaning mother-in-law as she picked up her fork and stuffed a bite of enchiladas into her mouth.

Madison merely laughed at her dramatics. "Believe me. Those greedy hands have a way of vanishing at meal time."

Genny mumbled something else over a forkful of Spanish rice.

"You know," Madison said, a sly look coming into her hazel eyes, "I feel silly saying 'this second one' or 'baby number two.' Aren't you ever going to tell me her name?"

Genny wasn't so easily fooled, not even while appeasing a craving. "Sure. As soon as she's born."

"That's cruel. I thought I was your BFF."

"You are. But you're waiting, just like everyone else."

"That hardly seems fair. I let you help pick names for the twins."

Genny rolled her eyes, unimpressed. "Because Gray and his mother wanted you to name one of them Archibald!"

"True. But it was your idea to shorten Blakely into Blake. Annette still hasn't fully forgiven me for naming him after Granny Bert's friend, rather than her favorite uncle."

"Did that uncle provide you with a home the way Juliet Blakely did? Without her, you wouldn't have the Big House," Genny pointed out with a cheeky grin.

"I hardly knew that at the time," Madison countered.

"This argument will have to wait. Preferably until *this second one* is born, or at least until I can wedge my belly out of this booth and waddle to the little girl's room." With a pointed glare, Genny warned, "Don't you dare touch my guacamole while I'm gone!"

Laughing, her friend assured her, "I wouldn't dare."

15

Genny had her 'dessert,' of a sort, on the way back to The Sisters. The antacid tablets weren't as good as the Mexican food but were every bit as appreciated.

Madison helped her friend into the house, watching in amusement as she all but snatched a sleeping Hope out of Cutter's arms.

"See?" Genny hissed. "He's hogging her again! He had all afternoon to hold her, and now here he sits on the couch, both of them dozing."

Cutter looked helplessly at Madison, wondering what he had done wrong.

"Forgive her, Cutter," Madison apologized. "It's the hormones talking. They make a woman crazy."

"They don't do much for a man's sanity, either," he mumbled. He unfolded himself from the couch as his wife crooned over the baby and scattered kisses upon her face. "I remember a time when she used to kiss me that way," he said, not fully teasing.

Genny frowned and lifted her face upward. "Sorry, sweetie. This one is for you."

He collected his kiss before straightening. "How was your day?"

"I missed Hope like crazy!" Genny said. She thought

to hastily add, "You, too, of course."

Cutter laughed at her fabrication. "Liar."

"I'll go, so the two of you can fight over who gets to burp the baby," Madison offered.

"Why? Does she have a tummy ache?" Genny asked in concern. "Has she been crying? Cutter, why didn't you call me and tell me to come right home? We didn't have to go shopping!"

"Reel in those hormones, girlfriend," Madison chided. "I was only teasing."

"Sorry. Between the hormones, the indigestion, and my due date being moved up a week, I guess I'm a little on edge."

"I'd say you're a lot on edge and justly so. But remember I'm as close as the phone. Call me if you need me. That goes for you, too, Cutter."

"Will do," he said. "Thanks again for helping out today."

"My pleasure." She dropped a kiss onto Hope's cheek first, then her best friend's. "He's a good man," she whispered in Genny's ear. "Go easy on him."

When Madison arrived home and found Bethani in the kitchen preparing dinner, she grew suspicious.

"I'd like to think you're simply being a thoughtful daughter," she told the teen, "but my Super Mom Spidey sense tells me you're up to something."

"Gee, can't a girl do something nice for her mother once in a while and not be accused of having an ulterior motive?" Bethani sniffed, managing to look both innocent yet offended at the same time.

"Sure, she can." Madison's tone was amicable before she added, "But she seldom does."

"I resent that!"

Madison bowed humbly. "My apologies to the chef. Let me take these packages up, and I'll come down and set the table."

"That's okay. I've got it."

The offer made her doubly suspicious, but Madison wisely kept her mouth shut. She disappeared up the back staircase to deposit the bags in her room and change into more comfortable shoes.

Halfway through dinner, Bethani eased a sly request into the conversation. As usual, they had their meal in the intimate kitchen nook, rather than the formal dining room.

"I wasn't sure I'd like it, but I'm really enjoying this art class. Mr. Raymond is very knowledgeable."

"I'm glad you're learning a new skill," Brash told her. "You never know when it might come in useful."

"Yeah," Blake scoffed. "She can now clothe her stick figures."

"Something you can't do with a football," his twin pointed out, keeping her tone even. Now wasn't the time to respond to his barbs and put their parents off on the wrong foot. "We're studying shading this week. Trenton is right. It really does make all the difference."

"It sounds like you're really learning about painting," Madison said, pleased. "I'm proud of you, honey."

"Thanks. Mr. Raymond wants us to study as many paintings as we can and pick up on the subtle nuances of shading and accenting. So, if you see me roaming around the mansion, looking at all the old paintings, think nothing of it."

"Thanks for the forewarning. It might startle me, seeing you finally notice we have artwork on the walls. For the past two years, you've been oblivious to it."

"Not at all," her daughter denied. "Trenton was right about the mural in the dining room. It is absolutely fascinating! The detail is so distinct. And the shading techniques make all the difference. Don't you think so, Daddy D?" She turned to her stepfather, her big, blue eyes looking guileless and sincere.

Blake coughed into his hand. "Overkill," he warned.

His sister flashed him an aggravated look, not at all appreciating his 'help.'

"I, uh, think it's a very well-done painting," Brash agreed. He sensed a trap.

"Trenton has told our teacher all about it. I used to tease him about only dating me because of the mural, but now that I'm learning more about shadows and light, I have to agree with him. The entire mural is fascinating! The fact that it was done over a hundred years ago makes it even more intriguing. Right, Mom?"

"There were actually several well-known artists back in the day," Madison said wryly. "I assume you've heard of Michaelangelo? Leonardo da Vinci? Vincent van Gogh? Pablo Picasso, to name a few. Art isn't exactly a twenty-first century invention, you know."

"I know but think of how crude the tools must have been back then! That mural was probably painted by candlelight. That took great talent, don't you think?"

"Actually, I do. Even when I was a little girl and came with Granny Bert to visit Miss Juliet, I was fascinated with the dining room mural."

"I understand now why Amanda Hooper insisted we restore it. It would have been a shame to paint over it."

"I would have never allowed that!" Madison huffed.

"But Granny Bert—"

"You know your great-grandmother. She was bluffing when she threatened that. She was just seeing how much she could get out of the show's producer."

"What a sucker," Blake smirked. "Amanda totally fell for that act."

"You have to admit, your great-grandmother is very convincing," Madison said.

"Beth may study the masters of art," he quipped, "but I prefer to study the master of trickery."

Madison eyed her daughter with knowing eyes. "Oh, I suspect your twin has picked up a thing or two from her, as well. You may as well spill it, sister. What favor do you need to ask?"

"Who said—"

"No need to bat the big baby blues. Just tell us what you want."

"Wellll," Bethani said, drawing out the word. "Now that you bring it up..."

"You're the one to bring it up but go ahead. You have our attention," Brash said when she faltered.

"We've talked so much about it, Trenton and I, that Mr. Raymond says he's just dying to see the mural for himself. He suggested we make it a field trip of sorts. We could bring the entire class over to study the mural and learn from the great Seymour whatever his name was."

Her brother broke in. "Hmm. You're so impressed, you can't even remember the artist's name?"

"Shut up!" she hissed from the side of her mouth. Somehow, she maintained a bright smile for her parents, still looking all sweet and innocent.

"And when would this field trip take place?" Madison asked.

Bethani winced a bit as she answered, "Friday?"

Madison shook her head. "Not happening. I'm hosting Genny's baby shower on Saturday. Here. There's no way I can have twenty students trampling through here the day before."

"There's not twenty in the class," Bethani assured her.

"How many? Nineteen?"

"More like twelve. Thirteen, counting the teacher."

Blake looked surprised. "We have that many dorks at school?"

"We're not dorks!" his sister snapped.

"Still," their mother said, "I'm afraid this week is out of the question. Probably next week, as well."

"But it's only a six-week class!"

"Maybe it could be an end of the class outing. Like a graduation party. Seriously, honey, now isn't a good time."

"This week, it's the baby shower. In four weeks, it will be the baby. Who knows—"

"Three," Madison corrected. "They moved her due date up."

"See? You definitely won't have time for it then! Please, Mom? Pretty please?"

"Not the puppy dog eyes," Madison begged.

"Why? Do they work?"

"No. They look ridiculous."

"I think they're kind of cute," Brash said.

Sensing weakness, Bethani swung her gaze to him and gave him her most pitiful look. "Please? Oh, please, please, please? It's truly important to me. If anyone can talk her into it, it's you, Daddy D."

"Maddy?" he asked, darting her a helpless look. No matter how many times Megan and Bethani pulled the same stunt, the puppy dog eyes got him every time.

"No. Not this week." She held steady, softening only to say, "I—I guess we'll see what next week holds. But definitely not this week."

"You're the best, Mom! You, too, Daddy D!" the teen beamed, bouncing in her chair happily.

Brash realized he had been played. "It was next week all along, wasn't it?"

She neither confirmed nor denied the realization. "This week, next week. Does it really matter? What matters is that I have awesome parents!"

"Suck-ers!" Blake hummed, not bothering to hide his taunt behind a cough.

Tossing her long, blonde hair over her shoulders, Bethani breezily replied, "It's called dual studies, brother dear. Art. *And* trickery."

Three days later, Blake grumbled, "I still don't see why you're kicking us guys out of the house. It's just a baby shower. You said it was only for Aunt Genny's closest friends, so what's the big deal?"

"Besides the fact that you'll eat all of the cake?"

"There's going to be cake?" he wailed. "And I don't get any?"

"Your sisters made it, not Genny."

"Eh. There's still a fifty-fifty chance it's edible," he decided. "I'm up for the challenge."

"We'll save you a piece. Now scram."

"Really? You're kicking Daddy D and me out, just like that?"

"You notice he's not complaining," Madison pointed out.

"But if there's cake, there's probably punch," the teen reasoned.

"We'll save some of that, too." Sensing another protest coming, she used an offensive move. "Do you remember the time you walked in on Granny Bert's geriatric swim class? The one they had without benefit of water, because something was wrong with the pool. Remember the wrinkles and skimpy bathing suits?"

"No matter how hard I've tried to unsee them," he said solemnly, slapping a hand over his eyes, "some things have remained burned into my cornea for eternity."

"A 'Mommy and Me' shower is sort of the same thing. Do you really want to hear about stretch marks and the healing properties of boob cream?"

"Aw, gross, Mom!" His hands moved to cover his ears. "Now I can never un*hear* that!"

Coming to his rescue, Brash tugged on his arm. "Come on, son. We'll go to the ranch and do something manly, like ear tag a few cows or practice shooting our bows. Deer season isn't far off, you know."

Cheered by the thought of going to the deCordova Ranch, Blake gave up his protest. A bonus was knowing his step-grandmother would offer him something more substantial than just cake and punch.

Kissing them both goodbye, Madison all but pushed them out the door. She still had finishing touches to put on the table.

Being that it was a special occasion, the shower would be held in the formal parlor, with refreshments served in the dining room. She used the infamous pedestal bowl as the centerpiece, filling it with an assortment of lotions, creams, and small favors clustered around a special how-to book for new mothers. She became misty eyed when she recalled Granny Bert had given her a similar book almost eighteen years ago.

Where had the time gone? How had her own babies become almost adults?

Seeing her mother's glassy-eyed gaze, Bethani frowned. "You're doing it again, aren't you? You're remembering your own baby showers, and you're going to start crying."

"No, I'm not," she sniffed.

"It's okay, Mama Maddy," Megan assured her. "I saw my mom doing the same thing. She's in the kitchen, pretending to get more ice."

"Just wait," she predicted. "One day, you'll both

have your own babies. And the very next day, they'll be all grown up, and you'll be doing the same thing we're doing!"

"Pretending not to cry?" Bethani teased.

Her mother could only nod, else there would be no denying the fact. She was relieved when the alarm binged, signaling an arrival. "I think Genny is here. Cutter is bringing her since she has so much to carry."

"What's to carry? A baby and a bag of diapers."

Madison tried not to laugh. "Obviously, you've never been around many babies."

Five minutes later, the front parlor was filled with baby paraphernalia. Cutter set up the baby swing in one corner, next to her portable bassinet. Tucked in among them were two diaper bags and extra diapers.

"Are they moving in?" Bethani whispered to her mother, eyes wide.

"No. Just visiting for the afternoon and staying for supper," Madison assured her breezily.

Soon after, the guests arrived. There were only twelve or so in all, making for a fun, intimate gathering. The women offered their best baby tips, writing them out on cards for Genny's later reference. They brought with them gifts of favorite products for newborns, favorite lotions and novelties for mom, and even a few pieces of lingerie any new father was sure to enjoy. They lingered over refreshments, sharing tales of their own birthing experiences, colic nightmares, and the best and worst of having a newborn.

Not once did baby Hope sit in her swing or occupy her bassinet. The women were too busy holding her, fascinated by her delicate features and exotic complexion.

After the last guest left, and Madison coaxed Bethani and Megan back downstairs to help with cleanup, she took a bag of trash outside. She was surprised to see Cutter still there.

"Cutter! Have you been here the entire time? I thought you were joining Brash at the ranch."

"I was, but..."

"Couldn't get that far away from your two favorite ladies?" Madison smiled knowingly.

"That, too," Cutter said, offering a lopsided smile. His mouth tightened as he admitted, "But, the truth is, I saw a suspicious-looking car circling the block. I thought it was best if I stayed nearby."

Madison's heart quickened. "Black sedan?"

He nodded. "I didn't want anyone slipping in, pretending to be an invited guest."

"Thank you, but I'm sorry you had to sit out here the entire time."

His crooked smile reappeared. "My whole world is inside that house. I'm not about to let someone in who doesn't belong."

Madison gave him an impulsive hug. "I'm so glad Genny found you. You and Brash are the best husbands in the world!"

"Speaking of Brash, here he comes now. We'll keep an eye out a little longer, and then we'll start grilling those steaks you promised."

16

Early Monday morning, not five minutes after seeing Brash and the twins off for the day, Madison's phone rang. Not recognizing the number, she answered with caution.

"Maddy?" a crackly voice said from the other end. "It's Virgie Adams."

"Oh, hi, Miss Virgie! I didn't recognize your number."

"I hope I'm not calling too early?"

"Not at all. I just saw the family off, and I have the morning to myself. What can I do for you?"

"Well, I remembered something. It may be nothing, but I thought it was worth mentioning."

"Of course. What was it?"

"I told you about the work Hank did out at Alpha's after the boys inherited the house. Remember?"

"Yes, I do."

"Well, now I remember something else. Something we found while we were out there. I thought you might like to see it."

"You have it there at your house?" she asked, hopeful she may finally have a lead.

The older woman's voice was hesitant. "Not

exactly."

"Oh? Then, where is it?"

"At Alpha's. At least, it was there. There's no guarantee it still is, but seeing as it was well hidden, I'd say there's a fair chance it's still in its hidey hole."

"That may be, but I don't have access to the mansion. That was a one-day sale, I'm afraid."

"Well, now, I may have a way in," Virgie said.

"Please tell me it doesn't involve an overturned bucket and a window. I've tried that before, and it's not as easy as it looks." She sounded like she was making a joke, but the truth was, she and Genny had done just that.

"Call me crazy, but I thought we might use a key."

"Keys are good."

"I thought Bertha might want to come along."

"Good thinking. I'll call her and see. When did you have in mind?"

So much like Granny Bert, the older woman said, "No use in wasting time. You want to meet me there, or swing by and pick me up?"

"I'll come by. You can fill me in on the drive to her house." Madison glanced at her watch, hoping her grandmother didn't already have plans for the day. "Even if she can't make it, I'll be there in about thirty minutes."

"Believe me, she'll make time for this."

Twenty minutes later, Granny Bert crawled into the front seat of Madison's SUV. Miss Sybil slid into the seat behind them.

"I knew you wouldn't mind Sybil coming along," her grandmother said without preamble.

As if I had a choice, Maddy thought. Aloud, she

said, "No. Not at all."

"See, Sybil? You worried over nothing."

"I didn't want to impose," the elderly woman said.

"You were as good a friend to Alpha as I was," Granny Bert insisted. "And you were as resolute as I was, refusing to go to that spectacle of an estate sale. It was nothing but a bunch of looky-loos, hoping to get an eyeful. Disgraceful, that's what it was!"

"Disgraceful," her best friend repeated with disgust, shaking her head.

"Didn't know a thing about the woman," Granny Bert continued to grumble. "They just wanted to see the blood stains."

Madison wondered if that weren't the same reason they both came now, but she didn't dare voice her thoughts. She swung into the Adams' driveway, not at all surprised to find Virgie ready and waiting at the kitchen door.

The three friends were so busy visiting, Virgie never did explain what she hoped to show them.

"Maybe we should go around back," she directed Madison as she pulled into the front entrance of the old estate. Her voice sounded oddly strained. "Pull up close to the garage."

Warning bells clattered in Madison's head. "Miss Virgie. Do we have permission to be out here?" she belatedly asked.

"I have the key, don't I?" the older woman replied.

"That sounds oddly like something Granny Bert would say when she's avoiding a direct lie."

"So don't ask a direct question." Virgie opened the door and slid off the seat. She tossed a look at her friends. "You girls coming?"

Granny Bert cackled in glee at the thought of a new and forbidden adventure. "Wouldn't miss this for the world!"

Sybil made a similar declaration.

Madison muttered a hasty, "Brash, forgive me for what I'm about to do!" Then, she followed behind the octogenarians.

"Better stick close to the side of the house," Granny Bert suggested. "In case there are cameras."

"Good thinking, Bertha. That's why you've always been our leader. You think on your feet. But we're not going far. I know a shortcut."

When Verna pulled a flashlight from her pocket, Madison groaned. "We aren't going through the front door, are we?"

"I figured the bank who repossessed the house changed all the obvious locks. The one I'm thinking of isn't so obvious."

"Better find a long stick, girls," Granny Bert advised. "Could be snakes down there."

While Sybil and Virgie fanned out to bide her instructions, Madison stared at her grandmother in horror. "Down *where*? Not a hidden tunnel!"

"Don't be so dramatic!" Granny Bert snapped. "The root cellar, child."

It wasn't much better, but Madison remained quiet as she returned to the SUV for a flashlight. While there, she found a curtain rod she had purchased but left in the car, intending to return it. It would make a good-enough snake-beating stick.

It took all four of them to coax the rusty hinges into moving, but they managed to get one of the cellar doors open. Before Madison could make the magnanimous offer to go first, Sybil stomped her way down the rickety steps, swishing a long stick in front of her. Virgie followed, her light shining ahead of them.

There was a crude door off to one side of the cellar, behind a few rusted cans and a gnarled snare of dried leaves, vines, and the remnants of old vegetables.

Granny Bert and Sybil cleared the debris away, warning the others to stand back in case a snake or rat considered the mess their home. Cringing at the thought, Madison was torn between running for safety and staying there to defend the older women.

Luckily, it never came to that. A big spider crawled its way out of the bramble, scurrying in the opposite direction, as Virgie slid the key into a simple keyhole wormed into the door. Without a door handle, the slot was easy to miss, but she knew exactly what she was doing.

"Where does this lead?" Madison whispered.

"Into the larder."

"What you would call a pantry," her grandmother supplied.

The door pushed inward, allowing the women into a dark, damp area that was surprisingly clean and sparse. Madison felt a moment of panic when Virgie shut the door behind them, but a sweep of her flashlight showed a set of five steps leading out of the space.

Just in case, she kept her curtain rod handy.

Granny Bert led the way into the primary pantry.

"There's still food in here," Sybil said needlessly, glancing around at the shelfing.

"And plenty of liquor," Granny Bert noted. "The boys must have used this as a party house."

Virgie pushed open the next door, which opened into the kitchen. The room was in sore need of an update but looked functional enough, assuming the appliances still worked.

"I had many a cup of coffee in this room," Granny Bert said wistfully, caught up in memories of the past.

"Remember that gingerbread Alpha used to bake?" Sybil mused. "It always came out perfect."

Madison followed Virgie's lead and switched off her

flashlight. It took a moment for their eyes to adjust in the dim interior. Even though the sun shone brightly outside, the shade on the kitchen window was pulled.

Bethani wouldn't be so fond of shadows if she saw these, Madison thought. They gave the house a dark, eerie look to go along with the dank, stifling odor of shuttered doors and windows.

Granny Bert led the way through the house.

"The house looks stripped down to its skivvies," Sybil said, the reproach evident in her voice.

"There was quite a turnout for the estate sale," Madison reminded them. "The bank probably took anything of value to an auction house."

"Looks plumb bare," Granny Bert tsked.

With heavy hearts, the women looked around the all-but-empty mansion. Their memories conjured up furniture and decor. They named off the pieces as they passed through the rooms.

"That's where the sideboard always sat," Sybil said, panning her hand to the empty space between two windows in the empty dining room.

"Remember that crystal punchbowl she had? She always kept in on display, right there on the sideboard. She was so proud of that piece," Virgie recalled. "It was a wedding present from the governor when her parents got married."

"Was her father a politician?" Madison asked in surprise.

"No," Virgie answered. "Just a wealthy supporter."

"Where did his money come from?"

"Old money, dear," she said, as if that explained it all.

"Fool though he was, it didn't take Lester Bodine long to figure that out," Granny Bert claimed. "He swooped in and charmed Alpha into marrying him, even though her daddy had plans for her to marry a boy over in Riverton. They were a better fit, both financially and socially, but for some reason I could never see nor understand, Alpha fell head over heels for Lester. They were married in no time."

"Lester may have been dumb," Sybil echoed, "but he was smart enough not to let her get away."

"Remember the chandelier that used to hang here? It was modest by Juliet Blakely's standards, but I always thought it had a simple kind of beauty to it," Virgie mused.

"Is that why it's so dark in here? They took all the light fixtures?" Sybil wanted to know.

"That. Or because no one turned on the switch," Madison observed.

"Better leave them off," her grandmother cautioned. "Just in case."

"Just in case what?"

"Just in case we trip an alarm. We don't want to call attention to ourselves."

"Because an oversized silver SUV and four women sneaking around an empty house aren't at all conspicuous," Madison muttered.

Sybil looked at Granny Bert, hooking a thumb toward the youngster among them. "Is she always like this?"

"I'm afraid so."

"Geez, Louise," she muttered.

"Hard to believe she's yours," Virgie agreed. "Even harder to believe she gets herself into so many scrapes, seeing how cautious she is."

"I can hear you, you know," Madison reminded them. "And I think you wanted to show me something?"

"It's upstairs. In what used to be one of the boys' room."

They had to enter the front parlor to access the

stairs. All eyes strayed to the barren floor in front of the fireplace. The carpet was gone now, but they all knew the spot where Miss Alpha's body had been found.

"Then let's go upstairs," Madison said, pulling their thoughts from the gruesome memories. "The sooner we see, the sooner we leave."

The older trio muttered about her lack of adventure as they trudged up the stairs. *Noisily*, she noted, although Madison kept the thought to herself.

"I think it was in this room," Virgie said, stopping at the first door on the right. "No, wait. Maybe it was that one." She pointed across the hall.

"Which was it?" Granny Bert wanted to know.

"It's been almost twenty years!" snapped Virgie. "I need a gosh-darn minute to recall."

Madison had forgotten that being so much alike in personality, her grandmother and Miss Virgie often had cantankerous moments like these. She supposed it was the hallmark of true friendship, but sometimes it wore on the nerves.

"We can search them all," Sybil said diplomatically. "What is it we're looking for?"

"A little hidden hidey hole alongside the hearth."

Sybil peeked inside the room on the right. "Not this one. No fireplace."

"There's a fireplace in here," Granny Bert said, swinging open the door opposite it.

"There was a loose board near the bottom," Virgie recalled. "Hank was about to nail it in better when we saw the edge of a piece of paper."

Madison squatted down, pushing and tugging on the lower boards on either side of the hearth. Nothing moved. "If it was loose then, it's not now. Maybe the wood swelled over the years."

"Or maybe it was a different room. There's four more doors between here and Alpha's room at the end of the hall."

One was another bedroom, devoid of a fireplace. After a break in the wall overlooking the entryway below, the second door accessed a small closet. The third led to the bathroom.

"If this isn't it," Virgie grumbled outside the last door, "I guess we're out of luck,"

The optimist among them, Sybil smiled. "At least it has a fireplace, so that's something."

Again, Madison bent to save the older women's joints. She pushed and tugged, but all the boards were intact on the right side of the hearth. The left side was their last resort.

She squatted again for the final time, hoping to find a weakness in the wood. When she felt the board give, she beamed up at her companions.

"Bingo!"

"That's it?" Sybil clapped her hands together in excitement.

"See? I told you it was there all along!" Virgie insisted.

"You thought it was way back at the front of the hall," Granny Bert huffed.

"Maybe I came in from the other direction," Virgie defended herself. She turned back to Madison. "Is there anything in there? Are the papers still there?"

Madison huffed out a sigh. "No. It's empty."

Their faces fell with disappointment.

"Well, it was a good try," Sybil said. "And I, for one, have enjoyed being back inside the house one last time, even if it does look like a chicken with its feathers all plucked out."

Madison stretched further inside the narrow opening, reaching as far as her arm would fit. "I think I feel something... Almost got it... Dang! I lost it."

"Try again, girl," her grandmother encouraged.

"Try holding your breath," Sybil suggested.

Madison shot her a dubious look, but she tried again. She used the curtain rod/snake-beating stick to pull the unseen item within closer reach. She stuck her arm back in the space, thinking with one more push, she could reach the elusive thing.

"I think I have it!" she announced. Twisting her fingers in a scissor effect, she secured the edge of something—a notebook, perhaps—and tugged it forward. She dropped it twice before she dragged it close enough to get a better grip. "Got it!" she called triumphantly, pulling it out into the open.

"What is it?" Sybil asked as the others crowded closer.

"A sketchbook of some sort," Madison said.

"That's it! That's what I brought you here for!" Virgie glared at Granny Bert for doubting her. "And you thought I was barking up the wrong tree. See? I told you it was here!"

While the two bickered about trivial details, Madison flipped through the pages of the sketchbook. Even in the dim lighting, she knew the images were grotesque.

"Oh my," she murmured. "These are... disturbing, to say the least."

"What are they? Let us see," Granny Bert said, abandoning her argument with Virgie.

"You may not want to. They're rather graphic."

"Nudies?" Sybil wanted to know; her voice was almost hopeful.

"Hardly." Madison stood, stretching cramps out of her long legs. "A flashlight will only make them that much harsher. Can someone open the curtain?"

Virgie hurried to push back the dust-covered draperies, allowing a stream of daylight through the grimy windowpanes.

"Don't say I didn't warn you," Madison said, handing the book to her grandmother.

Her friends crowded in on either side as she turned the first page.

"These don't look so bad," she said. "Birds. A decent sketch of a frog. A squ—oh, my! I see what you mean."

"Is that a squirrel?" Sybil asked, turning her head at different angles.

"It *was* a squirrel," Virgie said solemnly.

"These are horrible," Granny Bert breathed, thumbing through more pages. Each was more graphic than the last. "It takes someone truly sick to do those things to an animal. Someone even sicker to sketch them out on paper."

"Garwin, I imagine," Madison said. "I understand he took pleasure in torturing small animals."

"Like Lavonne's kittens?" Sybil spat.

"Among other things. Toward the back, the animals get larger."

"It's like he was practicing," Virgie whispered in horror, "working his way up to bigger and more challenging prey."

No one said the words aloud, but they all wondered the same thing. Was his eventual target a human being?

Could anyone, particularly a teenager, truly be that sick?

"I suppose it's a blessing," Granny Bert finally uttered in a shaky voice, "that Alpha didn't suffer any more than she did."

"Bertha!" Sybil said, aghast. "Are you saying that boy killed his own grandmother?"

"I think it's possible." Snapping the book shut, she handed it back to Madison. "Brash needs to see this."

"I agree." Madison took the notebook, handling it by the edge as if it contained a deadly virus. "Hold on," she said suddenly, holding up a finger in warning. "What was that noise?"

They all strained to hear shuffled feet.

"Help me pull the curtains shut," Granny Bert hissed. "Everyone, hide!"

17

The women scattered like quail.

Granny Bert stayed where she was, slipping in behind a long and heavy drape.

Sybil slid into the closet. Her dark skin blended easily into the deep shadows. As small and wiry as she was, she hardly made a bump beyond the wide doorframe.

Virgie grabbed Madison's arm and pulled her into the dark hallway.

"Trust me." She breathed out the words.

Cracking open the last door only a fraction, Virgie tugged Madison inside what was once the master bedroom. Even in the dim shadows, Madison could see the room was empty. How could they hide in here?

Virgie moved with sure feet, pulling her along. She stopped at the fireplace, pushing at the panel between it and a bookcase. To Madison's amazement, it slid open.

She kept her thought to herself, but mentally she rolled her eyes. *Geesh! I guess secret panels were standard issue back in the day! But if everyone had one, what was so secret about them?*

Before following the other woman into the tiny

space in the wall, Madison tucked the sketchbook into the waistband in the back of her pants. She had no idea who was inside the house or what they wanted, but she wasn't giving up the pad without a fight. Her faithful curtain rod would help defend it.

There was barely room for the two of them in the narrow gap, but somehow, they managed. Madison tugged the panel back in place and waited.

It seemed like a lifetime later, but she eventually heard footsteps coming up the stairs. Miss Virgie reached out to take her hand, squeezing it tightly in fear. Madison wanted to comfort the older woman, but she had no real confidence in their safety or the outcome of their folly.

What had they been thinking, sneaking into a house they had no business being inside?

Madison heard the muffled sounds of doors opening and closing. Whoever was inside, they weren't bothering being stealthy. She counted the number of doors as the person made his or her way down the door. Any minute now, the person would be in the room next door. The room where her grandmother and her best friend—

"Get your hands off me!"

Even through walls and the wooden panel she hid behind, Madison could hear the indignation in her grandmother's voice. "Who do you think you are, manhandling me like this!"

There was a gruff reply. A man's voice she couldn't hear distinctly enough to place.

"Otis Perry, I demand you take your hands off me!"

"Perry!" Madison whispered, uncertain if what she felt was relief or dread. It could go either way.

Madison pushed the panel aside and stepped out.

"Maybe we should wait?" Virgie suggested.

"I can't leave Granny Bert to fend for herself,"

Madison objected in a hissed whisper.

"Bertha can take care of herself, young lady. But maybe we shouldn't show our cards just yet."

Uncertain of what that meant, Madison crept to the far wall so she could hear better.

"What are you doing here, Bertha Cessna?" the lawman snarled. "You're trespassing on private property!"

She imagined her grandmother raising her chin as she said stubbornly, "Maybe I wanted to see the old house one last time, before it sold to the highest bidder."

"It's still trespassing. You should have come to the sale, just like everyone else in town." Madison's mouth turned downward when she heard him spat, "Including that trouble-making granddaughter of yours!"

"You leave Maddy out of this. She had as much right as anyone to be here that day."

"But she was the only one to assault another shopper!" he shot back.

"Did the man press charges?" she heard her grandmother demand.

Madison couldn't hear his muttered reply, but she knew the answer. There was a certain kind of satisfaction in hearing his silence.

"Where is the troublemaker?" he demanded suddenly. "I saw her car out back."

"Not that it's any of your business, but I borrowed it. My Buick is acting up."

Another muttered comment, probably something along the lines of 'I'm surprised it still runs,' Madison imagined.

"You're telling me you came out here alone?" Officer Perry demanded.

Madison heard Sybil's voice speak up, loud and clear. "She did not. *I* came with her." Her tone was emphatic.

"I should have known," he said in disgust. "Why do you let her drag you down with her, Sybil? You know she's a bad influence."

Madison couldn't help but smile, hearing the older woman turn on the charm. Miss Sybil still had it, so it seemed. "We didn't mean any harm. We just came to say goodbye to our old friend. We have a lot of good memories in this house, Otis."

"It's still trespassing. The bank owns the house now."

"No thanks to those grandsons of hers!" Granny Bert huffed.

Shaking her head, Madison moved toward the door. Her grandmother wasn't doing herself any favors, speaking out just when Miss Sybil was softening the ornery old lawman. It was time to intervene. With any luck, she could keep him from arresting them all on the spot.

"Where are you going?" Virgie hissed.

"To help."

She shook her gray head at such foolishness.

Madison stepped out into the hallway, but a noise down below drew her attention. Had Perry brought backup? *What if Brash were down there? How humiliating would that be?*

She couldn't imagine it being comfortable for either of them, though Perry would no doubt love it.

Deciding she wasn't there for the deputy's amusement, and she would face whatever wrath was in store of her, Madison moved forward. Just before pushing into the room, another noise stopped her.

Someone had bumped into a wall down below.

Brash isn't that clumsy, she thought. She tiptoed past the doorway, careful of where she stepped. She stealthily made her way to the open banister and peered down into the entry.

Nothing.

She waited a few moments, hearing her grandmother and Perry still bickering.

"You're here poking around in my case, aren't you?" the deputy accused.

"*Your* case?" Granny Bert raged. "You botched it so badly, there barely *was* a case!"

"I didn't see you doing much better!"

"I did everything in my power to find justice for my friend, even when it meant calling in outside help. *You* were too stubborn to admit we needed it!" her grandmother challenged.

"A fat lot of good that did! They couldn't help."

"They didn't hurt, either. Unlike *you*. You let key evidence go to waste!"

While the two of them hurled angry accusations at one another, Madison thought she saw a shadow moving below. She pressed back against the wall, holding in a gasp when she saw a shadowy figure cross the space. The person headed into the front parlor, toward the stairway.

There was no denying he wore a baseball cap.

Madison moved as quickly and quietly as possible. She motioned for Virgie to come with her as she stepped into the bedroom with the others.

"See!" Perry said with morose pleasure. "I knew she was here!"

"Shh!" Madison chided in a whisper. "That's not important. Did you come alone?"

"I'm the one asking the questions here, little lady."

"Answer my question!" she hissed, shaking the curtain rod in her urgency. "Did you bring backup?"

Even without the curtain rod she brandished, something in her voice gave him pause. "I'm alone," he answered quietly. "But don't think—'"

"Someone is downstairs," she whispered, cutting off any blustery remarks of him being able to handle the four of them. "I think it's the man from the sale. The one harassing me."

"You assaulted him," he reminded her, but he kept his voice moderately low.

"I know Brash reported the fact that someone has been stalking me. I think it's him. And he's headed our way."

Perry's demeanor immediately changed. As his hand moved to his service weapon, his voice took on a protective ring. "You ladies need to take cover."

"The drapes make my nose itch," Granny Bert complained.

"Come this way," Virgie urged, motioning toward the master bedroom.

As Deputy Perry crept forward into the hallway, the four women melted back into the shadows. Once inside the master bedroom, Virgie opened what looked like a closet door.

"It's the back staircase," she told them. "Hurry."

"But Perry..." Madison protested.

"We'll call for backup," Virgie said.

"Or we could charge the intruder from behind," Granny Bert suggested. "We'd have him cornered."

"Animals are dangerous when cornered," Sybil piped up as they descended the steep staircase. "I say we call for backup."

Madison wasn't certain what creaked more, the old wooden steps or the women's stiff joints. Inside the confines of the dark, narrow passage, the sounds were amplified and seemed loud enough for the intruder to hear from the other side of the house. It was a slow process getting three octogenarians down the staircase safely, but they finally made it to solid ground just outside the kitchen. Motioning for her companions to go out the way they had come in, Madison held back long enough to listen for sounds of movement.

Had the man made it up the stairs yet? Had Perry come down? Had they met in the middle and fought a silent battle? The scariest thought was that if the latter happened, who had won?

"Come on, Maddy!" Granny Bert urged. "We'll call for help."

The women hurried through the pantry, down into the lower larder, and pushed through the crude door into the root cellar. Again, it took the four of them to push open the rusty hinges of the outer doors, but soon they were blinded by bright sunshine.

"Get in the car!" Madison said heedlessly. "I'm calling Brash now."

The call went to voicemail, so she hung up and dialed 9-1-1. She gave Miss Sybil an extra boost to get into the SUV, crawled behind the wheel herself, and locked the doors.

"9-1-1. What is your emergency?"

"Vina! It's Madison! I'm out at Alpha Bodine's old mansion, and there's an intruder inside."

"Yes, Officer Perry is on the scene." Always professional, the dispatcher broke protocol to ask, "What are *you* doing there?"

"Never mind. There's someone else inside and—oh, wait! There he goes! He's on foot, running toward the woods behind the house. And there's Perry. He's in pursuit. He's okay," she reported in relief.

"I don't know about that," Granny Bert snorted. "Looks to me like he's huffin' and puffin'."

"Is that your grandmother?" Vina barked in disapproval. "You ladies get out of there! You could be in a dangerous situation. Get out now."

"But Perry—"

"Won't appreciate your interference, young lady,"

she retorted. Her voice brooked no argument. "Leave."

As Madison sped toward the police station, they met the other two deputies en route for Perry's backup. Brash's vehicle wasn't among them, making her wonder where her husband was.

Two minutes later, her phone flashed with his name on the screen.

"Maddy! Where are you?" he barked.

"Headed your way. Where are you?"

"Office. I just got out of a meeting. Do you want to tell me what in the hell is going on?" he bellowed.

She quickly warned, "You're on speaker, and I have passengers in the car."

"Good! Maybe someone can give me answers! Why were you out at the Bodine mansion?"

"You can yell at me later. Is Perry okay?"

"Since when are you so concerned about Deputy Perry?" he countered.

"Since we sort of left him high and dry," she admitted. "But Vina told me to!"

"I'm glad you listen to *someone*," he grumbled. "As for Perry, he's fine. The intruder got away, and Perry is hopping mad."

"I'm sure he is."

"I resent that!" Granny Bert butted in. "Who said I was involved?"

"With Genny out of commission, it only stands to reason."

"We'll be there in a few minutes and explain everything," Madison promised. "Love you."

In response, Brash only growled.

18

Brash sat at his desk, head propped onto his hands as he shook it back and forth. "Why, Maddy? Why?" he mumbled. "Why did you think breaking and entering was an acceptable way to investigate a case?"

"Technically," she said in a small voice, "we didn't break anything. We had a key."

"But you *knew* you didn't have permission to be out there."

Without a sound rebuttal, his wife remained silent.

"How am I supposed to explain this to the bank?"

"Why do you have to?" Granny Bert asked. "No harm was done. We didn't break anything. If anything, we did them a favor. We cleaned out the root cellar for them. And a few cobwebs here and there." She ran a hand through her hair to see if any lingered.

"I doubt they'll see it as a favor," Brash replied wryly.

"You're right. I'm sure they're much too busy to be bothered with such trivial details. If I were you, I wouldn't even mention it."

Known to make grown men quiver, his imperial smirk made no impression on the older woman.

Brash turned his attention to the other women in

the room. "Miss Sybil? Is there anything you would like to add to this fiasco of a situation we find ourselves in?"

"What fiasco, dear boy?" Sybil asked the chief of police serenely. She had helped Lydia watch him as a child and changed his dirty diapers. She was no more intimidated by his glare than her best friend.

Frustrated, he moved down the line. "Miss Virgie? Anything?"

"Absolutely!" she said, a bright smile lighting her heavily lined face. "I want to commend you for having a top-notch professional on your staff." She nodded her gray head emphatically. "Otis Perry has never been my favorite person. And yes, he was mighty sore at us and yelling at your wife and grandmother-in-law something fierce. But the moment he thought we might be in danger, he put aside his personal differences and protected us like any worthy officer of the law." She folded her hands together in satisfaction. "You can tell him I said so, too."

Brash struggled to keep his temper in check. "I'm glad he lived up to the expectations of the badge," he said. "I'm sorry to hear he raised his voice in anger but—" He shot his wife a sharp look. "I do understand his frustrations."

"Now that Virgie mentioned it, it did hurt my feelings," Granny Bert said with a discreet sniff.

"Not now, Granny," Madison warned from the side of her mouth.

Virgie raised her hand, as if they were in class.

"Yes, Miss Virgie?"

"I do feel I must mention I'm mostly to blame for what happened today. I was the one with the key. I was the one to call Madison."

"And why did you call her? I never got a straight answer about that."

"I remembered something I thought might be

relevant to the cold case. It was my idea to go out there. So, you see, it was my fault.”

“It may have been your idea, but all three of these ladies willingly accompanied you. I’d say you’re all equally at fault.”

“Once you hear why, you may say we’re all to be equally commended,” she predicted.

“And why is that?”

“If you don’t mind, I’ll let Madison explain the particulars. Hank must be worried sick about me. I left a note that said I’d be right back.”

“I’ve taken the liberty of calling your husband,” Brash informed her. “He’s outside, waiting to take you home as soon as we’re through.”

Sybil looked at her friend hopefully. “Think I can get a ride home? It’s about time for my program to come on.”

“Why, of course,” Virgie answered amicably. “Bertha, do you need a ride, too?”

“Ladies,” Brash broke in sternly, “we’re not done here.”

“What more is there to say?” Sybil asked innocently. “We left the house in better condition than we found it. We didn’t break or harm a thing. We attracted your wife’s stalker and left him dangling there for your deputy to arrest. We can’t help it if Perry let him get away!” She was quick to add, “But I do agree with Virgie. He was very chivalrous, telling us to take cover and let him handle the situation.”

“Are you suggesting you deliberately lured the stalker there, for Perry to intercept?”

The old woman ran the words through her mind, beaming brightly when she liked the sound of them. “That’s one way of looking at it!”

Frustrated beyond measure, Brash allowed Virgie and Sybil to leave but insisted they make themselves available for further questioning.

When Granny Bert would have followed them from the room, he spoke up, "Not so fast. Sit."

She turned back at him with her best look of innocence. "Are you speaking to me?"

"I certainly am. I may have gone easy on your friends, but they're first-time offenders. You two, on the other hand, are nothing but trouble!"

Granny Bert shrugged. "I've been called worse."

"For now, I'm willing to put the matter of trespassing on the back burner. I want to know what you found out at the house. Miss Virgie made it sound like something important."

Madison drew in a deep breath. "I think it could be." She pulled the sketchbook from her waistband, the cover a little wrinkled from wear. "Miss Virgie remembered finding this many years ago, in what I think must have been Garwin Bodine's room. The boy was seriously disturbed."

Brash took the book and flipped through its pages, his face tightening when he saw the graphic images.

"You're not kidding." He whistled lowly when he was done. "These are sick."

For once, neither woman had anything further to say.

Brash leaned back in his chair, looking first at the book, then at his wife. "I know what you're thinking," he said at last.

"Then you know I'm right. Anyone with that sick of a mind is a danger to society. He was a boy when he drew those, Brash. You can see that he graduated from birds and frogs to larger animals, like deer and sheep. Who's to say he didn't graduate to people after that? For all we know, this man is a serial killer. Brash, you have to find Garwin Bodine and bring him in for questioning!"

"It's not that simple, Maddy. This book is hardly an admission of guilt."

"I beg to differ!"

"Me, too," Granny Bert huffed. "That's proof of a sick mind right there. Evil."

"Or," he said, playing devil's advocate, "it could be proof of a creative mind. Have either of you ever sat through a horror movie? Watched a graphic video game that kids everywhere are playing these days? Those are just as sick, just as gruesome, yet they're considered entertainment. They rake in millions of dollars every year. Someone, somewhere, comes up with all those ideas and images." He plopped the sketchpad down on his desk, the sound echoing in the room. "For all we know, Garwin Bodine went out to Hollywood and made his fortune on this filth."

Before either woman could offer a rebuttal, there was a commotion outside Brash's door. It burst open unexpectedly, over Vina's frantic warning of "—can't go in there!"

"Dadburn it, Brash deCordova, that woman of yours is out of control!" Otis Perry pushed his way inside without invitation. Eyes glazed with anger and his face purple with rage, he never saw the two women sitting in front of his boss' desk.

Not waiting for her husband to reply, Madison came to her feet. Perry was short and wide, leaving her to tower over him. "I beg your pardon!" she glared back at him.

"I should have known you'd come running to your husband for protection! You and that grandmother of yours. Both of you are nothing but trouble." He jabbed his finger into Madison's shoulder as spittle flew from his mouth. "Stay. Out. Of. My. Case."

Brash had Perry backed up against the wall, his arm at Perry's throat, before the older officer had time to react.

"You, Deputy Perry," Brash told him in a deadly calm voice, "are walking on very thin ice. You *will not* touch anyone, particularly my wife, in such a manner again. Do I make myself clear?"

Perry's face lost all color. His eyes rounded, protruding from their sockets with fear. When he sagged against the wall, Brash thought for a moment that he had fainted. But when the deputy slurped in a deep breath of air and managed to nod, Brash eased his hold on the man.

"If you can behave yourself in a manner becoming to an officer of the law," Brash told him in a tight, carefully controlled voice, "you may take a seat and join us. If not, get out of my office and don't bother coming back."

Perry swallowed hard and took a seat.

Collapsed into a chair was an apt description, Madison noted. She moved aside and took another seat, allowing him to have hers.

"We were just discussing the incident at the Bodine mansion," Brash said, trying hard to control his anger. He settled into his chair and tortured a ballpoint pen, clicking the knob in and out, in and out. "I understand the intruder got away?"

Stubborn man that he was, Perry didn't know when to back off. "One of them did." He slid his eyes to the two women beside him, his accusation clear.

Brash chose to overlook it. "Did you get a good look at the man?"

"Average or above-average height. Average weight. Dark hair, best I could tell. He wore a baseball cap pulled low over his face."

"No distinguishing characteristics?"

"None that I could see."

"Was he carrying a weapon?"

"You mean like a curtain rod?" Perry asked, a snarl slipping into his words.

Brash was thrown by the reference. "Curtain rod? What do you mean?"

"Ask your wife. She brandished one against me."

Madison drew in a sharp breath but said nothing. When Granny Bert would have made a sharp retort, her granddaughter stopped her with a hand upon her arm.

Brash pierced his wife with a pointed look. "Madison? What is Deputy Perry referring to?"

"I had a curtain rod with me when I entered the mansion. To scare away snakes," she explained. She saw Brash fight back a smile at the visual. "I was still holding it when I insisted he stop bickering with Granny Bert and listen for a moment. I asked if he had anyone with him because I heard someone else in the house."

"Did you try to attack Deputy Perry with this curtain rod?"

"Of course not! I may have wiggled it to get his attention, only because he was too busy shouting that he was in charge." She relented by saying demurely, "But I agree with Miss Sybil and Miss Virgie. Once he realized the seriousness of the situation and the danger we could all be in, he acted very professionally."

Brash's eyes shone with satisfaction, silently thanking her for sparing the other man's pride.

"Deputy, is that when you pursued the intruder?"

"Uhm, yes, sir," Perry agreed, perplexed by Madison's gracious response.

Brash sat back in his chair, still giving the pen a workout. "I think I have a fairly clear picture of what happened today," he said at last, his anger dissipating. "Deputy Perry, do you have anything further to add at this point? I'll expect your full report on my desk, first thing in the morning."

"Just one thing," he said, a nerve working in his rounded jaw. "I think today is a prime example of the dangers of amateurs poking their noses in where they don't belong. As far as I'm concerned, that house still represents an active crime scene, and I'd thank you for asking your wife and her grandmother to stay away from it. Today could have gone quite differently if I hadn't intervened."

"I agree it could have gone differently," Brash allowed. "But I disagree about it being an *active* crime scene. Alpha Bodine's murder occurred almost thirty years ago. It's time to let it go."

"Never!" the man vowed.

"Now," his superior officer countered, his tone calm but final.

Drawing in a deep breath, Brash continued, "In fact, you should know that I have requested Madison and her team at *In a Pinch* to look into the very cold case of Mrs. Bodine's murder."

"You can't do that!" Perry protested.

"I can, and I have. To that end, these ladies uncovered something at the house that could become a key piece of evidence in solving this decades-old crime."

"That's impossible! I've been over that house with a fine-toothed comb! There's no way they found something I didn't," he insisted.

"And yet, they did." Brash motioned to the sketchpad on his desk.

When Perry made a move to take the pad, Brash stopped him. "I haven't finished looking this over. Be advised, I'm asking you to work with my wife and make available to her any information she requests. After nearly three decades, I think it couldn't hurt to have a fresh set of eyes on this case. I'm sure you agree."

Perry refused to answer. He glared straight ahead.

"Understand this, Deputy Perry. At present, I'm asking you to cooperate with the consultant of my choosing. If need be, I will make that an order."

The nerve continued to jump in Perry's cheek. Still staring ahead, he asked stiffly, "Am I excused?"

Brash's voice was like granite. "You are." When Perry reached the door, Brash added, "But hear this. Do not refer to my wife as 'that woman of mine' ever again. You will treat both her and her grandmother—you will treat *all* women—with respect and dignity. Do I make myself clear, Deputy Perry?"

"Crystal."

"Close the door on your way out."

19

Perry wasn't the only one on thin ice. Madison all but skidded from her husband's office, knowing she would deal with more cold treatment at home.

The entire morning was gone, and she still had work to do. She was in no mood to arrive at her office and find Derron on the phone, flirting with his latest Mr. Right.

"I hate to intrude," she said in a sweet voice, meaning no such thing, "but I need your help with something."

Derron turned his back to her, as if to shield his words. "Sorry, Nate. The boss is being needy today. Like I told you before, she's a mess without me here to line her out... Yes, exactly! So true... Yes, this weekend. See you then. Toodles." He blew kisses over the phone before disconnecting.

"I hope Mr. Hot Stuff Cutie didn't mind me pulling you back to work," she said with heavy sarcasm.

Derron shrugged. "He knows how it is. He, too, has a needy boss."

"What kind of job does he have?"

For a moment, Derron looked stumped. "You know what? I don't think the subject has ever come up."

Madison stared at him in disbelief. "Seriously? You think he could be 'the one,' and you don't even know his full name or what he does for a living?"

"We don't have time for such trivial nonsense," her assistant said.

"So, what do you know about him?"

"I know the important things. He likes the same music that I like, he likes the same food that I like, he likes the same clothes that I like. He likes *me*. That's all I need to know."

She threw her hands up in defeat. "Fine. He's a wonderful guy with fabulous taste."

"And he's handsome. Don't forget handsome."

"Got it," she said, stalking to her desk.

"What has you in such a snit?" he asked.

"Run in with Berry Perry," was her only reply.

"That'll do it!"

"Did you complete the display cases for Lamont Andrews?" she asked.

"Yes and made out his bill. It's on your desk for approval. I can drop it in the mail on my way out."

They were both working when the alarm binged with the arrival of a guest.

"Dollface? Do you know this lady?" He peered into the monitor. "She looks familiar, but I can't place her. Seventy-ish. Gray curls plastered with hair spray. Snappy dresser. She's wearing some divine vintage pieces!"

"That sounds like Janet McSwain."

"Does she have an appointment?"

"Forget the appointment. The question is, does she have a driver's license?"

"My guess is that she doesn't. She's parked half-on, half-off the curb. She walked up to the gate."

Madison sighed. "Let her in."

By the time Janet McSwain marched up to the Big

House, she was out of breath and out of sorts. Madison met her on the porch with a glass of iced water.

"Hello, Mrs. McSwain," she welcomed her. "What a pleasant surprise."

"Surprise? Didn't the principal tell you I was coming?" Janet straightened her hat and tugged her suit jacket into place.

Oh, dear.

"Oh, yes, of course," Madison lied smoothly. "What was I thinking?"

"That's the trouble, Sylvia, dear. You fail to apply yourself. You always were such a smart girl in school, but you don't apply yourself."

Madison's brow puckered. "Sylvia?"

"Would you prefer I call you Ms. Bodine? Keep things professional between us?" the elderly woman offered.

"Uhm, no. No, Sylvia is fine. Would you like to have a seat here on the porch? There's actually a breeze today," Madison said. She was loath to invite the poor woman inside and have Derron make fun of her. "I took the liberty of making you a glass of water."

"And with mint, just the way your grandmother makes it!"

Unsure whether she meant Sylvia's mother Alpha or her own grandmother Bertha, Madison simply smiled and delivered the glass into her hands.

"I'm afraid this isn't a social call, my dear. I came to discuss your son with you."

"Oh?" Madison thought it was best to allow Janet McSwain to guide the conversation wherever her wandering mind took it.

"He missed class again today. This is the second time this week. I simply can't allow this sort of behavior to continue. He's fallen behind in his studies."

"That's not good," she murmured.

"I know he was at school this morning. I saw him in the hallway. But when it comes to fourth period, he simply seems to vanish!"

"Is that before or after the lunch period?"

"Immediately after," the teacher supplied.

"I'll speak to him about his extended lunch periods," she offered noncommittally.

"He returned for his fifth period class the first time. I'm not sure about today."

"What other day did he miss?" Madison asked, for no reason. It simply seemed the thing to do. If it were Blake missing school, she would certainly ask as much, plus more.

"Why, it was the day..." The schoolteacher stopped abruptly, looking uncertain.

Oops. Another time warp? Madison wondered.

"That is to say... I'm sorry, dear. How very insensitive of me. I know you don't want to be reminded of that horrible, horrible day!"

"What, uh, what day is that?"

"The day your mother died, of course!"

The news stunned Madison. Garwin wasn't at school for all classes the day his grandmother was killed? Had anyone—namely Otis Perry—known that fact?

Her mind raced through the timeline. Fourth period must be around twelve-thirty or one, or there about. The crime scene photos showed Miss Alpha's body had been discovered shortly before 4:27. By then, her blood had started to congeal on the carpet. Three hours seemed like sufficient time for that to happen, didn't it? Could the teen have sneaked away from school, murdered his grandmother, gone back to class to create an alibi, and then pretended to discover her body at the end of the school day? The police report said the brothers found the body after walking home from school together as they always did.

It was possible, she thought. The strangest part of that scenario was the 'murdered his grandmother' part. The words just didn't make sense in her mind.

Then, again, neither did the pictures she had seen in his sketchbook.

Realizing the schoolteacher was looking at her with empathy, Madison cleared her throat and asked, "Have you discussed this with anyone else? The police, for instance?"

"No, dear. No one has asked."

"I—I'll speak with him."

"That's good, dear. I do hate to see my students fall so far behind."

"Absolutely. Thank you for stopping by."

"My pleasure."

Mrs. McSwain got to her feet and started down the steps. Halfway to her car, she called over her shoulder, "Tell Bertha I said hello."

"Granny! Granny, I have to talk to you! Right now!"

"Hold your horses. You've already dragged me out once today. Can't a body get a moment's peace?"

"I have some pertinent news about the case."

"Why didn't you say so? I'll be right over."

"Or I can come there," she offered, trying to be considerate of the elderly woman.

"Nah. I'm at the *Five and Dime* visiting Lerlene and that penny-pinching brother of mine."

So much for her complaints about not having a moment's peace! Madison shook her head and told her grandmother to come on over.

When she arrived, Madison shooed her into the kitchen.

"I had a surprise visitor today," she announced.

"Not the man in the baseball cap, I hope?"

"No. Janet McSwain. Scarily enough, she drove over here." Madison still cringed at the thought of the old dear driving.

"Donny Ray took her keys, but somehow, she always finds another set," Granny Bert grumbled.

"She had me confused with Sylvia Bodine."

"You two look nothing alike!" her grandmother scoffed.

"No. But I suppose with me talking to her about Miss Alpha in recent weeks, she got it confused in her head. Anyway, she came to talk to me—that is, to Sylvia—about Garwin cutting class twice in the past week."

"That doesn't surprise me."

"No. But listen to this. He missed her fourth period class on the day Miss Alpha was killed."

"Fourth period? After lunch?"

"Exactly. I'm certainly no expert, and I know it depends on temperature, exposure, and all kinds of scientific stuff, but I imagine three hours is plenty of time for blood to congeal after a stabbing death. Granny, what if he skipped school, came home to kill his grandmother, went back, and then returned with his brothers in time to 'find' her body?"

"I'm not sure the boy was bright enough for all that," her grandmother contemplated.

"*Mean* usually requires some sort of intelligence. Those sketches were very detailed. He had to have some knowledge of how things worked, to dissect them that way!"

"Maybe."

"You look skeptical," Maddy accused. She thought her grandmother would be as excited about this revelation as she was.

"I'm just thinking. You say Janet thought you were Sylvia? She came to discuss the boys with her?"

"One of them, at least."

"I didn't realize Sylvia was around during that time. What if Janet knew something we didn't know? What if Sylvia was here, in The Sisters, at the time her mother was killed? What if she was the one to do it?"

"I found a note in the files. According to it, she was in Waco at the time."

"According to what? An eyewitness? A credit card receipt? A paid alibi?"

"I—I don't know. It didn't say. It was just a hand-written note in the margin."

"Otis Perry," her grandmother huffed. "He did sloppy research and made sloppy notations. Doesn't prove a thing."

"Are you saying you think Sylvia did this?"

"I'm saying we still don't have enough information to make a solid arrest. Like Brash pointed out, those drawings, as disgusting as they were, don't point a definitive finger toward Garwin. We need more evidence."

"How do we get it?"

"If I knew that," Granny Bert said forlornly, "I would have seen justice served twenty-odd years ago."

"So now what? Where do we go from here?"

"I'm not sure what to do about the cold case, but right now, we have a hot case that needs our attention."

"A hot case?"

"The man in the baseball cap, girl! He's back, and he's obviously still carrying a chip on his shoulder."

"For the life of me, I can't imagine why he wants that painting so badly."

"I spoke with Jean Applegate today. She's agreed to come by and look at the painting. Maybe she can shed some light on this mystery."

"Jean Applegate is coming *here*?"

"I figured it was safer to bring her to the painting, than vice versa. You don't have a problem with that, do you?"

"Of course not! It's just that she's Jean Applegate. She's famous!"

Granny Bert rolled her eyes. "I've known Jean for years. She puts her panties on the same way you do. One leg at a time."

"When can she come?"

"She's speaking at the library on Wednesday, but she said she'd try to come by tomorrow afternoon if she gets in town early enough. If not, she can come across the street after the program."

"She can't come too late in the afternoon. Brash will be home. Remember, this is his Christmas present."

"Would you rather get to the bottom of this, or surprise your husband on Christmas morning?"

"Both?"

"That may not be an option, girl. Sometimes, you have to choose your battles."

"Ooh, that's a good one. I should have put that one down for Genny at her Mommy and Me Shower. I know I had to learn to choose my battles with the twins. Taking a bath every single night and wearing clean socks wasn't nearly as earth-shattering as I thought at the time."

"It takes practice, getting the parenting thing down. Too bad you had a double whammy. You didn't get to practice on one, then improve by the second or third."

"My father was your fourth child," Madison pointed out. "What's your excuse for how he turned out?"

"It took a while—fifty-five years, give or take—but he finally leveled out. But fourth and final babies are a breed all their own," her grandmother acknowledged.

"It sounds like Sylvia—or maybe it was Miss

Alpha—got it right by the third son. Gregg seemed to have turned out all right."

"Not bad, especially since, like you, the first two were a double whammy."

"Wait. Garwin and Gordon are *twins*? Why did no one ever mention this to me?"

Her grandmother shrugged. "I guess no one thought to. Does it matter?"

"I—I'm not sure. You know twins share a special bond."

"But do they when one is rotten to the core, and the other one just around the edges?"

Madison narrowed her eyes in consideration. "Good question."

Brash was still angry with her that evening.

"I still don't know what possessed you to think it was acceptable to take your geriatric crew on a scavenger hunt on someone else's property!" Brash told her after dinner. They sat outside on the porch swing, enjoying a pleasant evening breeze and the wide, open space of the outdoors.

Madison wasn't certain she could tolerate the reverberation from his anger within the confines of walls.

"I'm sorry, Brash. I know I don't always make the best choices when I'm working on a case."

"You think?"

"You don't have to be snide about it," she sniffed. "I get caught up in the moment, okay? In the excitement of closing in on the answers I'm searching for."

"More often than not, those answers close in on you!" he retorted. After a moment, he relented and sighed. "I understand excitement, Maddy. I understand enthusiasm. What I don't understand is putting yourself at risk, time and time again."

"You do it all the time."

"I'm a trained professional. And I go in prepared and armed with something more substantial than a curtain rod!"

"How were we supposed to know someone would follow us there?"

"I don't know. Maybe because that same someone has been following you around for several weeks now? Did you forget that, Maddy?"

She couldn't help but look sheepish. "I guess I sort of did," she admitted.

"Sweetheart, I'm trying to protect you. I'm trying to protect our family and keep us together. It would be whole lot easier if you worked with me, not against me!"

"I'm not working against you, Brash."

"Really? Because sometimes it doesn't feel that way. Sometimes, it feels like you're doing everything against the rule of the law."

"Some rules are meant to be broken," she mumbled beneath her breath.

"That's something Granny Bert would say," he accused. "And it's not an answer you would accept from our children." He stood from the swing and stomped to the edge of the porch. "If you won't do it for me, Maddy, at least do it for the three of them!"

"Where are you going?" she asked, alarmed that he would just walk away like that.

"I just remembered something I have to do at the office."

"Brash!" she protested.

"Let me be, Maddy," he requested in a resigned voice. "I won't be gone long. But for now, just let me be."

20

Jean Applegate arrived in time to stop by the Big House early the next afternoon.

"It's such a pleasure to have you, Mrs. Applegate! I'm a big fan of yours." Madison tried her best not to gush.

"Thank you, dear. I'm a big fan of yours, as well. My grandson Monte told me how you helped him retrieve his Pup. He speaks very highly of you."

"It was a pleasure to help him. Please, come in. I've got the painting right here."

Jean and Granny Bert seated themselves in her office chairs while Madison pulled the painting from behind her desk. Derron had the afternoon off.

"Oh my. This is very well done. Very well, indeed," the renowned artist said, quite impressed with the rendering.

"I thought so. I even entertained the notion that it could be one of yours."

"No, I didn't do this one. But I wouldn't mind claiming it! This is exceptional."

"As you can see, it's not signed. Do you have any idea who may have painted it? Is there any way to identify it?"

"I'm not sure. Let me study it for a bit."

"Can I get you some tea? Coffee? I'm sorry I didn't offer before. I was so thrilled to have you here, I simply forgot!"

"I'm fine, but thanks."

"Sure. I'll quit talking now and let you examine the painting."

"I'll take some coffee," her grandmother said. "In fact, I'll help you make it. You'll excuse us, won't you, Jean?"

"Of course."

On the way to the kitchen, Granny Bert chided her granddaughter. "What is wrong with you? You act like that's John Paul Noble in your office!"

"I've finally outgrown my crush on the actor," Madison admitted. "But, sorry. I guess I'm just excited to have her in my house. She's very well known in the art world. More importantly, she's very good. I love her work."

"So do I, but I don't smother her with attention!"

"Is that why we came all the way to the kitchen for coffee, even though I have a machine in my office?"

"Exactly. Give the woman some space!"

Madison prepared a carafe of coffee and carried it back into the office on a tray just in case the artist had changed her mind.

"Oh, you must have read my mind," Jean smiled. "I decided I needed some coffee, after all. It's been a busy day of travel."

After serving her guest, Madison waited patiently for her appraisal.

"I think I can conclusively say that the artist may have been one of my students. I see definite signs of the techniques I teach. Naturally, I can't be certain. Other artists may teach a similar method, but I think it's safe to say I may have had this artist in one of my classes."

"I don't suppose there's any way of knowing who the student was?"

"I'm afraid not, dear. Where did you find this, if you don't mind my asking?"

"Not at all. I discovered it at an estate sale at Alpha Bodine's."

"Alpha? I haven't thought of her in years! The poor dear. It was such a tragedy, losing her to such violence. They never did find her killer, did they?"

Granny Bert shook her head. "I'm afraid not."

"I'm sorry, Bertha. I know how hard you tried. And I remember what good friends the two of you were. In fact, I don't recall Alpha having a single enemy."

"She didn't. Everyone loved Alpha." The words sounded hollow, considering she had been murdered.

"Didn't Miss Alpha take lessons from you at one time?" Madison asked the artist.

"Yes, but I highly doubt... This was done by a much more advanced artist than Alpha," Jean answered diplomatically. "Unless, of course, she continued to study her craft," she added.

"Not that I'm aware of," Granny Bert said.

"Her grandsons, on the other hand, did take lessons from me," Jean continued. "They were all very talented. Garwin dropped out early on, and I only had the youngest boy in class for a short while, but Gordon continued to take lessons from me, even after he had started an art career of his own. There for a while, I believe he did quite well for himself."

"That's what I hear," Madison said. "Do you know if he still paints?"

"I'm afraid not. He opened an art gallery but when it failed, I understand that it completely soured him on the arts. I hear he's in another line of work now."

"Do you think this could have been one of his paintings? Or one of his brother's?"

Jean looked back at the longhorn painting. "Possibly. But if I were to guess, I would say Gordon's. Garwin preferred... darker subjects."

"So I understand," Madison muttered. "This may sound like a strange question, but are you aware of any paintings such as this one being stolen?"

"I'm not sure that's something that would be newsworthy," the artist replied. "I mean, this painting is good. Very good. But unless it's one of the masters' works or taken from a museum or gallery, stolen art very rarely draws that sort of attention. Outside of a police report, there's no way of knowing who might buy or sell—or steal—at will."

The news was disappointing, but Madison nodded. "I understand."

"If you're looking for a mystery," Jean offered, her eyes sparkling with jest, "I suppose there's always the possibility it could be a re-used canvas."

"You mean like in that movie John Paul Nobles was in?" Granny Bert asked, sparking at the thought of adding another layer to the mystery. "Thieves stole a bunch of art from the Louvre, painted over the pictures, and smuggled them back to America to sell on the black market."

"It's been known to happen," Jean assured them. Her eyes twinkled again as she added, "Of course, most often a re-used canvas simply means the artist started over. I've been known to do it myself, particularly on a poor first draft."

"Hmm," Madison said thoughtfully. "I've never thought of a painting in the terms of a first or final draft."

"Whether writing or painting, it's all an art form. Artists in any medium rarely get it right on the first try."

"That's why I'm no artist," Granny Bert proclaimed.

"I don't have the patience for it!"

"I do recall that you girls were more impressed with our male model than you were the actual class," Jean teased her old friend.

"Can you blame us? He was a hottie!"

After visiting a while longer, Jean noticed the time and said she must go. Madison thanked her profusely for coming and even offered to pay her for her expertise.

"Don't be silly. I enjoyed our visit. And seeing such a lovely painting was my pleasure."

Madison saw her guest to the door, but her mind was already spinning off in new directions. Was that why the man was so desperate to retrieve the painting? What if the longhorn were covering a Monet original? What if there were a long-lost Rembrandt beneath the leafy branches and docile setting?

It could happen.

And even if it weren't the work of the great masters, there could still be some other valuable painting under there. Perhaps that was why Gordon Bodine's gallery had closed. Perhaps he was guilty of pilfering stolen art. If that were the case, maybe Gordon truly *was* the one to use his grandmother's estate as collateral, even though the general consensus placed the blame on his twin.

"We may never know," she said mournfully.

"What's that, girl? Speak up," her grandmother said, waving a final goodbye as Jean drove away.

"I've been thinking."

"Oh, Lordy! What now?"

"What if that's what all this is about? What if the man wants the painting back because he knows there's a more valuable one beneath it?"

"That's a bit far-fetched, don't you think?"

"Is it? Why else is this man so persistent about

getting the painting back?" She went through her hypothesis with her grandmother, walking her through the thought process.

"I suppose it's possible." Granny Bert said when she was done presenting her case.

"Miss Virgie suggested Gordon was mixed up with some unsavory characters," Maddy said. "I think that makes this scenario all the more possible. I think that, for whatever reason, Gordon was keeping the painting at the mansion, and this man was determined to get it. I had the misfortune of seeing it first and getting in his way."

Granny Bert tsked. "Leave it to you, Maddy girl. Leave it to you."

"I'm bummed."

Bethani made the glum declaration as she threw her backpack onto the kitchen counter and headed to the refrigerator.

"I'm sorry, sweetie," Madison said, looking up from putting chicken on to boil. "What happened?"

"On the one hand, something good. On the other, something not so good."

"Let's go with the good hand first."

"Since there's no football game this week, our cheer coach managed to get us into a competition for Saturday. On the coast, no less. Beach time!" She did a little party dance before grabbing a container of yogurt.

"Sounds fun. So, what's on the other hand? Why are you bummed?"

"Because we're spending the night and have to leave during the day on Friday. *This* Friday, the day my art class was coming to tour the mural!"

"I guess we'll need to cancel the tour." Madison

hoped she sounded suitably sympathetic when all she truly felt was relieved. She wasn't looking forward to the tour.

"But the class was really looking forward to it," the teen whined. "Mr. Raymond is practically giddy!"

"I suppose you could not go to the cheer competition."

"Are you kidding? It's at the beach! No way I'm canceling. We'll just have to postpone the tour."

Before Madison could thank the heavens for small favors, the girl added. "*Postpone.* Not cancel."

"Fine," she grumbled. "We'll postpone."

Bethani glanced over her mother's shoulder to see the ingredients scattered out on the counter. "I see we're having King Ranch Chicken for supper. Still sucking up to Daddy D?"

Madison used the girl's previous words against her. "Can't a wife do something nice for her husband without being accused of having an ulterior motive?"

A cunning light came into the teen's blue eyes. "Sure. In fact, why don't I finish making the casserole, and you go put your feet up?"

"Uh-oh," Madison said, sensing a trap. "You don't have a third hand, but I think there's another not-so-good caveat coming."

"Not really." She looked sincere enough. "I thought you liked the beach."

"I do."

"Good! Then you'll be a chaperone for the trip?"

"I never said that!"

"Please, Mom? I know it's short notice but think of how much fun this will be. They're renting a place on the beach just for us, and you can stay there, too. How fun is that?"

"But that's only three days from now!"

"That's plenty of time to pack a bag. You don't even

have to ride the bus. You can take your own car, and Megan and I can ride with you to keep you company."

"I don't know, Beth. I have a lot of work to do…"

"Don't you deserve a weekend off? You've been under a lot of pressure lately, working on this cold case and all. This is your chance to get away and relax a little. Sunshine, sand, and surf. What could be better than that?"

The teen's smile was contagious. The thought of spending a weekend at the beach did appeal to her.

"But what will Brash say?" she wondered aloud.

Bethani's grin widened. "Good thing you're making his favorite dish tonight!"

21

The cheer team was thrilled with their accommodations for the weekend.

"Wow! Look at this place!"

Madison had to agree, the oceanside inn on Bolivar Peninsula was lovely. Three stories of sweeping views, all from wide verandas overlooking the Gulf of Mexico. A sandy beach just steps away. Water and blue sky as far at the eye could see.

The Mermaid's Retreat was the perfect haven and exactly what her overwrought nerves needed. Even playing last-minute chaperone to a boisterous group of cheerleaders and putting up with their on-going drama was worth a weekend at the beach.

It helped that the inn's owner, Sirenity Blue, was personable and attentive to their needs. Having ten giggling teenagers underfoot didn't faze the innkeeper in the least. She made them all feel welcomed and helped them get settled in. She served the girls evening snacks and promised a made-to-order breakfast each morning.

Madison liked the proprietor immediately, establishing a rapport that led to late-night conversations and what she hoped would evolve into a lasting friendship. Even after the girls and their cheer coach scattered for the night, cell phones in hand and ear pods to tune out the world, the two women curled up on the wrap-around porch and talked as the waters rolled into the gulf.

"Tell me. What led you to open an inn along the Gulf Coast?" Madison asked.

Sirenity tossed back her dark, pixie-styled hair and laughed. "With a name like Sirenity Blue, did I even have a choice?"

"Is that your real name?"

Hand resting over her heart, Sirenity nodded. "Honest to God. My parents have quite the sense of humor. My sister's name is Teal."

Madison clapped her hands in delight. "I love it!"

"She has a shop here on the peninsula, *Teal's Treasures*. You should stop by if you have a chance."

"I may do that. I can always use a few new trinkets."

"What girl can't?" Sirenity asked with a cheeky grin.

"Have you been in business long?"

Sirenity looked out toward the Gulf. Moonlight danced along the rippling waves, sparkling like jewels in the water. Her voice was reverent as she answered, "Long enough to know this is where I'm meant to be. Not long enough to truly make a difference in people's lives. But I'm working on it."

Madison's eyes twinkled with intrigue. "That sounds a bit mysterious. It sounds as if you have a story to tell, Sirenity Blue."

"I have a hundred stories. They come to me one at a time, looking for a place to escape. A place to retreat. To find the answers they're looking for." Her voice softly fell. "And I listen. That's what I do."

Madison raised her wine glass in salute. "What a lovely sentiment."

They fell silent after that, listening to the ocean's

whispered secrets.

What stories do the waters tell? Madison wondered. *If a picture paints a thousand words, what must an entire ocean divulge?*

She almost fell asleep on the chaise lounge, pondering that very thought.

The cheer team spent most of Saturday at the meet. Madison attended their first round of competition, clapped when they advanced to the next stage, and promised to be back when their turn came again. In the meantime, she was going shopping and checking out the oceanside community.

She made a point to stop in at *Teal's Treasures.*

The proprietor was as personable and easy to like as her sister. The two resembled one another a great deal, but Teal's hair was long and glossy black, with definable ruffles of blue for highlight. Teal blue, of course.

"Are you looking for anything in particular?" the woman asked. "As you can see, we have a little bit of everything."

"Yes, you certainly do. Suntan lotions, shades, beach apparel, umbrellas..." She walked along an aisle, naming off only a few of the items she saw. "Oh, and furniture, too!" Madison was surprised to see not just folding chairs and beach loungers, but upholstered chairs, consoles, shelves, and assorted ottomans.

"We're having a sale on some of our artwork," Teal told her. "We have some very talented artists here on the peninsula. I do try to specialize in local works, but I carry a varied assortment." She flashed a smile. "It helps that I have a friend with a brother in the business."

Madison saw several pieces of art along the back wall. "Okay. I'll make my way back there."

"Feel free to holler if you have any questions."

Teal returned to the front of the store to help other patrons as Madison worked her way through a maze of flip-flops, beach gear, and colorful cover-ups. Past the scented candles and seashell art, she smiled at the cute quotes emblazoned upon a collection of pillows and painted signs. The girls, she knew, would love the papasan chairs, and Blake would appreciate the chain-saw art deer head.

The paintings were much of what she expected. Seashells and seashores, gorgeous sunsets, and carefree sailboats. The parrot painting made her think of Derron's Tango, and the pastoral scene could have come straight from the deCordova or Montgomery ranches. There were cityscapes of Houston and Galveston, and a plethora of oil refineries in silhouette. She didn't care for the modern hodgepodge of colors and shapes, but she thought the field of Texas wildflowers was very well done. She was interested enough to thumb through the small stack of canvases leaning against the wall, some of them with frames, some without.

And that's when she saw it.

An almost perfect companion to the longhorn painting currently residing in her hidden passageway.

The style was the same. The colorization was the same. This painting was of a longhorn cow facing to the left, its coat a creamy white with random red spots.

The exact opposite of the bull.

Together, the perfect pair.

A squeak emitted from her throat.

Madison gulped and looked around, hoping no one had heard the strange noise. She made a similar sound when she saw the price tag.

Two hundred and forty dollars! There was no way she would pay that for the painting, no matter how good it was.

"Find something you like?" Teal asked, seeing her stare at the painting.

"Uhm, yeah. Yes. This painting is very well done."

"Isn't it, though? My friend's brother painted it. I think it's magnificent!"

"Is it—Is it by chance on sale?"

"As a matter of fact, it is. See the green dot? Forty percent off."

Madison did a quick calculation in her head. "Oh. That's still over my budget. My husband and I promised not to spend more than a certain amount on each other."

"Anniversary?"

"Christmas. I'm looking ahead," Madison admitted.

"Very smart. The holidays will be here before we know it! According to my friend, that was originally part of a pair. Somehow, they got split up, so I'll tell you what... I'll knock another ten percent off. And since you're staying at my sister's inn, I'll make you an even better deal. How does sixty percent off sound?"

"Seriously? That would make it only about a hundred dollars!"

"Hey, I've had it for a while now," Teal confided. "Most people are shopping for remembrances of the coast, not Western art. Take the bargain, and we'll both be happy."

"You're on!" Madison said without hesitation.

"Perfect! Here, I'll carry it to the front for you."

Madison followed behind her, reluctant to let the framed canvas out of her sight. She had already been down that path once, and she didn't want to repeat it. As Teal rang up her purchase, Madison asked, "Do you think your friend would object to you giving me his name? I notice the painting isn't signed, but I'll love to know more about the artist."

"Sure. I know Gregg wouldn't mind. He's a school counselor not too far from here. He and his wife visit the peninsula often. Give me a second, and I'll find his number."

Madison's mind screamed with excitement. *Gregg, the school counselor! The youngest of the Bodine boys. Which meant his brother, most likely Gordon, had been the artist.*

"Thanks, Teal," she beamed. "That would be great. I appreciate it."

On the way back to the competition, Madison wondered whether this reinforced her theory about the stolen art or negated it. If her previous assumption was correct— that Gordon's gallery was involved in pilfering stolen art— that meant he was directly involved with the heist. If this was his painting, he was the one knowingly painting over a stolen piece.

If that weren't the case, then it poked holes in her entire theory.

But what else could it be, she wondered, *if not that?*

Was Gordon Bodine's work impressive enough to push someone else into stealing it? According to Jean Applegate, he was good but not that good. Not so good that the man in the baseball cap would go to such lengths to possess it.

So, what if, she considered, *Gordon* had been the one to steal it from another artist and passed it off as his own work? Maybe the man in the cap was simply trying to get his own artwork back.

If that were the case, there had to be more to the story than what she saw. She doubted earning a seller's commission was the issue. If the painting were worth thousands, Gordon might try to sell it on the sly to avoid giving the artist his or her cut. But the commission payout on a couple of hundred dollars would hardly be worth such trouble.

Madison couldn't help but think she was missing something. Some link that tied it all together and explained why the man in the baseball cap was so desperate to get his hands on Brash's present.

"Geez," she said aloud. "First the chair I bought for him and now the painting!" She puffed out her cheeks on a sigh. "From now on, I may stick to giving my hubby gift cards. They're less trouble and definitely less drama!"

The weekend trip to the coast proved to be exactly what Madison needed.

She managed some rest and relaxation, played in the still-warm Gulf with the girls, made a new friend, and found one more link to not only the mystery behind the painting, but also to the whereabouts of the Bodine men.

Best of all, two nights away from her husband was the perfect ice breaker between her and Brash. His anger had cooled considerably by the time she returned, and he was the same loving, attentive husband as normal.

By Monday afternoon, Bethani was once again begging to set up the tour for her art class.

"Okay, fine!" Madison finally relented. "Let's just do it and get it over with."

"Thursday, then?"

"What happened to Friday?"

Bethani looked at her mother incredulously. "There's a game this week. I have to cheer."

"Fine. Thursday after school."

Her brother was concerned. "What am I supposed to do while the geek squad is here?" Blake wanted to know.

Madison rolled her eyes. "There's another way into the kitchen, son. They won't interfere with you getting to eat."

"And we're not all geeks!" Bethani insisted, popping him upside the head.

"Hey, watch the hair," he said, ducking away. "I have a date later."

"A date?" Madison questioned. "It's a school night."

"A study date," he assured her. "I cleared it with Daddy D."

"Oh. Well, then, okay."

"Cool." He hugged his mother with one arm as he snagged an orange with the other. "You're the best."

Madison fought back tears as she took the back way to her office. She would miss moments like this when the kids went off to college. She might even come to miss their constant bickering, the way Granny Bert predicted.

Hoping her timing was right, Madison dialed the number Teal Blue had given her. With any luck, Gregg Bodine was home from school but hadn't sat down for dinner yet.

A masculine voice answered on the third ring. "Hello?"

"Mr. Bodine?"

His voice came out a bit cautious. "This is Gregg Bodine."

"Hi. My name is Madison deCordova. I hope you don't mind, but your friend Teal Blue at *Teal's Treasures* gave me this number. Do you have a moment to talk?"

"I suppose. What's this about?"

"I purchased one of the paintings she had gotten from you. I don't know if you'll remember it, but it was of a longhorn cow grazing in a grassy field."

"Oh, I remember the painting." His voice sounded quite emphatic.

"It's a gorgeous piece. I was wondering if you could tell me more about it."

"I'm not sure what there is to tell. It's a cow in a field." She thought she heard a shrug in his words, but his tone finally relaxed. "I think my brother took a snapshot while visiting our hometown," he offered, "and painted it from the photo."

Madison decided to play innocent. "Your hometown? Is that here in Texas?"

"Yes. Tiny little town called The Sisters. Technically, they're two different towns, but it's hard to know where one ends and the other begins."

"The Sisters?"

"Yeah, up in River County. You've heard of it?"

"You may find this hard to believe, but I actually *live* in The Sisters! Juliet, to be precise."

"Really?" He sounded stunned. "What a small world! Who's your family? Wait. Did you say deCordova? Isn't that the name of the football guy? The one who played pro and then coached at Texas A&M and Baylor?"

"Yes. Brash. Brash deCordova. He's my husband."

"You're kidding!"

"Not at all. You may not remember her, but my grandmother is Bertha Cessna."

"Granny Bert? Of course I remember her! She and my grandmother were good friends."

Madison debated on how to best reply. She played it safe by saying, "I don't think I know any Bodines here."

"You wouldn't. There's hardly any of us left, and none of us live there anymore."

"That's a shame. Do your siblings live around you?"

"No. One brother is in Austin. The other? It's been

so long since I heard from him, I'm not sure where he is these days."

She pressed her luck by asking, "Your parents?"

"Just my mom, and she's somewhere in the Louisiana swamps. We don't talk very often. But forgive me for getting off track. You wanted to know about the painting, not my life history."

If only you knew! Madison thought to herself.

"Yes. Right. The painting. Teal mentioned it was part of a pair. I'd love to buy the other one, too, if it's available."

"Sorry, but it disappeared years ago."

She pretended to be disappointed. "Oh. So, this is an older painting?"

"I'd say at least fifteen years or so. My brother painted it after we got the house back. My grandmother... that is, we inherited her house after she died and we all came of age. Me, mostly. I was the baby of the family."

"And the painting just came up missing?"

"Yeah, I think so." He sounded unsure of the details. "I remember seeing the companion piece. It was of a bull, lying in the pasture. For a while, it hung on the wall in the game room. Even though Gran was dead and gone, we knew better than to hang Western art in her prized rooms. We decorated the game room for our own tastes. For Garwin, that was neon beer signs." His laugh sounded hollow. "But one day, I went back to the house, and the bull was gone. I guess one of my brothers sold it or something. They were always doing stuff like that. Whenever they needed a little extra money, they just sold off another piece of our past."

"That's a shame," Madison said, meaning it.

"I figured if they could take one, I could take the other. More information than you wanted to know, I'm sure. My wife tells me I'm still bitter and need to learn to let it go, but sometimes it just gets to me, you know?"

"I'm sure it does," she commiserated. "Is the house still there?" Now she *was* pressing her luck.

"Yes, but it no longer belongs to us. Darn fool brother of mine used it as collateral and lost the whole thing!"

"I truly am sorry to hear that, Mr. Bodine. It sounds like you got the short end of the stick."

"Comes with the territory of being the youngest, I guess," he said. "They always did boss me around."

"Maybe it's a good thing I was an only child, after all," she mused.

"When I talk to my brothers again—which won't be anytime soon, I can assure you—do you want me to mention you're interested in the second painting? They may remember what happened to it."

"Uhm, yes. Great. That would be fine. Thank you." It was an awkward response, but her mind was at work again.

What if the man harassing her turned out to be his brother? She and Genny had tossed the thought around that very first day, but she had moved on to other scenarios by now. What if her first impression had been the right one? The Bodines had been banned from attending the sale. Perhaps Gordon had known the painting was somewhere in the house and wanted it badly enough to take drastic measures in getting it back.

Madison worried she had just made matters worse.

Way to go, Maddy girl, she sulked to herself. *Nothing like volunteering your phone number to your stalker!*

22

"I'm so confused."

Madison made the admission to her grandmother as they sat staring at the two paintings side by side.

"What's so confusing?" Granny Bert scoffed. "That one on the left is a bull. You don't have to see the equipment underneath to know he's got extra muscle and a thick, masculine neck. The one on the right is a cow. Even if the udder isn't a dead giveaway, her bone structure is more feminine."

"I'm not talking about the art subject!" Exasperated, Madison ran her fingers through her hair, tugging on the roots. "I'm talking about the case. About the mystery *behind* the paintings. I have so many different theories floating around in my head that I've gotten them all tangled up in my mind."

"Well, then, let's talk it through," her grandmother said pragmatically. "Maybe we can get this sorted out."

"I don't even know where to start," Madison said, almost in a whine.

"Start with the paintings. What do we know about them?"

"I know that someone, probably Gordon Bodine, painted them several years after Miss Alpha's death. I know that the brothers had enough respect for their grandmother's memory that they hung the Western pieces in the game room, rather than in what they called her 'prized' rooms."

"That says something about their raising, at least," her grandmother mumbled.

"I know that at some point, the painting of the bull disappeared. What I don't know is how it reappeared during the estate sale, or why the man in the ballcap wants it so badly."

"Theories?"

"At first, I thought maybe the painting of the bull contained a secret message. But Derron and I examined it with a magnifying glass and couldn't find a thing. When I found the second painting, I felt compelled to buy it. I thought seeing them together as a pair might tell me something. But even side by side, I can't see a pattern or any sort of story being told in the background."

"I think we can rule out the possibility of them being a map to hidden treasure," her granny nodded.

"Agreed. My next theory was the stolen art angle. It makes the most sense, since we know that Gordon owned a failed art gallery, and the house was used as collateral for a loan. My guess is that he got caught doing something illegal—probably fencing stolen art— and lost everything."

"So does that make the man in the baseball cap Gordon Bodine?"

"It makes sense, don't you think?" Madison sounded anything but certain.

"I reckon. But if he's already been caught and shut down, why the urgency?"

Madison's face was glum. "I don't have an answer for that."

"So, let's move on to the cold case. What have you

learned on that front?"

"Other than speculation and gossip? Very little. The usual motive—and the only theories that make sense—are theft, anger, and greed. Nothing was stolen, no one seemed to have a raging vendetta against Miss Alpha, and, if greed were the motive, it was a weak and wasted effort. The boys couldn't claim it for another several years and even then, it's not like they immediately sold out, split the money, and ran. The house pretty much sat empty for twenty or so years."

"Like your husband always says, murder never makes sense. What about the reasons that defy logic and good sense?"

Maddy's mouth twisted in thought.

"I explored the cult angle. There's no definitive proof that Sylvia was part of one, but I think it's highly possible. The thing is, the group she belonged to wasn't into devil worship, so the marks carved into the dead animals and the creepy signs don't fit in. Honestly? I think those were the work of kids, trying to stir up trouble and cause panic."

"Sounds like something that Garwin would think amusing," her grandmother harrumphed.

"Exactly. Which brings me to the other reason for murder that defies all logic: pure meanness. The unexplainable workings of an evil, psychotic mind."

"Again. Garwin."

"Yes, but there's still the fact that Gordon was no angel. Maybe the two of them were in on it together."

"The twin connection?"

Madison shrugged. "Maybe. It's hard to say. To be honest, my brief conversation with Gregg Bodine proved more helpful than all the rest of my research put together. Their family completely fell apart after Miss Alpha's death, and there's been little contact between the brothers. He's lost contact with Garwin. Gordon lives in Austin. And Sylvia is in the swamps of Louisiana, of all places."

"Louisiana?" Granny Bert barked. "As in the last place her father and brother were seen alive?"

"Yes, ma'am, that's the place. Makes you wonder about those rumors floating around all these years, doesn't it? Rumors that Leroy and Benny may have faked their deaths. Maybe they were right. Maybe it was all a scam, and Sylvia was in on it, too."

"I wouldn't put it past Leroy, that's for sure and certain!" her grandmother snorted. "And I wouldn't put it past him to have come back and killed Alpha, thinking Sylvia would inherit everything and share with him." She thumped the table emphatically. "So, we still can't rule out greed."

"True. But if he did have something to do with her murder, it did him no good. Sylvia's boys inherited everything," Maddy mused. "I'm not sure if or how it works into Miss Alpha's death, but I know that Gordon and Garwin sold off pieces of their inheritance bit by bit. The estate belonged to the three of them, but they never seemed too worried about shortchanging their youngest brother. He's still resentful of that fact, even though he seems to have a loving wife helping him work through his anger."

"You're right. I'm not sure that fits in with anything."

"I know. But something keeps nagging at the back of my mind, saying the murder and the painting could be connected. There's something I'm missing. Something that makes this painting important enough to steal. Something that in some weird way has to do with Miss Alpha's death."

"I thought it wasn't painted until years later."

Madison blew out a miserable breath. "Oh, yeah. I forgot that small detail."

After a moment of dejected silence, Granny Bert had a question. "How attached are you to those paintings?"

"What do you mean?"

"Would you be heartbroken if one of them got messed up?"

"Well, they were supposed to be Brash's Christmas present. And together, they cost me over a hundred and fifty dollars." She considered the original question. "But I suppose I could live without them. Why? What did you have in mind?"

"What if Gordon Bodine did paint over an old canvas? If he did it on one, he may have done it on both. Like everything else, maybe he planned to sell them one at a time. Could have been to throw off suspicion, could have been on an as-needed basis for cash." She abruptly asked, "Which one is your favorite?"

"I suppose the bull."

"Then let's see if we can scrape off some of the paint on the other one. Just in one corner. Just enough to see if there's something under there."

Madison sounded skeptical. "I don't know, Granny. I think we'll just mess it up. That sounds like something for a professional."

"Give me a little vegetable oil, and I bet I can prove you wrong," the older woman said with confidence.

After a moment of contemplation, Madison relented. "I guess I don't have anything to lose. Other than a hundred bucks, that is." Grumbling, she added, "And a really cool present for my husband."

"Look at it this way. If there's a valuable painting under there, maybe there's a reward. Then you can buy him something even better."

Still looking doubtful, Madison held out her hand. "Just give me the cow."

After loosening the back of the picture frame,

Madison realized the painting had been done on a canvas board, rather than a traditional stretched canvas as she first assumed. "I don't know if this is a good sign or a bad," she muttered. "At least we won't stretch the canvas when we destroy the painting."

"Stop your complaining. And watch what you're doing," Granny Bert cautioned. "You dropped it!"

Madison shot her a sharp look and argued, "No, I didn't. I have it right here in my hand. See?"

"Then what fell on the table?"

"Whatever it is, it fell face down." Frowning, Madison set the canvas with the cow aside and reached for the fallen object. "That's weird. It looks like another canvas board. For whatever reason, I think they doubled the boards.'"

"Maybe to make the frame fit better," Granny Bert suggested.

"Maybe." She scooped up the board and flipped it over, expecting it to be blank.

Madison gasped when she saw the second painting. It was not nearly as well done as the longhorn, but a decent-enough rendition that she had no trouble recognizing what it depicted.

She recognized the setting first. *Miss Alpha's parlor! Complete with Persian rug and mantel clock.*

Her eyes focused on the people in the painting. The woman with the gray bun and the dress was Miss Alpha. The other was a teenage boy, judging from his white t-shirt and sneakers, and the baggy set of his jeans. He was close to the same height as the woman but heavier. No doubt stronger.

Madison leaned in closer to study the details. The elderly woman had something in her hand and seemed to be arguing with the teen. Her face looked angry. Madison couldn't be certain, but she thought the papers in Miss Alpha's hand contained the picture of a bird.

The sketchpad!

Beside her, Granny Bert paled. "Is that... Is that Alpha?"

"I—I think so." Madison's answer was breathless.

"And is that what I think it is in her hand?"

"Garwin's sketchpad? Yes. I think so."

"So, Alpha discovered the gruesome sketches and confronted the boy."

"It looks that way."

Granny Bert's voice filled with sadness. Madison didn't remember ever hearing her grandmother sound so defeated. "The boy killed her?"

"Not—Not necessarily. We don't know what transpired next," she was quick to say. "Maybe this was a form of self-therapy. Maybe he used his art as a way to express his anger."

It could have been true. Perhaps the painting was nothing but fantasy. Perhaps it was nothing but his imagination running free. A way to express his darkest thoughts and to work through his anger toward his grandmother.

It was possible.

But neither woman believed it.

Madison peered more closely at the painting. The hands on the clock showed a few minutes after ten. Morning or night, she wondered. The window beyond looked shadowy, so she guessed it was nighttime. Had Miss Alpha waited up on him one evening, confronting him when he came home? The painting didn't show the boy's face, but Madison could see his hands clenched in anger.

After a long moment of dread, Granny Bert spoke. "I reckon we need to see what's behind the other one."

Dread pooled in Madison's stomach. What if it was as she feared? What if this next painting was of Miss

Alpha's actual death? How would her grandmother react? Alpha Bodine had been her friend.

There was only one way to know.

Like with the first painting, there were two boards in the frame, one on top of the other. Madison slowly separated them, carefully revealing the hidden painting at the back.

Whether fantasy or fact—whether it happened only in his mind or in reality—Garwin had painted a graphic rendition of a fight between himself and his grandmother. And in this painting, there was a knife and blood.

Granny Bert cried out in horror, the sound mangled.

Madison's mind screamed in its own silent protest.

There were no words.

The proof, however, was there on the canvas. Miss Alpha had fallen to the floor, a wooden-handled knife sunk into her chest. Blood was already pooling on the floor around her. The teenager had blood on his hands and on his striped t-shirt. Maybe the most telling fact was the face of the clock. 1:05.

Enough time to leave school, murder his own grandmother, and return to campus in time for fifth period, Madison realized.

The thought was chilling. Sickening.

Madison put her hand over her mouth to hold in the horror of it all.

Had her murder been premeditated?

Did it matter?

Garwin had done it. Garwin Bodine had killed his grandmother!

23

In the silence following their horrible realization, the buzz from Madison's phone seemed especially harsh.

With effort, she dragged her eyes down to focus on her screen's message.

The words jolted her. "Oh, no!" she cried. "I forgot Bethani's art class is coming over. They're already on their way."

Her grandmother looked stricken. Her voice was filled with angst. "We can't stop now! Not after almost thirty years! I finally know the truth. I have to see this through."

Madison gently touched her arm. "Not stop, Granny Bert. Just postpone. I promise." She tried out a weak smile. "What's one more hour, after all this time? Please. I'll put this back in the secret panel for safekeeping, and the minute they're gone, I promise we'll call Brash. But we need to hurry now. The class is almost here."

Granny Bert's sigh was heavy. "I'll do it. I'll put it away. You stay here and try to hurry them along. The sooner they leave, the sooner we can make the call. The sooner we can see justice served."

"Are you—Are you sure?" It was like asking her grandmother to carry her friend's dead body to its grave.

Face pale and drawn, Granny Bert pulled slowly to her feet. As Madison laid the painted burden in her arms, the older woman moved with the same heavy footsteps of a pall bearer. She looked every bit her age and more.

Granny Bert disappeared through the back hallway as the front door chimed, announcing Bethani's arrival with her class.

Company couldn't have come at a worse time.

"Mom? Mom, we're here!"

"Be right there!" Madison called back. "Show your guests in."

She did her best to calm her thoughts as she tidied up and straightened her hair. The dark- chestnut strands were a mess after torturing them so earlier.

Even from the connecting butler's pantry, she could hear Bethani's excited chatter about the mural on the dining room walls. Trenton's deeper voice chimed in with thoughts about the shading techniques.

Madison expected to see a dozen teenagers in the formal dining room. To her surprise, there was only Bethani, her boyfriend, and a man with his back to her, bent close to examine a particular scene Trenton called to his attention.

"Hello," she greeted the tiny group. "Where is everyone? I expected the entire class."

"There was some sort of mix-up, and no one understood we were coming today," Bethani explained airily. "We'll have to reschedule, but I told Mr. Raymond it was fine for him to come on over. He's been dying to see it for himself. Here, come meet him."

Madison was pleased to see her daughter so excited about her art class. She hooked an arm around the teen's waist and followed her around the long table.

"Mr. Raymond, I'd like for you to meet my mom Madison deCordova. Mom, this is our art teacher Mr. Raymond."

The man straightened and turned, a smile on his lips. He extended his hand for introductions and said smoothly, "Mrs. DeCordova. How gracious of you to allow me to come today. I've been quite anxious to see your impressive work of art."

He said something more, but the buzz in Madison's head drowned out his words. Her mind was stuck in slow gear, barely churning to process her thoughts.

Standing before her was the man who had been harassing her for weeks. The man from the estate sale. The man who followed her to Granny Bert's and tried breaking into her car. The man who posed as the exterminator to get into the house.

And now, here he was. Inside her home and acting as if his presence was perfectly normal. Acting as if he had never seen her before.

Madison wasn't sure how she responded. She shook his hand, making the physical contact as brief as possible. She thought she mumbled some sort of greeting. If Bethani and Trenton thought her welcome less than gracious, she couldn't worry about it now. Her mind struggled to keep up.

The man was *here*. Inside the house.

She had to protect the kids. And Granny Bert.

She had to keep her family safe.

Her frantic thoughts warred back with questions.

Who was this man? He called himself Mr. Raymond, but who *was* he? Was this Gordon Bodine?

How could he look at her so guilelessly, as if this were the first time they had met? He had stalked her on and off for over a month. She had hit him in the face with a bowl, for Heaven's sake! Granny Bert had threatened him with a shotgun. He *had* to recognize her!

How could she get the kids out of harm's way? She had to get a message to Brash, without alerting suspicion.

The art teacher's words dragged her away from her thoughts.

"Bethani and Trenton have been telling me about this mural for weeks, but I had no idea it was so magnificent."

"Uhm, yes," she managed to say.

"Tell him about how Granny Bert wanted to paint over it, Mrs. D," Trenton said, having heard the story from his girlfriend. "It would have been a great travesty. I'm so glad she didn't!"

"That—That was just a ploy. She wouldn't have carried through with it," Madison assured the teenager.

"Granny Bert?" Mr. Raymond questioned, looking amused by the odd name.

Madison was proud of herself for answering without a stutter. She gradually gathered her wits about her again. "My grandmother, Bertha Cessna. She has a flair for the dramatics." *You remember, don't you?* She thought silently. *Like pulling a shotgun on you when you tried breaking into my car?*

He never batted an eye.

Madison deliberately stepped closer to the mural, placing herself between the man and her daughter. Determination kept her voice steady. "Experts tell me it's one of Seymour Addison's largest and best works still in existence today. A rare treasure, so they say."

"And I agree. It's truly stunning."

If he wanted to play nice, so could she. She could act like a normal, congenial hostess. Surely, he would reciprocate like any normal, gracious guest. It was the Southern standard of good manners.

"Beth, why don't you and Trenton go to the kitchen and make Mr. Raymond a glass of iced tea?" she encouraged. It would get the kids out of immediate danger, and she could somehow get an SOS to Brash.

The teacher thwarted her efforts. "Thanks, but I'm good."

Maybe small talk would soften him up, Madison decided.

"I understand you're quite an accomplished artist, Mr. Raymond," she said with a forced smile. "Bethani tells me you've sold several of your paintings. Where was your studio?"

"I've had several over the years. I started painting when I was quite young," he asked.

"Oh? Did you take lessons, or is yours a born talent?"

"I'd like to think it was more of the latter, but my art teachers would appreciate me giving them much of the credit. I've had several of those, too," he volunteered before she could ask.

He was being deliberately evasive. Madison tried again.

"From what I understand, we're very fortunate to have someone with your talent involved with this new program. How did you hear about it?"

At last, the teacher offered something she wasn't forced to drag from him. "Quite by luck," he told her, his facial expression changing to one of enthusiasm. "I have several friends in the teaching profession, and one mentioned this innovative new program starting at your school. It sounded intriguing."

He sounded so convincing that Madison had to question herself. This *was* the same man, wasn't it? Granted, she had never gotten a good, long look at her stalker's face. He had been wearing the baseball cap most of the time. In the few seconds before swinging the bowl, she hadn't exactly been studying his features.

Could she be mistaken? Was her mind playing tricks on her? She thought she had seen the man again at the hospital. But, like the teacher, the man in the hospital hallway had appeared not to recognize her. What if she had it all wrong?

"As luck would have it," Mr. Raymond went on, an odd light coming into his eyes, "everything worked out, and I was available."

Something about his smile tickled the hairs on the back of Madison's neck. The cunning light in his eyes was deliberate, daring her to challenge him.

He was playing with her. He knew that she knew. He knew that she suddenly doubted herself. He threw out this little tidbit because he was *enjoying* this game of cat and mouse!

She hadn't been mistaken. This was the man. This was Gordon Bodine.

"Luck, indeed," she muttered. Manipulation was the better word. But, *how?* How had he managed to manipulate his way into the brand-new program at Sisters High? And to be the first person on the docket, to boot?

A random image came to mind. The crumpled front fender of a dark sedan. The sedan she thought was following her. The one idling down the street from Granny Bert's house. She remembered the surge of relief she felt when she saw the dent, proof in her mind that it was a different car than the one driven by the man in the baseball cap.

She couldn't have been further from the truth, she now realized.

She needed to know the particulars.

"How did you manage to get the honor of kicking off

the entire program?" she asked, subtly shifting on her feet. She put another inch or two of her body in front of Bethani's. "I understood the first class was assigned to a photographer."

"Yes, but the poor sucker was in a crash right in front of the inn where I was staying. I was one of the first on the scene. He mentioned the job he was due to start that same week, so I offered to take his place."

"What an amazing coincidence," Madison murmured, knowing it was no coincidence, at all. The accident had been called in as a hit and run. He no doubt stashed his vehicle nearby and ran to the scene, pretending to be a concerned onlooker.

Her blood chilled. If that were the case, Gordon Bodine was even more callous and calculating than she first imagined. He was as deranged as his twin! He had arranged an accident—hurting another individual and potentially himself—to worm his way into the school program. Posing as a teacher, he could then use her children to gain access into the mansion. They were simply pawns in his game.

Biting back a small gasp, she struggled to speak in a conversational tone. "What—What brought you to town?"

He looked surprised by her question. It was the first ripple in his glossy act of innocence.

"You said you were staying at the *Bumble Bee Bed and Breakfast*," she pointed out. "What brings you to our little town? We don't get a lot of tourists, especially at this time of year."

"Just here for a brief trip down memory lane," he replied, already recovering from his surprise. "I came here as a boy."

"Oh? You have relatives here?"

"No one you know," he assured her. He seemed done with the conversation. "Trenton, tell me what you like best about the mural."

The teen brightened, eager to discuss the painting with an art aficionado. "What's not to like?"

As the two engaged in conversation, Madison saw an opportunity to whisk her daughter to safety. She turned toward her and said, "Beth, do get refreshments for our guest. I know we'd all love some tea while studying the mural." She made a shooing motion with her hand, hoping the girl would understand her urgency.

Naturally, she wouldn't.

She *couldn't*. In Bethani's eyes, Mr. Raymond was nothing more than an enthusiastic art teacher, eager to see the famed mural painted upon the Big House's dining room walls some one hundred years ago. She had no idea the man was dangerous. She had no way of knowing he had been stalking her mother for weeks, looking for a way into the house.

Bethani had no way of knowing she had played right into his hands and led him directly there. By invitation, no less.

"Huh?" the girl asked in confusion, trying to make sense of her mother's frantic sign language. "What..."

"Bethani?" Mr. Raymond called, seeing through Madison's attempts to get her daughter from the room. "Trenton made an excellent point about the technique used here. Why don't you tell me what you see in this vignette? You may need to step closer to see it."

"She'll just be a minute," Madison said quickly, stepping in front of the girl's path. "She'll—"

"Mo—om—mm! What is *wrong* with you?" Bethani hissed, pulling the word into three syllables of pure humiliation. "He said he didn't want anything."

"But I do. I'd love some tea." Her words came at a fast, nervous pace. "And I'm sure Trenton would, too." She turned to present the boy with a bright smile, begging him to see the desperation her daughter was blinded to.

He was even more oblivious than his girlfriend. He was blinded by admiration for their art teacher. He and Mr. Raymond shared a passion for fine art, something that not even Bethani, as much as he loved her, understood. It baffled him why her mother acted so strangely now.

"I'm good. I just want to hear Mr. Raymond's thoughts on the mural and the way Addison used shadows and light to create such realism."

"Excellent point." Their teacher smiled. "Bethani, come closer, and let's explore the technique together."

When the girl moved around her, the teacher seared Madison with a victorious glare.

"Beth—" she protested, only to have her daughter shake her hand away.

"You don't have to stay in here, Mom. This is stuff we're studying in class and will probably bore you. You go on and get your tea. We may be in when we're done here," Bethani said.

Her blue eyes sent out a different message, altogether. *Mo—om, you're embarrassing me*, the look said. *Stop acting so weird!*

Madison wasn't about to leave her daughter alone with a madman. She wasn't budging.

"Not at all," she said with false brightness. "I'd love to learn more! I told you how I've always been fascinated with this mural. Maybe now I can understand the artistic significance of my fascination." She wedged her way in beside her daughter. "Tell me, Mr. Raymond. What do you paint?" she asked. "Do you paint murals?"

"Nothing so grand, I'm afraid."

"But you must have a specialty," she pressed. How long would they play this game? How long before he admitted why he was truly here? "I was recently in a shop that had some gorgeous seascapes," she went on, "as well as some impressive Western art. What do you paint?"

He turned toward her, the cunning look in his eyes chilling by several degrees.

"As a matter of fact," he said, a sneer twisting his mouth, "I do appreciate a good Western piece now and again."

<h1 style="text-align:center">24</h1>

Granny Bert slowly made her way to Madison's office.

She had failed her friend Alpha in so many ways.

Alpha had come to her, all those years ago, worried about her grandson. While refusing to offer particulars, she admitted he displayed some disturbing tendencies. Bertha had assumed she meant the boy was a randy teenager; after rearing four sons of her own, she knew the challenges of raging male hormones.

What if she hadn't listened closely enough? Had Alpha dropped clues she might have missed? Granny Bert vaguely remembered the trouble with Lavonne's feline population. Both women had come to her after a heated discussion left a wedge in their friendship. She remembered now that Lavonne claimed Garwin was abnormally cruel and inhumane. Alpha had complained that the boy was misunderstood. She was doing the best she could, raising three boys alone at her age, but folks around here were too judgmental. They didn't understand the emotional damage done to a child when abandoned by a parent.

Had Alpha said more, and she just hadn't listened? There had been a lot happening in her own life at the time. Charlie had gone off on another of his tangents, fancying himself a race car driver. As if putting himself in mortal danger weren't enough for a mother to worry about, he was willing to uproot his wife and child, dragging them around the country with him at whim.

Madison was barely a teenager at the time, too young and impressionable to be exposed to the lifestyle of the racing circuit. For once, Charlie and Allie realized the effects their life choices made upon their only child. They realized their daughter needed a steady home. A place to set down roots and feel settled.

They simply didn't feel they were the people to give her the needed stability. They came to Joe and Bertha, asking if they would take the girl to raise.

There was no question. No hesitation. Of course they would take her and gladly so. It was the least she deserved. But it didn't mean the decision didn't disrupt their lives. It was an adjustment for them all.

Had Bertha been so caught up in her own life, that she had missed clues Alpha sent about hers? Had Alpha sensed she was in danger? Had she known her grandson was sick enough and deranged enough to do something as vile as commit murder?

It sickened Bertha to think she might have missed the signs. That she left her friend alone to fend for her own safety.

And to top it off, she had failed to seek justice for Alpha's death! Almost thirty years had elapsed, and her friend's murderer was still on the loose. How had she missed the clues? How had she mangled the case so royally?

Granny Bert stashed the canvases back inside the hidden panel. Her hands shook as she deposited the gruesome proof of Garwin's demented mind. The paintings were so graphic and detailed, she half-expected to see blood upon her hands.

Just in case, she rubbed her hands on her legs to cleanse them.

On a whim, Granny Bert decided to step into the secret passage and follow its hollow walls back toward the kitchen. She was in no mood to meet up with a boisterous brood of teenagers and their art-loving teacher. She would keep to the inner passage, get back to the kitchen, and perhaps even leave. She felt a sudden need to get away and clear her head.

For once, she didn't ponder memories of the many times she had moved through this passage with her brother and their friend Hank. As children, they wasted away the hours while their parents worked for Juliet Blakely, entertaining themselves the best they could. The secret passages were especially fun for the trio, giving them access to overheard conversations and quickened routes.

But on this sad journey, her thoughts were still heavy with grief.

Poor, dear Alpha. To be murdered by her own flesh and blood! What thoughts went through her mind, Granny Bert wondered, as her grandson thrust the knife into her chest and watched her fall? Had she suffered long, or was death imminent? She hoped for the latter. No one, least of all sweet Alpha, deserved to bleed out on the carpet at her grandchild's feet.

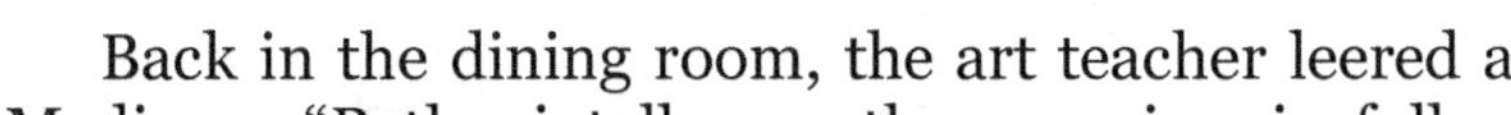

Back in the dining room, the art teacher leered at Madison. "Bethani tells me the mansion is full of interesting artwork. I'd like to see it."

"I'll show you," Madison volunteered quickly. "The kids can stay here and study the mural, while I show you the other pieces."

"No, I'm sure there's a lesson to be learned in the other works, as well," Mr. Raymond insisted. "They'll come with us."

Trenton looked confused. He motioned toward the mural. "I thought we were here to study the walls. There's so much to be learned, right here in this room!"

"There is," the man agreed. "But a nice Western piece might be the perfect counterbalance to put this work in perspective."

"Western? There's no Western art in here that I've ever seen," the boy insisted.

"I beg to differ," Mr. Raymond said, his eyes trained on Madison. His voice was cold and flat. "I know there happens to be one piece that resides within these walls. I'd like to see it."

"Maybe we define Western differently, Mr. Raymond," Madison feigned ignorance. "Let's you and I take a walk, and you can educate me on the different classifications of art." She took a calculated risk, half-turning, leaving her daughter exposed as she encouraged him to follow.

It was a risk she shouldn't have taken.

"Not without them," the teacher said, grabbing for Bethani's arm.

"Hey!" the teen said, startled by his rough grip. She tugged, but he held her arm steadfast. "Mr. Raymond, you're hurting me. Please lighten up."

"Sorry, Bethani, but that's not possible." He didn't bother looking at her as he spoke through clenched teeth. He pulled her forward, unconcerned when she stumbled. "You're coming with us."

"Let my daughter go!" Madison demanded.

"Yeah, Mr. Raymond. What's gotten into you?" Trenton asked. He put his hand on the teacher's other arm, only to have it slung away.

Raymond's voice turned angry. "I. Want. To. See. The Western. Piece," he said, biting out the words.

Bethani's blue eyes turned frantic. "Mom! What's

he talking about?"

"Nothing, Bethani. He's confused. Come over here to me, and your teacher and I will work this out."

"The girl goes nowhere!" he barked. His arm shifted without warning, moving to hook around Bethani's throat. She clawed at his arm to get free, but to no avail. When Madison and Trenton would have fought him, his grip at her throat tightened.

"Stop! He's—He's choking me!" the girl gasped.

"That's right," the teacher barked. "Both of you. Step back! Take another step, and I cut off her air supply."

"No! Don't do that. I'm backing away. See?" Madison put her hands up and took a step backward.

"Me, too," Trenton said, his face pale and his voice unsteady. His eyes were trained on his girlfriend.

"Why do you want the painting so badly?" Madison demanded of the man. If he wanted to prove his twin killed their grandmother, she could take care of that for him. She planned to turn the paintings over to the police as soon as they were done here.

"Wha—What painting?" Bethani managed with limited breath.

"The one your mother has," her capture snarled. "The one that belongs to *me*."

"If it was so important to you, why did you leave it at the house? You should have taken it before the bank repossessed!"

"It *was* out," he insisted. "I know it was. That stupid brother of mine stole it back and hid it somewhere in the house." He snorted with disdain. "Gordon always was a pompous fool."

Madison blinked in surprise. "Wait. You're... You're not Gordon?"

"You think I'm Gordon? That's rich!" He threw back his head and howled with laughter, the sound bitter.

It was worse than she imagined. The bottom fell from her stomach. Her daughter was in the clutch of a madman. A known killer. A man who enjoyed torturing his prey before killing it.

"That... that makes you..." Already a mere whisper, Madison's voice fell with horror. "... Garwin?"

"And what if it does?" he snapped.

"But you—you killed your grandmother!" Forgetting his threat to choke Bethani, Madison charged toward him, her arms flailing as she tugged and pulled, clawing at his arms. "Let my daughter go! Release her!"

"Back off, or I swear... I'll kill her, too." With one tug, he lifted the girl off the ground, her body dangling from within the hook of his arm. Bethani sputtered out a faint squeal as she blindly kicked her legs.

"Don't!" Madison begged.

Trenton tried wrenching his girlfriend free, but Garwin only tightened his grip.

"I've done it before, and I'll do it again," he vowed. "Back away. Both of you!"

On the other side of the wall, Granny Bert heard the commotion in the dining room. She put her ear to the wall, the same way she had done as a mischievous child.

This wasn't idle gossip over tea and dainty sandwiches.

She heard the frightened quiver in Madison's voice. Then she heard the threat in some unknown man's words. It was enough to send her back down the passage, much more quickly this time. She had to call Brash and get word to him.

"Hurry! Maddy's in trouble!" she said when he answered. "Come in quiet. Someone's in the house. He has Bethani."

"Who? Who is it? Where are they?" Brash demanded, already spurred into action.

"Dining room. I'm in the secret passage. Just get here." She cut the call, not wasting time with details.

Even though the fireplace was now fueled by a gas insert, there was a polished brass toolset for looks. Granny Bert grabbed the hooked poker and made her way back through the secret passage.

She wasn't going in unarmed.

Her feet back on solid ground, Bethani sputtered and coughed around large gulps of air. "Mom!" Her voice was but a squeak. "What's he talking about?"

"This man isn't who he says he is. His real name is Garwin Bodine. He's a murderer. He killed his own grandmother almost thirty years ago."

Trenton swallowed hard and stepped back. "D— Don't hurt Bethani," he begged of his teacher. "She didn't do anything."

"Neither of them did," Madison was quick to point out. "This is between you and me. Let the kids go."

"So that they can call your husband? I'm not stupid! You said you were married to the chief of police. No way I'm letting them free," Garwin hissed.

"They're just kids. They don't have to be a part of this."

"Too late for that. Like it or not, they're part of it."

"You don't have to choke her, though. At least ease up on her," Madison pleaded.

To her surprise, he did just that. He didn't release the girl, but he did ease his arm back from her throat, allowing her to breathe freely.

Bethani managed a nod but said nothing. She seemed preoccupied with the act of breathing.

"Why, Garwin?" Madison asked. "Why did your grandmother have to die?"

"She saw the sketchpad. She was angry. Angry and yelling. Threatening to call the authorities." A frown creased his forehead, giving him a troubled look. "Gran almost never yelled." Caught up in the painful memory, he sounded vulnerable. He sounded more like a lost, frightened boy than a cold-blooded killer.

"She was upset." Madison tried reasoning with him. "You can understand that."

"None of this would have happened if she had just stayed out of it. If she hadn't snooped around and found the sketchpad." Garwin ran his free hand over the back of his head, his expression distressed.

He looks human, Madison thought, *instead of the monster I know he is.*

The thought disappeared as his voice hardened. "Now, look at the mess we're in!"

"We can get out of it. We'll find a way," she promised soothingly.

"No. Too many people have died. It's too late."

Madison instinctively pulled Trenton behind her. She only wished she could pull her daughter free. Somehow, she had to find a way to save Bethani!

"P—People?" she questioned warily. "What people?"

"Everyone thought Gordon was the good twin. They thought he was so sweet and innocent. But he wasn't. He was greedy and devious. He deserved everything he got! He was stupid enough to try to blackmail his own twin. He stole the painting back and tried to use it against his other half. Can you imagine the gall that took?"

"You... Garwin, what did you do?" Killing his

grandmother was horrific enough. But to murder his own twin? She felt ill at the thought.

His face took on a mocking expression. "You never win, double-crossing your twin." He laughed again, the sound short and brittle. "I heard that one enough growing up. They were always spouting that one off."

A slight noise drew Madison's attention.

Granny Bert? Blake? She prayed neither walked into this mess. She had her hands full as it was, trying to save three people's lives!

"We've wasted enough time," he said in a sudden about face. "I'll take the painting now, Mrs. deCordova. In fact, I'll take both."

"B—Both?"

"Yes. Both. And don't bother acting like you don't know what I'm talking about. You know exactly what I'm talking about. You told me so, yourself."

Madison stared at him in disbelief.

Snippets of their conversation circled in her head.

You said you were married to the chief of police… They were always spouting that one off.

"You—You said you were Garwin!" Madison accused.

"*I* never said that," the man corrected. "*You* said that."

"But… why?"

"Why didn't I correct you? Why bother?"

This time, Madison definitely heard a loud *thump!*

Another knock or two, followed by a watery-sounding voice speaking from the other side of the wall.

"Gregg Raymond Bodine!" the voice said in a haunting tone. "I am ashamed of you!"

It was disguised, but Madison recognized the sound of Granny Bert's voice. She forced her eyes not to widen the way Bethani's did.

Ever so subtly, Madison pressed her elbow against

Trenton, cautioning him to stay quiet. She sent the same silent reprimand to her daughter, using her *Mom look.*

The art teacher didn't notice. His face lost all color. His eyes looked glassy. Glazed over with something akin to fear.

Mingled, perhaps, with the tiniest bit of hope.

"Gr—Gran?" he whispered. His voice strengthened. "Gran, is that—is that you?"

"Who else do you think it would be, boy? And what do you mean, man-handling that young lady beside you? You mind your manners and let go of her this minute, young man!"

Gregg gulped and moved his arm from around Bethani's throat, still trying to assimilate in his mind what was happening.

While he stood rooted in shock, Madison whipped her arm out and snatched Bethani away from his side. She all but dragged the startled teen to her, shoving her into Trenton and well behind the shield of her own body.

"Go!" she hissed to the two. "Get out of here!" She knew they wouldn't heed her plea, but it was worth a try.

Gregg was still too stunned to notice. "Gran? Gran, wh—where are you?"

"In puredee misery, that's where!" Granny Bert harped, imitating the voice of her old friend. It was convincing enough, at any rate, to make the man believe his grandmother's ghost spoke to him. "It was bad enough, seeing your brother's sketches. Knowing what he was capable of. Watching him plunge a knife into my heart!" In typical Granny Bert fashion, she couldn't have sounded more dramatic. "But *this!*" Her voice quivered with disgust. "I thought you, boy, were better than this."

"I—I didn't know what else to do. Honest, Gran, I didn't know what else to do!" He put his hands to either side of his head.

"What did you do, boy? I need to hear you say it."

Gregg hung his head in shame. "You always did make us confess," he grumbled. "You never did let us get by with a thing."

"Then say it, boy. Tell me what you did. These old bones can't rest in peace until I hear you confess."

"It was them, Gran," he said, starting to whine. "The twins! They were always bickering. Always trying to one-up the other. It's like you told them. Like they always told each other. *You never win, double-crossing your twin.* But this time, their double-crossing backfired on us all. They took it too far."

"How far?" the ghostly voice in the walls asked.

"Gordon knew what his twin had done. He knew that he—he had killed you. He used it to blackmail Garwin. It went on for years. Garwin knew a lot of shady people, and Gordon needed them to keep his business afloat. They were both mixed up in some bad things—honest to God, I don't know who or what, and I wanted to keep it that way—until Garwin finally had enough. He killed Gordon. Took him on a fishing trip to Galveston and dumped his body in the Gulf."

He raked his hand across his mouth as if to rid the bitter taste of the words from his lips.

"You know how much they looked alike. How much we *all* looked alike. Momma said we could have been triplets, no matter the age difference. We were as handsome as our father was, Momma always said, even if we never knew who he was." He was rambling now. All but blubbering, confessing his soul to what he believed was his grandmother's ghost.

"It was easy for Garwin to take over Gordon's life," he continued. "No one much cared what happened to

Garwin, so no one missed him when he just vanished. He stepped into Gordon's shoes and took over the gallery. No one thought to question him. But he wasn't the businessman Gordon was. Or the schmoozer. Without Gordon's smooth lies and silver tongue, the gallery went belly up. Gordon had already mortgaged the house to buy the gallery. He talked Garwin and me into signing away the deed, promising to make us partners, but we never saw a dime." Gregg tapped on his chest like a pouting child, his voice a whine. "Like every other time, he cheated me out of my part of the inheritance. Both did!"

"What did you do, child?" the walls wailed. "What did you do to Garwin?"

The eerie, sing-song voice rattled him into a barked admission. "What do you think? I fed him to the sharks, the same way he did to his twin! He deserved that much and more!"

"When? When did you do that?" Granny Bert, aka his long-dead Gran, demanded.

"After the estate sale. I heard he was there, stirring up trouble. He told me the whole sordid story. I swear, I didn't know until then. He wanted my help. Begged for it. Promised me half of what they had stolen from me over the years."

"Don't stop now, boy," Granny Bert cautioned from beyond the wall. "Confess the rest of it!"

"Being a school counselor, I knew about the new program at Sisters High. We cooked up the idea of causing a wreck with the photographer. I thought it would shake him up, and I could volunteer to take his place. It would give me an in. A reason to be in town and find a way into the house." His voice turned defiant. "I studied art, too, you know. It wasn't just my brothers. I was qualified to teach an art class, too."

"Keep talking, boy. I'm growing weak, and I can't

rest until I hear it all." With her flair for dramatics, Granny Bert allowed her voice to wax and wane. "Don't make me face eternity, not knowing the truth of your deeds."

"I didn't know Garwin would botch the job. He hit the guy too hard. Broke the guy's arm and his own nose. Stupid idiot," Gregg complained. "He had to go to the ER to get it to stop bleeding."

Madison broke in with a gasp. "That *was* you! And that's why you didn't recognize me at *Texas General*! That's why you didn't have a black eye."

Gregg ignored her interruption. He was bent on confessing to his grandmother's spirit.

"Garwin was hyped up on pain pills and booze. Started confessing to more than just killing family. I didn't want to know. I wanted no part of it. I drove down to the coast, took him out on a boat, and pushed him over. It was the only way to stop him. He was evil. As far as I'm concerned, the world's a better place without Garwin Bodine in it."

"Garwin always did have a mean streak," the voice through the wall acknowledged. "But you? You were better than this. Why did you stalk this lady? You tried to break into her house. And look how you treated my good friend Bertha! You knew what a good woman she was. Salt of the earth! She was kind to you when you were a boy. Took you fishing a time or two. Why did you harass these good people?"

Madison tried not to roll her eyes. Leave it to Granny Bert to bolster her own ego, even when coaxing a confession from a killer!

"You don't know what it was like, Gran." The man started to whimper. "My brothers were always so mean to me. They ganged up on me, two against one. They stole everything from me! First you, then my inheritance. All I had was the life I made for myself.

Don't you see? I had to get the painting back. I had to hide what Garwin had done! It—It would have ruined my career, having a killer for a brother."

The sadness in Granny Bert's voice was real. "So, you became a killer yourself," she said, her voice waning again. Madison imagined this time was due to pure heartache. Heartache for her old friend, and for so many lives ruined and lost.

Gregg Raymond Bodine crumpled against the wall. The fight had gone out of him. "Gran, don't go!" he begged, pressing his cheek to the wall. "I'm sorry! You have to forgive me. I—I never meant for this to happen. You have to believe me!"

Even as Brash and Otis Perry rushed into the room, slapping handcuffs onto his wrists and reading him his rights, the grown man continued to blubber, "Gran, don't go! Say you forgive me!"

The walls, however, remained eerily quiet.

25

After almost three decades, the mystery of Alpha Bodine's murder was laid to rest. With Gregg's full confession to the sins of all three of her grandsons, a sense of normalcy slowly returned.

Bethani and Trenton were healing from the trauma of being manipulated by their teacher and used as bait. Even though Gregg Bodine offered a few valuable contributions to their art education, he had used them for access into the Big House. Trenton took the betrayal the hardest, particularly since he blamed himself for placing his girlfriend in danger.

Granny Bert had a wonderful time re-telling the story of her portrayal of Alpha's ghost. She remembered how her friend had often used the art of confession on the boys, making them come clean on their deeds of mischief. She feared those forced confessions may have contributed to her demise by a demented grandson, but it had also worked to solve the mystery of her murder.

Bertha found special satisfaction in knowing Alpha's soul truly could rest easy now, having found justice for her death.

Otis Perry apologized to his old nemesis for fueling

the feud between them all these years, based primarily upon their shared inability to solve Alpha's murder. He promised to do better going forward. He even apologized to Madison for treating her with anything less than respect.

Maddy was skeptical about his promise to change, but Brash asked her to give him the benefit of the doubt. As Otis Perry's superior officer, he made it clear that such disrespect toward women would not be tolerated. As his brother in arms, he congratulated him for his part in helping to solve the decades-old cold case.

Publicly, Brash gave him a special commendation, along with special recognition for the former justice of the peace and their civilian consultant. Pictures of Perry, Granny Bert, and Madison appeared in the local newspaper, alongside a long article about the case and the key components to solving the crime.

Sybil and Virgie were delighted to see their names mentioned for coming forward with information vital to the case. No mention was made of their trespassing escapades. Along with Madison and Granny Bert, the women were even more delighted when they received a small stipend from a local crime reporting program. It was enough to treat everyone, even Wanda, Derron, and Arlene, for margaritas and dinner on the next Fish Friday at *Montelongo's*. Neither Tango nor Lucky Ducky were allowed to join them.

The downside to solving the cold case was that, after finding the perfect Christmas gift for Brash, Madison had to expose it three months early. He told her not to bother replacing it, but she vowed to find something even better. It had become a sort of competition between them, finding the perfect gift for as little money as possible.

"I'll have to start all over," Madison lamented.

"As if you mind shopping," he scoffed.

"Seriously, I'm not that fond of shopping."

"Our bank account begs to differ."

"You're just worried, because you know I would have won this year."

"I consider myself the winner," Brash insisted. "Once the DA has the case all sewn up, I get the paintings back. I've already found the perfect place for them in my office. Plus, we've solved a cold case and delivered justice after almost three decades. A win, any way you look at it."

"I think Genny and Cutter should be proclaimed the all-time winners," Madison decided.

The crowning event of the month was the birth of the Montgomery's daughter, Faith. The eight-pound, four-ounce baby girl was the picture of health, with a head full of blonde curly fuzz, big blue eyes, and dimples in her cheeks, elbows, and knees.

From her hospital bed, Genny gazed down at the two babies she and Cutter held in their arms.

"Our first bundle of joy gave us hope that we would someday have a family," Genny told her audience. "Our second bundle of joy is a testament to our faith that it would happen."

"She's adorable, Genny. The exact opposite of her sister, and yet the perfect complement to her," Madison proclaimed.

Not on the roster that day but unable to miss the blessed event, Laurel was there with Cade beside her. "You have an absolutely perfect family," she said.

"Yes, I do," Genny beamed happily. "*We* do." She looked up at her husband adoringly, ashamed of all she had put him through in the last nine hormone-crazed months. "Thank goodness this wonderful man stood with me through it all, bringing us to this moment."

"You may have had a little to do with it," Cutter

joked, his fingers measuring an inch or so. Turning his smile to their friends, he bragged, "This lady right here was brilliant in there. Never complained a bit. Handled the whole birthing thing like a champ."

"It's not like I had a choice," Genny pointed out modestly. "It was a little too late to change my mind about it."

"But the result is always worth it," Madison agreed, "no matter how much pain is involved."

"You two did it the smart way," Laurel mused. "One pregnancy, one birthing process, two babies. Two for one."

"I do pride myself on efficiency," Madison smiled.

"Ah. That explains how you solved a cold case and your stalker mystery with one single painting," Cade said. "In case I haven't said so before now, nicely done."

"You may have mentioned it, but I'm not opposed to hearing it again."

"Neither is her grandmother," Brash informed their friend. "She's so impressed with her own part in the effort, that she's thinking of offering seances as a sideline for Snoop 'n Soup."

"Snoop 'n Soup?" Laurel asked. "What is that?"

"Something I no longer have time for!" Genny said, looking down at the two babies in pink. "Sorry to leave you in the lurch, Maddy, but my sleuthing days are on hiatus for a while."

Her best friend offered an indulgent smile. "Believe me, I do understand. Twins—or almost-twins, in this case—have a way of keeping you busy."

"I'm sorry to say that Granny Bert has foreseen your dilemma," Brash added, not entirely in jest, "and offered to substitute Sybil and Virgie in your absence."

Cutter hooted with laughter, imagining the chaos that would create. "Maddy, you may have to change the name of your business to '*In a Pinch and a Creak*.'" He laughed again at his own wit. "Your knee pops enough on its own, Brash. Imagine all their joints popping and creaking."

"Try sneaking down a staircase with them," Madison muttered. "I can assure you; it can't be done silently."

"I'd make you pay for that knee comment," Brash threatened, "but I'll take it easy on you. You're now the father of two girls. Believe me, your time is coming."

As the conversation turned back to the babies and the bright future that laid ahead for them all, laughter and camaraderie flowed easily among the friends.

"Don't forget to send me the pictures you took!" Genny reminded everyone once again.

"Sending them now, including the picture of all of us that the doctor took," Laurel said. It helped that she was friends with the OBGYN and could convince her to take a picture of the six of them around the babies.

"Perfect."

Madison scrolled through the dozens of photos she had taken so far, selecting the best of the best to send to her friend.

"You'll love this one of the four of you," she predicted, bringing it up on her screen. It was too good not to show off right now. "It's a perfect shot. The new daddy, smiling down at his girls."

Genny's eyes grew moist when she saw the photo. "You're right. It's perfect," she agreed. "I don't need a thousand words for this picture. One word will do."

She smiled at the handsome man beside her and the two babies they held, one fair and one dark.

"Bliss," Genny said. "Pure and simple bliss."

Note from Author

Thank you for reading, and for sharing this special event!

It's true, I think of all my books as my babies. It's exciting to watch them grow and evolve from a mere spark of my imagination into a story I can share with you. Thank you for indulging my fantasies and allowing my imaginary friends to come to life. Your support means more to me than you can ever know! Please, keep those personal notes, public reviews, and reader recommendations flowing. (It takes a village to raise these babies, you know.)

There's more to come in 2022 for Madison and her family and friends in The Sisters, so stayed tuned! I hope to have more *Texas General* stories for you, in addition to a new series. Or two.

To stay in the loop, check out www.beckiwillis.com often, and be sure to sign up for my not-so-monthly newsletter. Drop in for an e-visit anytime at beckiwillis.ccp@gmail.com. I love visiting with readers!

Again, THANK YOU for reading!

ABOUT THE AUTHOR

Becki Willis, best known for her popular The Sisters, Texas Mystery Series and Forgotten Boxes, always dreamed of being an author. In November of '13, that dream became a reality. Since that time, she has published over twenty books, won a Silver Falchion Award for Best Cozy Mystery, the RONE Award for Best Paranormal Fiction,   first place honors for Best Mystery Series, Best Suspense Fiction, and Best Audio Book, and has introduced her imaginary friends to readers around the world.

An avid history buff, Becki likes to poke around in old places and learn about the past. Other addictions include reading, writing, junking, unraveling a good mystery, and coffee. She loves to travel, but believes coming home to her family and her Texas ranch is the best part of any trip. Becki is a member of the Association of Texas Authors, the National Association of Professional Women, and the Brazos Writers organization. She attended Texas A&M University and majored in Journalism.

Connect with her at http://www.beckiwillis.com/ and http://www.facebook.com/beckiwillis.ccp.   Better   yet, email her at beckiwillis.ccp@gmail.com. She loves to hear from readers and encourages feedback!

BONUS EXCERPT!

If you haven't started their story yet, here's your chance to catch up on Laurel and Cade's blossoming relationship in *Texas General Cozy Cases of Mystery*.

From Book 1, *A Case of Murder by Monte Carlo*.

CHAPTER ONE

"Yum," the lab tech murmured, stuffing a chip laden with spicy avocado and shrimp dip into his mouth. "This may be the winner right here." He closed his eyes to savor the explosion of flavors upon his tongue. "Perfection."

"Thanks!" Laurel Benson beamed. "I hear Ayla in Respiratory has a spinach dip to die for, so I'm anxious to see how this one compares."

It had become a tradition here at *Texas General* on Game Day, a sort of 'competition behind the competition.' While thousands of college football fans trekked to Kyle Field for their grand scale tailgating parties, each department within the hospital hosted a party at their prospective nurses' station. The Emergency Room where Laurel worked was no exception.

The hospital itself—fully embracing the time-honored tradition of Aggie football—provided health-conscious versions of fan favorites, but it was up to staff members to bring "the good stuff", the dishes oozing with cheese and calories and enough cholesterol to guarantee job security for health professionals worldwide. Creamy dips, gourmet salsas, and calorie-rich finger foods fought for space among the platters of veggie sticks and salt-free chicken wings. Decadent desserts weighed down one end of every table, tempting even the staunchest dieter with sugary fruit toppings, cream fillings, and the lure of a chocolate-induced coma. The offerings were so diverse (and so delicious) that it quickly became a competition to see who could bring the best and tastiest dish. Just one year in, and the highly anticipated contest already had a coveted trophy worth fighting for: a massive maroon and white wreath awarded to the station providing the best snacks.

"If I weren't already married," the technician claimed, eyes still closed in reverence, "I would propose marriage, right here on the spot."

"A marriage can't survive on dip alone, my friend," Laurel reminded him, reaching around his extended belly to swipe a cookie. "And if you weren't married to Glenda, I couldn't indulge in these scrumptious cookies of hers. *These*," the petite nurse proclaimed, palming a second cookie as reserve, "I could survive on."

"We may have to send the trophy home with you, Jim," a second nurse agreed, moving in behind him to fill her plate. "Glenda is like our very own secret weapon."

"Small bit of compensation," he agreed around another mouthful of dip, "for having to put up with Football Fandemonium."

It was a term they coined for the added influx of patients each Game Day, one of a half dozen or so sacred Saturdays strung between August and December when the fighting Texas A&M Aggies hosted their opponent for the week. Saturdays were naturally busy in the ER, but with tens of thousands extra footballs fans in town, the excessive celebrations, after-parties, and snarled roadways always doubled, if not tripled, their load. The bigger the school rivalry, the crazier the reason for the ER visits.

Laurel checked her watch, sinking into the rolling chair behind the desk. "It's been relatively quiet, so far," she said. The cookie made a satisfying *snap!* as she sank her teeth into it. "But I imagine the Fandemoniums will start rolling in within the hour."

The words barely cleared her lips before they heard the ambulance's wail.

"Thanks a lot," Mary Ann said, already abandoning the plate she just filled. "Look what you did."

Laurel had the grace to look apologetic, needlessly taking blame for the incoming. "Sorry. You eat. I'll take this one," she offered.

"I'm already up," Mary Ann said, motioning her to sit back down. She gave one last mournful look at her abandoned plate. "I didn't need the extra calories, anyway."

The siren's sharp trill grew louder, bleeding in ahead of the gurney as the sliding doors flew open and paramedics rushed their patient inside. "Hit and run victim!" one of the medics called over his shoulder. "Heart rate 288 with 12-lead showing V-fib, blood pressure unsteady. In and out of consciousness. Bring a crash cart, stat!"

Laurel jumped to her feet, just as a familiar chime announced the door opening from the waiting room, most likely to admit a walk-in patient. Even as she heard the rustle of fabric and voices approaching from the front, she would have abandoned her post and offered aid to the hit and run victim, had someone not beat her to it. The on-duty doctor and two more nurses rushed toward the gurney before she could round the counter.

Satisfied that the hit and run had adequate help for the moment, Laurel turned her attention to the walk-in. A thin woman followed timidly behind the medical assistant from Admissions, her steps unsteady. One glance told her that the woman was as much frightened as she was in pain.

Before returning home to the Bryan-College Station area, Laurel started her nursing career in Houston, working in one of the busiest and most acclaimed hospitals in the nation. Over six years of experience had honed Laurel's assessment skills. Almost unconsciously, she could look at a patient and make an immediate assessment call. Today was no exception.

One hundred-ten pounds soaking wet, poor posture, stooped shoulders. Possible early signs of osteoporosis. Sallow skin color, dark circles under eyes. Could be exhaustion, could be drug use. No visible signs of injury or physical trauma, so must be internal. Looks more nervous than in pain.

Either way, in dire need of a hot meal and a hot shower, not necessarily in that order.

Laurel suspected the woman's hair had once been dishwater blond, but the dishwater definitely needed changing. Unkempt locks hung in disarray, streaked now with gray and a layer of grease. Her clothes weren't the tattered rags of a homeless person, but the dirt had been there long enough to set in. Making a mental note to offer a shower and change of clothes before releasing her, Laurel was thankful *Texas General* took a holistic approach to health care. The woman looked forty if she was a day, but Laurel suspected she might be several years younger. Hard living had a tendency to age women before their time, and something in her weary eyes and lined face told Laurel that life hadn't been easy for this woman.

A lanky boy in his teens trailed behind them, his eyes enormous as they found the commotion on the other side of the corridor. Intent on the buzz of activity around the hit and run accident, he walked past the room the assistant led his mother into.

"We're right here," the assistant said brightly, redirecting the youth.

With a sheepish expression, he shuffled into the small space, but his eyes never quite left the other room.

Well aware of the drama unfolding across the hall, Laurel put as much warmth as she could into her smile when she greeted the newcomers. She knew how disconcerting it could be for other patients when they heard a crash cart mentioned.

Helping the woman settle onto the narrow bed, she noted how her small frame barely made a shadow, much less an indentation.

"My name is Laurel. Can you tell me your name and date of birth?" She read the printed information on the hospital band, waiting for verbal confirmation.

The woman's voice was scratchy and wavered with either pain or fear—Laurel would bet on the latter—but the words were clear. "L…Lily Moses. 2-25-1982." Sure enough, younger than the forty she looked.

"What brings you in today, Lily?"

Lily darted a nervous glance toward her son. "Uhm, I got a hurting in my gut and all," she said. Almost as an afterthought, she clutched at her mid-section and offered a grimace. "It hurts something powerful."

Laurel suspected something wasn't quite right with her new patient. As she fitted the blood pressure cuff around her skinny arm, winding the binding a second time to hold it in place, she asked, "How long has this pain been bothering you, Lily?"

"Oh, uhm, it started a few days ago." Another darted look toward her son, who seemed to be more concerned with what happened across the hall than what happened here with his mother. "But it got real intense about an hour or so ago. Ain't that right, Harold?" When the boy made no reply, she called his name again sharply. "Harold!"

"Huh?" He reluctantly dragged his attention back to his mother.

She repeated her claim as Laurel clamped the oximeter onto the tip of one finger. "I said ain't that right?" There was a pointed insistence in her voice as she needled the boy with her laser-like glare.

"Oh, uh, yeah," the boy said. "'Bout an hour ago. I remember, because we were watching the game. On Channel 3."

Laurel studied the numbers on the monitor, watching as they made a valiant effort to record a stable blood pressure. She was careful to keep the look of censure off her face; even though Harold made a point to mention the channel, their local network couldn't carry the game. The boy obviously wasn't telling the truth, but why? She overtly checked for needle marks on Lily's arm as the machine failed to get a reading. When the pressure built and the cuff tightened for a second time, Laurel saw the first real look of pain cross Lily's face.

"Sorry. Sometimes it has to pump a second time. Can you describe your pain for me?" she asked, wondering if the woman was experienced in the art of hiding signs of drug abuse. She knew some addicts preferred to shoot up in the soft tissue between their toes. While she contemplated a way to talk Lily out of her shoes, the woman offered a very vague description of what she called 'terrible bad' abdominal pain.

Maybe she's just nervous. Heart rate slightly elevated and pressure 178/86. Neither necessarily indicative of severe pain or drug use, but I'll give her the benefit of doubt. The vagueness could be attributed to nerves. Emergency rooms had a tendency to do that to patients.

"Is Harold your son?" Laurel asked, offering the teen another warm smile. His attention had wandered back across the hall, where things were obviously deteriorating. The Code Blue warning still echoed in the corridor, muffled only by the sound of running feet and hurried bodies. One glance across the hall told Laurel that their patient was in dire condition.

"My oldest. Got three more at home, and all," Lily offered.

"Oh, my. Four children. What a blessing!"

Lily's quiet harrumph spoke volumes, but her son was too busy watching the other room to notice the slight.

"How old are they?" Laurel asked.

"Harold's sixteen, Danny's thirteen, Paulie's twelve, and Jill is ten."

"Is their father at home with them?" The question came out innocent sounding enough, as Laurel listened to the steady thump of the woman's heart.

"Ain't seen none of their fathers in at least five years," Lily snorted. "Don't know where two of them are, and don't care. Know exactly where Harold's old man is. State Penn in Huntsville."

"And none of them pay child support? I could put you in touch with—"

Lily interrupted her before she could finish her offer of help, doubtful though it was. "Ain't none of them got a dime to their name, much less the gumption to claim their own blood." She raised her chin a fraction and made a bold claim. "We've done just fine without 'em. Don't need the likes of none of them, coming around after all this time. Not after all the hard stuff's done been done, changing diapers and wiping snotty noses and losing a night's sleep to teethin' babies. No, ma'am, I don't need them now." She set her jaw stubbornly, but Laurel saw the slight quiver in her chin.

"Good for you, Lily," Laurel said softly. She made another mental note, this one to find a business card for an organization that specialized in helping single mothers in need. "If you'll answer a few more questions for me, I'll let you settle in and rest for a few minutes until a doctor can see you. Are you comfortable, or do you need a few more pillows?"

"Nah, I'm fine." Now Lily craned her neck, trying to see across the hall. "What's the commotion and all over yonder?"

"Car accident, I believe. Now, Lily, tell me more about this pain. Would you say it's more of a stabbing pain or a radiating pain?"

"Ain't never been stabbed before, so don't know how that would feel, and all." She nibbled on her lower lip, still watching the hustle of activity taking place across the way. "You reckon that fella's gonna make it?"

It wasn't unusual for one patient to be curious about another. Often, it helped to ease their own fears by transferring their worries to a stranger. Other times, any sign of bad news— even if applied to a stranger— was enough to send a patient into a panic attack.

No matter the reason for Lily's pointed concern, she was in no position to supply her nosy patient with answers. Strategically positioning herself in Lily's line of sight until she could tug the curtain fully shut, Laurel's answer was non-committal.

"I certainly hope so, but my concern at the moment is for you. I need you to tell me more about the reason you came in this afternoon, Lily."

A wary look moved into the woman's eyes. "Why? You don't believe me? You think I'm making all this up? I got better things to do than come down to some emergency room, I can tell you that!"

"I'm sure you do. And I'm not suggesting your pain isn't real. I just need to know more about it, so we can help you feel better."

"Maybe I oughta put on one of those gowns you offer," Lily said, cutting her eyes to her son. "Harold, step out in the hall while I change, and all."

The teen scrambled out of the chair, moving faster than Laurel had seen him do so far. No doubt, he was eager to be on the other side of the curtain, ogling the scene as it unfolded across the way.

"Do you need help changing?" Laurel asked, retrieving a folded gown from an upper cabinet and placing it on the foot of the bed.

"Nah. Never did like anyone seeing me in my skivvies," Lily said. "I'll be fine. You trot on along and see if you can help that man yonder. He looks to be in bad shape."

"Use this button here to call me if you need anything."

"Just go, and don't mind me none."

Laurel stepped out of the room, a frown crinkling her forehead. Most patients demanded prompt attention, yet Lily Moses insisted she leave her alone to tend another patient. Somehow, Laurel suspected it was hardly a magnanimous act of selflessness on her part. She couldn't help but remain skeptical.

Harold had wandered closer to the hub of activity. While he stood just far enough away not to interfere, his avid curiosity pushed the bounds of propriety. Privacy was the least of the ER team's concern as they fought to save the man's life. The curtain hung abandoned, as personnel rushed to and from his bedside.

Grabbing the plate Mary Ann had recently abandoned, Laurel took a 'round about path to meet Harold head on and herd him back in the right direction. "I thought you might enjoy a bite to eat," she said, deliberately walking between the nosy teen and the disturbing scene no one should have to witness, particularly an impressionable youth.

He craned his scrawny neck out to see around her, the irritation plain upon his face. *Dark hair, pale skin, poor muscle tone,* Laurel assessed. *Spends too much time indoors, probably on some gaming device, without getting proper exercise. Pockmarks on his face could be acne, could be drug abuse. Ripped jeans, faded black t-shirt, shaggy haircut. Among my peers, slouchy. Among his peers, borderline stylish.*

The change in fashions always made Laurel feel her age. Twenty-nine still seemed young, until little things like loud music and trendy clothes started bothering her. Still, she doubted his classmates viewed Harold Moses as a trendsetter. *Could be because he, too, needs a hot shower.*

He started to decline her offer of food, until he caught sight of the offering. The heavy-duty plate fairly sagged with the weight of the delectable game day fare piled upon it. "Well, maybe just a bite."

"Why don't you follow me to the desk, and we'll get you a drink to go with it? I can find you a chair, too, until your mom gets changed."

"Uhm, okay." He turned to follow but threw a mournful look over his shoulder. He was clearly torn. Should he watch the horrific spectacle playing out across the hall, or give in to the heady aromas wafting up from the plate?

His stomach eventually won out, and he followed Laurel without incident. She faced the chair away from the activity and offered him a soft drink, but by the time his plate was empty (mere minutes later) he had inched it slowly around and was again able to watch the comings and goings in the other room.

"Is that guy gonna make it?" he finally asked. Despite his morbid fascination with the real-life drama, the quiver in his voice belied his detachment.

Laurel knew better than to offer empty promises. "He's certainly getting the best care available," she assured the teen. "Can I get you anything else? Another piece of cake? A brownie?"

"Maybe a brownie," he agreed. He shot a look toward the abandoned table. Other than Laurel, everyone was huddled around the gurney across the hall. His eyes wandered back toward the activity. "Who hit him?"

"I don't know any of the details." She placed a brownie on

a fresh plate and added a cookie for good measure. "Tell me about your mom's pain. Is this the first time she's complained about it?"

"Uh, yeah, I think so. It just came out of nowhere." He leaned back in his chair, trying to see around the technician blocking his view. His voice was distracted as he dipped his chin, then swiveled it at an angle to get a better glimpse around the interference. "Started moaning and groaning. Grabbed her stomach and said it hurt something terrible."

"Was that before or after that amazing quarterback sneak? That was quite a play, wasn't it?" Judging from her smile, there was no way to know Laurel was making it all up. She simply wanted to know if Harold had been watching the game, or if he had been wrong about the channel.

"Uh, yeah, crazy," he agreed, but without enthusiasm. He forced his eyes back to the plate she offered him. "It was after, I think. Yeah, definitely after."

Just as I suspected. He wasn't watching the game.

Aloud, she asked, "Do you know what your mom had to eat today?"

He shrugged his thin shoulders. "I guess she ate Fruit Loops, same as us."

"Did anyone else have a stomach ache?"

Harold stuffed the brownie into his mouth in one bite, speaking around the chocolate. "Didn't say so, if they did."

"Are you okay here, while I go check on my patients?"

"Yeah, yeah. I'm good." He waved her away, seemingly eager to be rid of her questions and her watchful eyes.

"Please stay here at the desk, Harold. We don't want to be a bother to doctors and nurses while they try to help other patients."

"What other patients?" he scoffed. "There's only one closed curtain, besides my mom and that guy."

"Hear that tone just now? That means someone else is coming in. So, do me a favor and stay where you are. Okay?" She was smiling, but her tone made it clear that it was not a request.

Taking his harrumph as consent, Laurel checked first on the still-dozing Mr. Chen, and then on Lily. She found the latter rummaging about in the cabinets, reinforcing her earlier suspicions of drug use.

"Lily, why aren't you in bed?"

The woman whirled around guiltily. "I, uh, was cold," she stammered. "I was lookin' for a blanket. Yeah. Lookin' for a blanket, and all."

Laurel plastered a smile onto her lips. "That's not a problem. Here's one right here at the foot of your bed. I think if you'll lie back down, you'll find the bed is much warmer on your feet than the cold tile floor."

"Maybe so," she agreed placidly, allowing Laurel to help her back onto the mattress.

"The doctor will be with you as soon as possible." Laurel spoke as she worked, making a show of opening the blanket and spreading it over her patient. "Now. Isn't that better?"

"Much warmer," Lily agreed. "Where's my boy?"

"He was having a few refreshments while you changed. Would you like for him to come back in now?"

"Yeah. And leave that curtain open, will you? I'm feeling a bit closet-phobic with it pulled shut, and all."

It was a flimsy excuse, butchered word and all. Laurel compromised by pulling the curtain half-way open.

To Lily's dismay, it was the wrong side to see into the other room.

CHAPTER TWO

"Harold, your mom is ready for you now," Laurel informed the teen in the hallway.

True to his word (if a grunted harrumph was considered a promise), he was still seated, but the chair was at least six feet further out into the corridor, allowing for an unobstructed view of the room across the hall.

"I'll just finish my drink," he said.

"If you don't mind, I'll have to ask you to step inside with your mom. There's another chime, so yet another patient is coming in." The Fandemonium was right on schedule now, bringing in one patient after another. She wanted to know Harold was inside the room before she checked on the newcomer.

"They took some chick in that room," he offered, pointing to the first room. "Looked like a cut on her arm."

Laurel gave the boy a firm look. "Please remember to respect the privacy of other patients, or I'm afraid I'll have to ask you to return to the waiting room."

"Hey, it's cool." The boy stood, lifting his palms into the air. He offered a sheepish smile, but his eyes slid off to the side. He was obviously more concerned about losing access to events across the hall than he was with keeping his mother company. His foot hit the leg of the chair as he turned, but he made no offer to return it to the desk, or to pick up his abandoned plate.

Irritated by his rude behavior and his nosiness, Laurel opened her mouth to ask him to leave. She had taken pity on the teen and his mother, sensing their nervousness and thinking she was doing them a favor by keeping them together, but she had little tolerance for insolence. Before she could say a word, a woman stormed down the hallway, her voice frantic.

"Where is he? Where is my husband? What have you done with him?"

Shifting her priorities, Laurel gave Harold the briefest of glances to assure he was back where he belonged, before turning her attention to the woman barreling down the corridor.

"May I help you, ma'am?"

"You can tell me where my Raul is!" she retorted, jerking open the first curtain and peering inside. A stifled cry of alarm greeted her. Undaunted, the woman moved along and swept aside the next curtain, where Mr. Chen still softly snored.

"Ma'am!" The tone of Laurel's voice was sharp enough to give the woman pause. "Please! Control yourself."

"My Raul!" the woman lamented. "Where is he?"

Fifty-five, too old and too heavy to be wearing neon pink leggings, Laurel quickly assessed. *Not sure I can take her if she turns confrontational. More table muscle than arm muscle, but all those diamonds could put an eye out. May need a hefty dose of Valium on standby if the husband doesn't pull through.* Hurrying toward her, Laurel mentally calculated the effective dose needed for a woman of her heft.

Laurel reached for the woman's arm, intending to pull her aside to stop her tirade down the hall, but had her hand shaken away. "They say a car hit him! Drove right over him and fled like a coward!"

Harold stood frozen in his mother's half-opened room, his face void of all color as the hysterical woman's frantic march reached their room. The teen stood aside and stared at her, mouth hung open, as she swept her gaze across the space. Lily hovered there on the bed, her face as pale as her son's, the blanket drawn up to her neck. Something akin to fear flickered in Lily's eyes before she quickly looked away.

I can't allow this woman to terrorize our patients. Behemoth or not, this has to stop! Laurel stiffened her spine and took the woman's arm in a firm grip, refusing to turn loose this time. "Ma'am, I must insist that you come with me. Can you tell me your name?"

"Esmeralda Gonzales. You have my husband, Raul. Why won't you lead me to him?" The woman rounded on Laurel, staring down at her in challenge.

There were times, like now, when Laurel's petite frame put her at a disadvantage. At five four, she was several inches shorter than Mrs. Gonzales, who was tall even without the spiked heels. Laurel suspected she was also about a hundred and thirty pounds lighter than the woman, give or take ten pounds. She refused to let that intimidate her, however. Worried or not, the wife had no right barging into *her* ER and frightening *her* patients! Laurel had seen the look that crossed Lily's face. Noted the way Harold had shrunk back in fear, his face slack and his eyes wide. She had taken an oath to protect her patients, and protect them she would! Even against whirlwind wifezillas like Esmeralda Gonzales.

"We had a patient brought in by ambulance about fifteen minutes ago. Please wait here, while I check our records and see—"

For the first time, Esmeralda noticed the activity spilling out from the other room. She took off at a lope, her heels making a racket on the tiled floor as she reached out her arms and wailed in dramatic fashion, "I'm coming, Raul! Hang on, baby, Mama's on her way!"

Laurel had to jog to keep up with her, trying, in fact, to beat her across the hall. Again, her shorter legs were at a distinct disadvantage as the other woman's long legs gobbled up the distance. Laurel skidded to a stop just behind her, as Esmeralda Gonzales burst her way through the personnel gathered around the gurney.

"Raul! My God, Raul, wake up! Is he dead? He's dead, isn't

he? I insist you tell me what's happening, right this instant!"

Laurel lifted her hands helplessly, mouthing an apology to the doctor at the brunt of the wife's demands. With a simple acknowledgment to Laurel, Dr. Baek gave his full attention to the woman still spewing one question after another. Her words were now coming out in a fast, jumbled mix of English and Spanish. Thankful to turn the wife over to the attending team, Laurel murmured an inquiry to the nurse rooted out into the hallway.

"What's the story?"

"Hit and run," Danni Barrington said, keeping her voice low. "He's in bad shape, but I think we have him semi-stabilized for the moment."

"Was he in a car, or on foot?"

Laurel's stomach sank when she heard the reply. "On foot. If he pulls through, he'll likely lose one or both legs. The bones are crushed beyond repair."

"How tragic."

The tone sounded again, alerting the arrival of another walk-in patient. "Do you need help?" Danni offered.

Laurel tipped her head to one side, the loose curls brushing the side of her face. "Thanks, but I think I hear sirens, too. Sounds like we've got another ambulance on the way."

Danni blew out a weary sigh. "Definitely Game Day."

Picking up the pace, Laurel headed for the first room. She hated making patients wait, but sometimes, like now, it couldn't be helped.

Halfway there, she saw the medical assistant leading the latest patient around the corner. Two men staggered behind her, seemingly holding the other up. Both were huge men, tall and muscled, and could pass for football players themselves, especially dressed in maroon and white jerseys as they were. At first glance, she wondered which one was the patient and which was the support, until she saw a trickle of blood making its way down one of the men's faces.

Three hundred pounds, easy. Excellent physical condition. Possible pro ball player. Could easily bench press me without breaking a sweat, despite being obviously inebriated. Laceration near the periorbital area. Frontal sinus fracture could be a concern. Doesn't seem to be in pain, but wait until the party afterglow wears off. A tiny smile tickled the corners of her mouth. *Appears to have a Siamese twin, except that his twin is white and bald, as opposed to black and sporting dread locks.*

She spoke as she passed, promising to be right with them. The injured man offered her a lazy, drunken grin.

"Where ya goin', nurse? I neeeed you," he protested.

Laurel spoke over her shoulder. "Bridgett will get you settled in, and I'll be with you shortly."

She stepped into Room 1, where a young woman held a bandage onto her bleeding arm.

Early twenties, possibly a college student. Looks frightened, so probably first time in ER without momma. Doesn't appear to be a bleeder. Moderate pain, above-average fear.

"Oh, my, it looks like you have a nasty cut. I'm Laurel, and I'm sorry it took me so long to get here." She gave the young woman a warm smile as she gloved up. Moving close to the bedside, she wanted to assure the girl with her presence before proceeding. "What's your name, sweetheart?"

"C...Carly. Carly Acosta."

"Do you mind if I take a look at your arm?" When the girl thrust her arm out for inspection, Laurel carefully pulled the bandage away. A bit of blood still seeped from the gash, which looked about an inch and a half long. "Oh, my. How did you acquire this?"

"It was stupid, really. We—a big group of us in the dorm— were watching the game on TV, and I was about to slice another stick of summer sausage. We made a touchdown, everyone cheered, someone spilled a drink, someone bumped into me, somehow I got cut. Stupid, but it happened."

"Let's get this cleaned up really well and we'll see what we have. I think it might need a couple of stitches, but luckily for you—" she paused for effect, using exaggerated flair to make the bold claim "—I am an excellent seamstress." She felt the girl's arm relax, just as she hoped, as a timid smile stole across her pale face.

As Laurel gathered the supplies she would need to clean the wound, she tried to ease the girl's fears with casual conversation. She learned the girl was an engineering major from Odessa. Even though she was now a sophomore at the University, being almost seven hours from home, she still battled a severe case of homesickness. And yes, this was her first visit to the ER without one of her parents present.

Sometime around the antiseptic, Carly felt comfortable enough to ask a question of her own. "If you don't mind me asking, why did Mrs. Gonzales open the curtain earlier? She looked like she was searching for something."

Laurel looked up in surprise. "You know her?"

"Of course. She owns *Mama G's Taqueria*. They have *the best* fish tacos you can imagine. They will blow your mind."

"I don't believe I've ever eaten there. Where are they located?"

"They have three locations, but we always eat at the one on Holleman. I hear her husband runs the one in downtown Bryan, and it's really good, too. The new one is out on Rock Prairie."

Three locations. Could explain all the diamonds.

"I hear they're going through a nasty divorce, and that the husband is trying to get control of the Rock Prairie restaurant," Carly continued.

Hmm. She certainly seemed distraught earlier. Maybe this accident will bring them closer and make them remember why they got married in the first place, Laurel thought to herself.

To her patient, she said, "I'm sorry if she frightened you. I have no idea how she got back here, or why she thought it was appropriate to look into each room. I do apologize for that."

"It's okay. I just hope nothing is wrong?"

Laurel offered a noncommittal smile. "We directed her to the right place." With no further explanation, she began cleaning up her trash. "I'm going to let this air out for a bit. It will probably continue to bleed a little, so dab it with this gauze as needed. There's plenty, so don't be afraid to get a fresh piece. If it starts to bleed more than this, be sure and hit the call button." She adjusted covers and made certain everything was within the girl's reach. "Can I get you anything else? Maybe some ice water? It may be a few minutes before the doctor can come in and take a look."

"I'm good for now. Thanks."

"Sure. Buzz if you need me."

Stepping into the hall, she encountered Bridgett coming from the Fandemonium's room. The medical assistant hesitated for only a moment before rushing into an apology. "I'm really sorry about earlier. That woman just pushed her way past me. I didn't even have time to warn you. I normally like to walk the spouses back, but she was having none of that. She was like a bulldozer, just plowing her way through."

Laurel placed a comforting hand on the other woman's arm. "I understand. Don't take it too personally. Let's just try to do better in the future, okay? We can't have that scene repeating itself."

"No, ma'am. I'll make sure that it doesn't. Again, I'm really sorry."

"Thanks, Bridgett. How's it looking out there?"

"Filling up, as expected."

Drawing in a deep breath of encouragement, Laurel pasted a smile on her face as she entered the next room and donned fresh exam gloves.

Wow. The fumes are strong enough in here to get drunk on. That must have been some tailgate party!

"Hello, again. I'm Laurel. And let me guess. *You* are the patient." She pointed to the black man sitting in the chair, while his white friend sprawled on the bed.

"Got a little scratch on my head is all," he said. He wore the same goofy grin as before.

"I have an idea. Let's have you switch places with your friend, so I can take a look. What's your name?"

"They call me Knuckles."

His friend roused from the bed, glaring at him in contempt. "That's what they call *me*, you dimwit! They call you Block."

The huge man actually giggled. "Oh, yeah. They do."

Rolling her eyes, Laurel knew these two would be a handful. She used a no-nonsense voice to bark out instructions. "Knuckles, off the bed. Block, give him your chair."

Block swayed precariously as he stood. For one awful moment, Laurel thought he might fall forward and crush her beneath him. With one hand on the wall, the big man steadied himself until he regained his balance. Laurel stood back while the two men moved about the room, crowding the space with their bulk. It took far longer than it should have for the patient to settle upon the bed and swing his tree-sized legs onto the mattress.

"Made it!" he cried in triumph, still grinning.

"Yes, you did." In spite of herself, Laurel smiled. His delight was genuine, even if ridiculous. "Can you tell me your real name and your birthday?"

"Harold Bevans."

Two Harolds in one day. What are the odds? Laurel mused. She was still waiting for his second answer, which required considerable thought. After two close guesses, he finally got his birthday correct, so she presented him with another question.

"So what happened? What brings you in today?"

For the first time, his silly grin faltered. A sheepish look replaced it as he admitted, "I fell off a barstool."

On a scale of one to ten of *Crazy Reasons to Visit the ER,* Laurel gave it a five. Working in a college town full of bars and drinking establishments, she had heard the complaint before.

"The old spinning barstool, huh? And I guess you hit the floor a little too hard with your head?"

"Nah. Got this on the way down." He pointed somewhere in the general vicinity of his head, even though his actual aim pinned the pillow behind him. "The chick beside me had some wicked chains and a big, shiny buckle on her boots. Musta hit one of them when I fell."

Knuckles hooted with laughter. "It wasn't her *boots* you had your face buried in, bro!"

"Wouldn't have bothered for such a little scratch," the big

man continued, the silly grin resurfacing, "but her scream scared the bartender."

"Scared him worse when she fainted from the sight of your blood," his buddy snickered.

"He says you gotta sign a release form, sayin' I ain't really hurt and I can't sue him for neggi—negli—negligee." The butchered word ended on a hiccup.

"Negligence," Laurel supplied. "And that isn't up to me, my friend. Can you turn your head for me, so I can get this cut cleaned up? By the way, it may sting just a little."

Judging from the big man's toe-curling scream, it did just that.

CHAPTER THREE

Laurel was still chuckling as she pulled off her exam gloves.

You would think I poured undiluted alcohol into his wound. What's that they say? The bigger the man, the bigger the baby? On the bright side, he did sober up rather quickly.

His friend, however, was another matter. He was still asking for Laurel's number as she pulled back the curtain and stepped into the hall. She was eager to get a breath of fresh air.

Too much testosterone and alcohol for these delicate lungs!

Laurel promptly collided with a warm, solid form. Surprise warred with embarrassment, and she jerked her head up to see the object of her discomfort.

Great! Even more testosterone! A sinking feeling settled somewhere near the bottom of her stomach, where something else had already started to swirl. That swirl meant nothing but trouble. *This time, testosterone in a very handsome package. Six one, slender build, excellent muscle tone. Healthy skin, good teeth, gorgeous brown eyes. Can't imagine what he's doing in the ER. Every inch a healthy, virile male.* A silly adaptation to an old memory came to mind. *Run, girl, run, fast as you can. Gotta outrun the testosterone man.*

"I'm so sorry. My fault," she said gracefully, trying to pull back. Never mind that her traitorous body was quite content, smack dab against his muscled chest.

"No, it was mine. I wasn't watching for cross traffic."

It was a strange thing to say, until she made a belated observation. *Blond hair clipped short and neat. Khaki pants, starched blue shirt. No tie but wearing a suit jacket. No-nonsense set to his jaw. Stern look on his face, no smile whatsoever. Definitely law enforcement. Either a Texas Ranger or a detective. I repeat. Run, girl, run.*

"No problem." Laurel forced a smile. "After you, Officer."

His spiked brows spoke volumes.

"You have the look," she explained.

"Very observant." He thrust out a hand. "Detective Cade Resnick, College Station Police Force."

She tucked her small hand into his, bracing for the zing of electricity she knew would come. She wasn't disappointed. "ER Charge Nurse Laurel Benson, *Texas General Hospital.*"

"In that case, you may be just the woman I'm looking for."

From anyone else, the words might have sounded like a come-on. The brisk tone in Detective Cade Resnick's voice made it anything but that.

Before Laurel could answer, Knuckles poked his bald head from between the crease in the curtains. "Don't bother, officer," he advised. "She'll break your heart. She left mine in pieces, not to mention what she did to my buddy. He's almost in tears."

Laurel rolled her eyes at the dramatic claim, delivered amid a haze of alcoholic fumes. "That's because he sobered up and could feel the full sting of the antiseptic."

"See? See? She's coooold," Knuckles complained.

"In that case, Nurse Benson," the detective replied smoothly, "could you warm your friend up with a nice cup of strong, black coffee? If that doesn't work, I may have a pair of handcuffs that will do the trick."

Instead of being threatened, Knuckles was amused. A broad grin, not unlike his friend's formerly goofy smile, stretched across his face. "You may have found your match, little lady. And with that, I graciously bow out."

Laurel winced when she heard the racket on the other side of the curtain. *Not sure about the gracious part.* She suspected he tripped over the chair—or perhaps his own big feet—but a stern shake of the detective's head kept her from checking on him.

"He'll be fine," he said with calm certainty. "If you can tell me where to find a recent hit and run victim brought in by ambulance, I'll let you get to making that coffee."

Laurel immediately bristled. *Is he being condescending? Assuming my skills only extend as far as making coffee?*

Another clatter from the other side of the curtain reminded Laurel that the detective was right. Knuckles needed help sobering up, and now wasn't the time for her pride to rear its ugly head. The hospital couldn't release Block into his care if both men were under the influence.

"I believe you're referring to the patient in Room 6. First room on the left hall, where all the... oh. Looks like they've already moved him. They must have taken him up to surgery, second floor."

"You weren't the nurse in attendance?"

"No, that would be Nurses Beene, De Marco, and Barrington." She looked around to catch a glimpse of someone who had helped with Raul Gonzales. Even Esmeralda Gonzales and the band of personnel had vanished while she cared for the other patients. More time must have passed than she thought. "Dr. Baek was the attending physician," she offered, "but I believe he's in with another patient at the moment."

"I'll wait, if you don't mind."

"Of course not. In fact, we have refreshments, if you'd care to have a bite while you wait." She flashed a smile, this one sincere. "Game Day tradition," she explained.

A curt nod acknowledged the invitation. "I saw the table in the waiting room. I remember now that *Texas General* has a reputation for being a bit unorthodox."

He made it sound like a bad thing. Instead of bristling, Laurel turned up the wattage of her smile and quoted the hospital's tag line. "Unique health care. For Texans, by Texans." Dropping her voice to a conspiratorial level, she confided, "I've seen what they offer out there. This is where we keep the good stuff."

The detective instinctively leaned in when she dropped her

voice. The woodsy scent of his cologne was a welcome change to *Eau du Coors*, but it wreaked havoc on her breathing just the same. She struggled to keep her voice light as she continued, "Help yourself to the microwave in the break room, right through there, if anything needs warming up. If you'll excuse me, I need to check on my next patient."

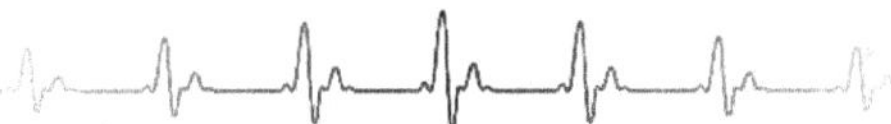

Busy readying Mr. Chen for a move upstairs, Laurel had no way of knowing that the detective had missed lunch that day and found the Game Day smorgasbord particularly tempting. She didn't know that he filled his plate and carried it to the break room for a quick zap in the microwave.

And she certainly didn't know that, once inside the privacy of the secluded room, the no-nonsense detective indulged in a huge smile, thoroughly amused by the refreshing Nurse Benson.

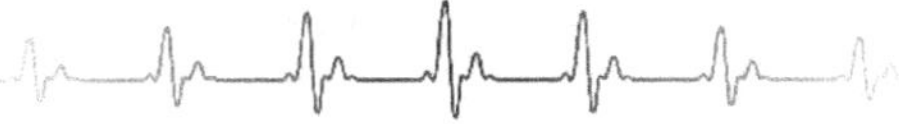

Two Fandemoniums later, Laurel had all but forgotten about the handsome detective.

That was the story she was going with, anyway. Even with herself. Who had time to fantasize about tall, gorgeous men who blew the testosterone meter completely off the charts? He hinted that he didn't approve of *Texas General's* innovative approach to holistic health care, and that he thought her best suited for kitchen duty. She wouldn't waste valuable brain cells on cave-man mentality, even if it belonged to the sexiest man she had seen in some time. She had patients to care for and work to do. *Run, run,* she would.

She proved her seamstress skills to Carly Acosta and sent Harold 'Block' Bevans home with a spiffy new bandage and a semi-sober, broken-hearted friend. (Personally, she thought her rebuff hurt Knuckles' egotistical pride, more than it did his feelings.) With Mr. Chen checked into a room upstairs and Lily

Moses still complaining of pain that didn't show up on X-rays or toxicology reports, Laurel checked an expectant mother for false labor pains and reassured an armchair coach that his chest pains and severe indigestion were most likely a result of eating too many hot wings during a nail-biting win for the Aggies, rather than the heart attack he suspected. By the time she made it back to the desk for the first break in over three hours, she was exhausted.

"Another Game Day lives up to the hype," she moaned, sinking into the first chair she found. The cushions, though thin, welcomed her weary bones as graciously as the finest feather bed.

"Thirty more minutes," Danni grinned. "Then we hand over all the fun to the night shift. That's when the real doozies come out, anyway. Plenty of time to get good and drunk and celebrate another Aggie win in style."

"I see we have reason to celebrate, as well." With a smile, she nodded to the huge wreath on the break room door.

"They said your spicy shrimp dip tipped the scales."

"Cool. What's the word on Raul Gonzales?"

"He pulled through surgery, but it's still touch and go."

Laurel winced in empathy. "His legs?"

Danni shook her head in regret. "Had to take them both."

"That's horrible! Did they find who hit him?"

"No, but there was a really hot detective here, asking a ton of questions."

"Oh, I ran into him," Laurel assured her friend. "Literally."

The monitors went off on the panel, alerting them to a problem in Room 5. "That's Lily Moses' room," Laurel said. "*Again.* This is the third time we've gotten an alarm, but when I get in there, she looks perfectly fine. No signs of distress, no matter what the monitors say."

"Maybe it's a faulty machine. What alarms?"

"First, it was the blood pressure cuff. Her pressure dropped drastically, but when I took it manually, it was fine. I changed the machine. Right after that, it was her heart monitor. Sky high, erratic beat. I get in there, she looks perfectly calm and relaxed. Now it's her blood pressure again, all wonky. I don't know what is going on with her. Nothing shows up on any tests, but she insists she's in tremendous pain."

"Want me to go this time?"

Laurel pushed out of the chair with a sigh. "No, I've got it. Thanks, though. On the other hand, if you'd like to help with my charting…" She offered her best smile, hoping her co-worker would take pity on her.

As she opened the curtain to Lily's room, Harold shuffled away from the bed and back to his chair, tugging on the arm of his t-shirt. The boy looked as tired and weary as she felt.

"Lily? Are you feeling alright?" she asked in concern.

"Uhm, I still got the hurting, and all. And—And I threw up again."

The news surprised Laurel. "Again? I didn't know you *had* thrown up."

"Oh, yeah, yeah. Several times before we left the house. Once after we got here and all, and again now."

"This is the first you've mentioned it, Lily." The reprimand was in her tone. "Why didn't you tell the doctor you were having trouble keeping things down?"

"I—I guess it slipped my mind." Her eyes slid away almost guiltily, making Laurel wonder once again if she were making up some of her symptoms.

"You should have called me. I would have helped."

"That's okay. Harold helped me clean it up and all."

Laurel turned her gaze to the boy. "How did you dispose of the vomit, Harold?"

Looking squeamish and slightly green at the mere mention of the word, the boy made a grimace and pointed toward the restroom. "Flushed it down the toilet, quick as I could."

"Hmm. If it happens again, please call me. I'd like to see the volume and content."

The teen's lip curled in repulsion. "Whatever," he said, a shimmy moving through his thin shoulders. The worn-out collar of his t-shirt sagged with the motion, offering a glimpse of an angry red mark near his collarbone. Laurel noticed another red mark near the bottom of his sleeve. She wondered if the boy had been in a recent fight.

"I know you must be exhausted, Harold. Have you had a chance to move around and get a bit of fresh air?"

"A little."

"Did you find the vending machines?"

His shrug made her wonder if he had money to put in them, even if he found them.

"I think we have a few cookies and drinks left," she offered. "I'll bring you some in before I go off shift."

"What about me?" Lily wanted to know. "Don't I get nothing to eat?"

"Not if you're sick at your stomach, I'm afraid. Actually, I came in because your blood pressure alarm went off again. Does your cuff feel all right?" Laurel checked the fittings, finding it was on upside down. She frowned her disapproval. "Did you take this off, Lily?"

The woman's eyes darted to her son. "Uh, yeah. When I upchucked. Didn't want vomit to get on it and all. Harold musta put it on wrong."

"That's what we're here for, Lily. To help you with things like that. Don't be bashful about pressing that button."

"Sorry, nurse. I'll try to remember."

"Is there anyone we need to call, to check on your other children? Someone's with them, right?"

"Oh, sure, sure. My neighbor keeps an eye on them for me. We single moms have to stick together, and all."

"I'm sure you'll be back at home with them shortly."

Instead of looking relieved, Lily looked alarmed. "You mean... they ain't keeping me overnight?"

"That's up to the doctor, but so far, all of your tests have come back negative. I'd say there's a very good chance you'll be sleeping in your own bed tonight." Laurel offered a warm smile, hoping to reassure the woman. "Doesn't that sound nice?"

"Uhm, yeah. Swell." Her lie was so obvious, Laurel's brows drew together in concern.

"Lily, is there some reason you don't want to go home? Do you not feel safe there?"

"Of course I feel safe!" the other woman huffed. She pulled the covers up around her in a defensive manner. "Why on earth wouldn't I?"

"I don't know. But if there is a reason, you can talk to me, you know." Laurel's voice was soft and full of compassion. "I'll do my best to help you. And your children."

"I just want to find out what's wrong with me, and what this hurtin' is about," she insisted. "That's the only reason I want to stay tonight. To find out what's wrong with me."

"I'll update the doctor on this latest news of vomiting and see what he has to say. If it happens again, please press the buzzer. Okay?"

"Yeah, sure."

"I'll stop back in one last time before I leave," she promised. "Harold, if you'll come with me, I'll get you those cookies."

Someone had cleared away the refreshment table, but Laurel rummaged around in the refrigerator until she came out with half a sandwich, a small container of dip, and two soft drinks. She grabbed her secret stash of Glenda's cookies and brought it out to give to Harold.

To her surprise, Detective Resnick was back at the desk, scribbling in a small notebook.

"Hello again, detective. Harold, here you go. These should tide you over until you know what's happening with your mom. If she stays overnight, you have a ride home, right?"

"Got our car," he mumbled, avoiding looking at the detective. Laurel wondered if he had a valid driver's license or if, like most teens, he was naturally nervous around law enforcement. He turned away without thanking her, making her almost regret her decision to give up her coveted cookies.

"Who's the kid?" the detective asked as Harold shuffled away.

"His mom came in about the same time as Mr. Gonzales, complaining of a stomachache. Poor kid's been here all afternoon. If he's like most teenagers, I know he's starving, even though I made him a plate earlier."

"You've got teens at home?" he asked, his eyes flickering down to his notebook. Along the way, they may have skittered over to her ring finger.

"Brothers," she grinned, sinking back into her chair. "I remember the hunger years, all too well."

Instead of sharing something about himself, the detective offered as an aside, "I saw him up on the second floor, wandering around the waiting room where the Gonzales family is gathered."

Laurel's tender heart went out to the teen. "Like I said, they came in about the same time as Mr. Gonzales, and he saw most of the drama unfold. I think he was pretty shaken up. Like many people, he seemed to have a morbid fascination with what was happening, but I think it affected him more than he's letting on."

"Could be," Detective Resnick said, but he didn't sound convinced. "I have a few more questions I'd like to ask, if you don't mind."

"Sure, but I doubt I can be of much help. As I said, Danni helped attend. I wasn't part of the care team."

Danni beamed up at the handsome detective, obviously more than willing to cooperate.

Not for the first time, Laurel envied her friend's voluptuously full figure and easy, dimpled smile. While both women were about the same petite height and sported a head full of short, natural curls, that was where the similarities ended. Danni's corkscrew ringlets were a fun, vibrant rust color and danced around her face with a life of their own. Laurel's looser curls were so dark they were almost black. Not even thirty years old yet, and a few wiry gray strands were already weaving their way amid the dark silk. Danni was full of curves and knew how to wear clothes that enhanced her best features. Laurel was slim and straight, but in all the wrong places.

She moved on to her chair, preparing herself for the

inevitable. Men always gravitated toward Danni. She had the personality to go with the looks.

Sometimes, Laurel feared the same could be said for her. She fell flat in so many ways.

"I've already taken Miss Barrington's statement. I'd like to talk with you, if you can spare a few moments."

Clearly surprised, Laurel blinked up at him. "Okay."

If the detective expected her to stand and join him for a private conversation, he underestimated her exhaustion. He looked slightly irritated when she continued to sit there, waiting for the questions to begin. The muscles tightened around his mouth, but he flipped his notepad to a new page and began.

"I understand you were the first to speak with Mrs. Gonzales."

"Yes, that's right. According to Bridgett in registration, she more or less pushed her way in and stormed down the hall, searching for her husband."

"Can you describe to me what happened?"

Laurel had been too busy to give the incident more thought, but now that she had time to reflect on it, it made her angry all over again. She felt the huff building within her.

"She stopped at every single room, jerking open the curtains and peering inside. I heard one patient yelp in fear. I saw another patient shrink back in shock, obviously frightened. By that time, I had reached her and tried to pull her aside, but she knocked my hand away."

An odd light touched the detective eyes. "Are you saying Mrs. Gonzales assaulted you?"

"What? No, of course not! The woman was obviously distraught. She didn't mean me any harm, but she was frightening my patients. I had to stop her."

By now, the light had clearly turned to amusement. "And did you?"

He's laughing at me? He's obviously wondering how little ol' me stopped big ol' her!

"Did I what?" she fairly snapped. She refused to make it easy for him, not if he was going to make fun of her.

"Stop her."

"She didn't open any more curtains," Laurel said, a prim expression upon her lips. She neglected to point out that there had been no more along that hallway. "I was attempting to calm her down and reason with her when she spotted her husband's room and all the personnel gathered there."

"And then what?"

A smile itched at her lips as she recalled the way Esmeralda had loped off like a horse, her spiked heels clattering like horseshoes upon the tiled floor. She had been quite the spectacle, a woman of her bulk in neon pink leotards, a leopard skin top, and arms flailing above her head, diamonds catching and sparkling in the light. Stifling a giggle, Laurel tried her best to give the grave situation the seriousness it deserved.

"She ran all the way to his room," she finished simply.

"And you were…?" He left the question open-ended.

Laurel offered a rueful smile. "Trying to catch up. Quite frankly, her legs were longer than mine."

"And once she reached the room? Do you recall anything she said?"

"She demanded that her husband wake up. She thought he was dead. She had a steady barrage of questions after that, but I thought the doctor and the attending team were better suited to answer them, so I left and came back to my side of the hall."

"Your side?"

"We generally divide the workload by hallways. Since we had two serious patients on the left hall, I had the right hall primarily on my own today."

He asked a few more questions, following up with a request for her business card. "I may have more questions in the future."

"Certainly," she agreed. She pulled out a second card so that she could give it to Lily. "Why all the questions about Mrs. Gonzales?"

"Just being thorough." Cade Resnick slipped a business card from his pocket with long, nimble fingers and slid it across the desk. "And here's my card, in case you think of something else you may have forgotten."

"Absolutely, although I doubt I have anything to add."

"Just in case," he reiterated. His brown eyes held hers for the briefest of moments, before he swept his gaze across the space to include Danni. "Ladies, I appreciate your cooperation. Again, if you think of anything you may have forgotten, please don't hesitate to call. Have a good evening."

"You too, Detective," Danni called in a singsong voice, the giggle just below the surface.

"Have a nice evening," Laurel added.

The man had barely turned his back before Danni broke out in silent laughter and whispered, "I'm green with envy! Detective Hot Stuff just asked for your number!"

"He did not!" Laurel hissed, just a little too loud. She lowered her voice and repeated, "He did not. He simply wanted to know how to get in touch with me."

"Exactly! He didn't ask for *my* card."

"Well, I am Charge Nurse," she reasoned. "It's probably a chain of command thing."

"Sure it is. I think he's just got the hots for you!" Danni clapped her hands together in glee, enjoying teasing her blushing friend. "Detective Hot Stuff has the hots for Laurel!"

"Shh! Would you keep your voice down?" she hissed. "He's going to hear you!"

They both stared after the man, judging if he was within hearing range. When he stopped and turned back toward them, Laurel thought she might go into cardiac arrest.

"And by the way. My congratulations to whoever made the spicy shrimp dip with avocado. It was superb."

"Laurel!" Danni said, hopping up from her chair with an excited clatter. "Laurel made it!"

"Good job, Laurel."

Laurel stared after his retreating back, uncertain of what shocked her the most. For all his no-nonsense by-the-book protocol, his informal use of her first name came as quite a surprise.

On top of that, the man had actually smiled at her.

And Detective Hot Stuff has a very attractive smile, she acknowledged.

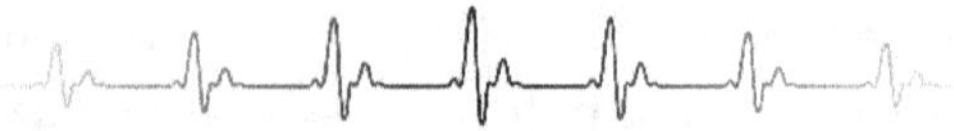

Read more at *Texas General Cozy Cases of Mystery,* and the companion series, *Texas General Cozy Cases of Romance!*